PRAISE FOR THE NOVELS OF SORAYA LANE

I Knew You Were Trouble

"Readers will fall head-over-heels in love with Nate and Faith. Lane's latest is filled with a huge dose of Southern Texas charm." —*RT Book Reviews*

"First-rate writing and memorable characters prove that sometimes things are worth the trouble as demonstrated by Ms. Lane." —*Jenerated Reviews*

"A fun, endearing, yet heartbreaking read that kept me eagerly turning pages just waiting to see how everything works out for Faith and Nate." —*Romance Junkies*

"For those who love a Texan man and some good flirtation, I recommend *I Knew You Were Trouble*." —*Harlequin Junkie*

Cowboy Take Me Away

"A sexy, charming Southern read." —*RT Book Reviews*

"Soraya Lane keeps the story going and exciting to the very end." —*Reader to Reader Review*

"If you like steamy cowboy romances you'll love this book." —*Bitten By Love Reviews*

All Night with the Cowboy

Soraya Lane

St. Martin's Paperbacks

This is a work of fiction. All of the characters, organizations, and events portrayed in this novel are either products of the author's imagination or are used fictitiously.

ALL NIGHT WITH THE COWBOY

Copyright © 2018 by Soraya Lane.

All rights reserved.

For information address St. Martin's Press, 175 Fifth Avenue, New York, NY 10010.

ISBN: 978-1-250-13103-4

Our books may be purchased in bulk for promotional, educational, or business use. Please contact your local bookseller or the Macmillan Corporate and Premium Sales Department at 1-800-221-7945, ext. 5442, or by e-mail at MacmillanSpecialMarkets@macmillan.com.

Printed in the United States of America

St. Martin's Paperbacks edition / June 2018

St. Martin's Paperbacks are published by St. Martin's Press, 175 Fifth Avenue, New York, NY 10010.

10 9 8 7 6 5 4 3 2 1

For Yvonne Lindsay—I couldn't have written this book without you!

Acknowledgments

There is so much that goes on behind the scenes before a book hits the shelves, from writing to editing (and more editing!) and design. I'm so grateful to have such a wonderful team working with me at St. Martin's Press, and I'd like to make special mention of my editor Holly Ingraham for all her work on this novel. I'd also like to thank my copy editor, proofreader, and the entire publicity team for everything they've done for me—they are the true stars behind the scenes! It's been so exciting seeing my River Ranch series come to life, and it's because of these extraordinary people that it was able to happen. I would also like to thank my literary agent, Laura Bradford, for her support, as well as fellow novelist Yvonne Lindsay for being my daily writing partner.

Writing a novel can be an unusual process . . . there's the initial excitement of coming up with a shiny new idea and new characters, the thrill of writing that first scene or chapter, and then the panic that sets in when you realize you have to write an entire novel! And then it's always sad to reach the end, because it means saying good-bye to characters that you've fallen in love with over months of living and breathing their stories. But the best part of the process is hearing from readers after they've read the book, and I truly hope you've enjoyed reading this novel as much as I enjoyed creating it.

Fiji is one of my absolute favorite places in the world to visit—it truly is the most magical holiday destination. If you ever get the chance to travel there, I promise it'll be just as magical in real life as it sounds on the pages of this story. The people there are amazing, and the islands are breathtaking.

I love to hear from readers, and if you'd like to be notified of any news or new releases, please sign up for my newsletter on my website sorayalane.com or find me on Twitter @Soraya_Lane.

Until next time xx

Prologue

Professional Bull Riders World Finals, Las Vegas

November 4

TANNER FORD shut his eyes for a nano-second before signaling for the chute to open. His fingers were clenched tightly around the rigging, glue helping to hold him in place as the bull emerged full throttle into the arena. He heard the roar of the crowd but blocked out everything else, counting in his head, listening only to the grunt of the beast beneath him and the powerful thrust of his enormous, unpredictable bucks.

Holy shit. The bull swung sideways, living up to his reputation, lurching back and forth as he shook the hell out of Tanner. Thunder Cat was known for being gnarly, but then that's precisely why Tanner had been thrilled to draw him. He was going for the win, and he wanted to take home the title for the second year in a row.

He was at five seconds. He was so close, and he tucked his spurred boots firm against the bull, wanting him to buck harder, wanting to score the best damn points in the—

Tanner lurched back, the whip-fast movement popping something in his wrist and sending pain shooting through his arm. He held as tight as he could, but something wasn't right. He couldn't keep his balance.

Thump. He hit the ground with a cruel thud, the snap of his ankle a noise he'd never forget—if he survived to tell the tale. His arms flailed as he tried to protect himself from the charging bull, the insistent fall of his hooves was too close for comfort as Tanner tried to roll away and failed.

"Arrghh!" he screamed as he tried to use his leg and his ankle refused to oblige. The sickening flop of his foot made vomit rise in his throat at the same time as twin horns descended toward him.

Thunder Cat gored him, going straight into his side. Tanner screamed as burning hot pain exploded through his chest, and the bull lunged for him again, piercing him a second time, his helmet peeling off his head as he desperately tried to protect himself.

He lost all feeling in his hand when the big beast careened over his wrist, then stomped on him again as he charged off. And just as Tanner tried to breathe again, tried to suck in some air that just wouldn't fill his lungs, everything went black.

Chapter 1

November 22, Thanksgiving

TANNER took a deep breath before entering the room. From the moment he'd woken up in the hospital and started his long stay there, he'd imagined Thanksgiving afternoon; the smell of turkey roasting, the sound of his family talking, the feeling of finally being able to walk into a room again. He glanced down at the cast still covering his lower leg and clenched his fingers tightly around the crutches. Not exactly walking, perhaps hobbling was a better description for what he was doing, but it was close enough.

"Tanner?"

He stood up as tall as he could and gave his younger sister a grin, ignoring the blast of pain in his right wrist as her little toddler threw her arms up, excited to see him. "Hey, Mia. Hey, Sophia."

"Tanner!" Mia exclaimed, leaping up and throwing her arms around him. Her pregnant belly squished against him and he struggled not to groan as she held him. Everything hurt still—his chest, his back, his wrist and his leg. He was a goddamn mess all over, but he wasn't about to let anyone else in the room know that. Even his little niece, Sophia, toddle-walked over to him and held onto his leg in a big cuddle. Thankfully it was his good leg, so he wasn't wincing in pain the entire time.

"Hey, it's not that exciting having me home, is it?" he asked, grinning down at Mia and pressing a quick kiss to her cheek, then ruffling Sophia's hair before she toddled off again. "You'd think I'd been gone for a year."

"Honestly, you haven't been home a minute and I'm ready to strangle you," Mia muttered. "Of course it's exciting! You scared us all half to death when you ended up in the hospital like that."

He hadn't meant to tease her—she'd lost her best friend to a riding accident and he wasn't trying to trivialize what had happened—he just didn't particularly want to be the center of attention. Not here and not at the hospital—all the fuss was embarrassing.

"Hey, Tan," Cody called out, raising his beer bottle. "Ready for a drink?"

"Hell yes," Tanner answer, throwing his brother a grateful smile. "Hey, Sam," he said when his brother-in-law shook his hand, slapping him on the back and passing the beer over from Cody. Mia hadn't been married to Sam for long, but Tanner already felt like he was part of the family. It helped that they both shared a solid love for Quarter Horses.

"It's good to have you home, Tanner." His older sister Angelina had been talking to their dad on the other side of the room but she was by his side now, giving him a long, warm hug. She was so unlike Mia, who was usually always dressed down in jeans and a T-shirt or her riding attire. Angelina was more often wearing tailored pants and silky blouses, making her stand out like a sore thumb whenever she returned to the ranch.

He always loved Thanksgiving—it was the only time their entire family was ever together. Cody might be the complete opposite of him and Angelina was as interested in the ranch as he was in clothes shopping, but they'd always gotten along well and he missed the hell out of them when they weren't around. As kids they'd been more similar, it was only as young adults they'd slowly drifted apart when it came to their careers and interests.

"Good to have you home, son." His dad, the one and only Walter Ford, spoke in his trademark booming voice from the other side of the room.

Tanner raised his beer to his father and took a long, cool sip. It was like heaven in a mouthful as he stood there, propped up on his crutches.

"Come sit," Cody ordered. "Put that leg up and watch some football."

He let Mia fuss and take his beer while he settled himself down, grimacing when he lifted his leg up and placed it on the coffee table. It was good to get the weight off it, but it still hurt like hell most of the time—a dull, never-ending thud of pain that he was almost starting to get used to.

"You feeling okay or putting on a brave face?" Mia asked, her brows drawn together, concern written all over her expression.

"If I told you the truth, you'd only start fussing."

Mia nodded. She was his ally in this whole thing— Mia was a professional show jump rider, and although not as dangerous as what he did, it was still a high-risk

sport. Not to mention the fact that he'd stood her ground
with her when their entire family had protested about
her continuing to ride while she was pregnant with
Sophia and now again with her second pregnancy. She
owed him a debt big time.

"You let me know if you need anything, or if all of
this," she said, waving her hand around, "gets to be too
much."

She left him then and went back to Sam, and Tanner
grit his teeth and tried to get comfortable. He'd been
hurt before, but damn, this was something else. Perhaps
he should have heeded his doctor's advice and stayed a
few days longer.

"So how'd you convince the docs to let you out of
the hospital so soon?" Cody asked as he sipped his beer.

"Bribed a pretty nurse," Tanner replied with a wink.

"I should have guessed." Cody laughed and Tanner
joined in, pleased he'd decided to come home. It was
Thanksgiving and the last thing he wanted was to sit
alone in a hospital bed, wishing he was at home with
the rest of his family.

"Any thoughts about rehab yet?" Cody asked. "And
please don't tell me you're hoping to get on a bull again.
Surely you've got all that out of your system? It's been
ten years of risks, Tan, it's time to give it up and grow
up a little. Get a real job."

Tanner took a big pull of beer. "We're not all cut out to
be pen pushers," Tanner replied, knowing how badly
that would grate his brother.

"You know what? Screw you," Cody muttered. "At
least I'm not trying to kill myself every time I go to work."

Tanner wasn't so sure about that. He'd feel like he
was trying to kill himself if he went to work in an

office each day, but he decided to keep his mouth shut instead of retaliating.

For the next half hour, Tanner managed to ignore Cody and watch the game, and before he knew it, his sisters were calling them in for dinner and everyone rose. Tanner hauled himself up as best he could, accepting Cody's hand when he steadied him and held out one of the crutches to him.

"Thanks," he muttered.

"You know I do actually give a damn about you, right?" Cody asked. "It's the only reason I keep at you about doing something different with your life."

"Yeah, I know." Tanner moved into the adjoining room where the big dining table was set. "It just ain't gonna happen." A huge turkey was in the middle and smaller dishes surrounded it—Tanner's mouth was watering just looking at the feast. His brother needed to learn when to shut his mouth, and right now would be as good a time as any.

"But when is enough going to be enough, Tan? What do you have left to prove?" Cody asked. "I think you owe it to us."

"Just leave it," Tanner ground out, not wanting to ruin a damn fine meal because his brother wouldn't get off his back.

"You know," Mia said, obviously having heard the conversation and trying to deflect the argument. "The best thing you can do is to heal your body properly. If you do decide to go back to riding, and that's something only you can decide, you're less likely to injure yourself if your body's in top form. Maybe you can promise us all that you won't go back until you're in top shape again?"

"See, words of wisdom over here," Tanner said with a laugh, eternally grateful for Mia. "I need to heal, then find a top physical therapist. I'll be back on a beast in no time, but I will give you all my word that I'll wait until I'm good and ready before I go back. Maybe I'll stick with broncs awhile before returning to bulls." It wasn't a question of *if*—in his mind it was only a matter of *when*.

Mia gave him a look and he stared back at her, but then she smiled and leaned over to take his plate. He ignored the raised eyebrows from his father and didn't bother looking at his other siblings.

"Everything?" she asked, gesturing toward the dishes of food.

He nodded. "The works." He'd been fantasizing about this meal all week as a way to survive the disgustingly bland hospital food. Angelina passed him another beer and he took it gratefully, although it would have to be his last. He didn't want to mix the pain meds he was on with too much alcohol.

Everyone started talking and Tanner reached forward to take the plate from Mia, sucking in a sharp breath when he engaged his stomach muscles without realizing. The bull had gouged straight through his flesh, into his ribs and tearing through his side, and the pain there was still hard to manage.

"Thanks," he said, trying not to hiss with pain as he set the huge plate of food down.

"You know," Mia said, leaning toward him a little as she filled her own plate. "I think you need to go away somewhere for a few weeks. You can go somewhere relaxing, take a physical therapist with you, and just focus on healing. I think a long rest away from here would do you good for your recovery."

He grunted. "Why is it that you and I are the only people in this family who speak the same language sometimes?"

She laughed. "Seriously, Tanner, can you trust me to organize it for you? I've been talking to some PT's and investigating options for you. I really want to help."

"Damn, girl, sounds like you've been busy while I've been lying around in a hospital bed."

There went that look again. Mia never sucked in her bottom lip, yet she'd done it twice now and he had no idea why. He raised an eyebrow and stared at her, long and hard. "Mia?"

"I need you to be open-minded," she said. "But I've tentatively booked accommodations for you, and the jet is available. You can leave the second week of December and come back in the New Year."

Tan took a sip of his beer. "What's the catch?" He couldn't exactly see what was so bad about taking a vacation.

"I've also booked the physical therapist." She hesitated and he set down his beer, waiting for her to finish. "There was one who clearly stood out from the rest, so I took the liberty of making sure she was available, too."

"Cody, how about you say grace this year," Walter Ford, Tanner's dad, suggested from the other end of the table, interrupting the conversation Tanner was having with his sister.

"It's Lauren," Mia whispered as Tanner went to bow his head.

His head shot up so fast he got whiplash. "What?" he demanded in a loud voice.

"Tanner!" His father scolded.

"Lauren Lewis," Mia repeated, her voice barely

audible. But he knew what he'd heard, and he knew why she'd said it so quietly, too.

"You've got to be goddamn kidding me," he muttered.

Tanner sat silently, head dipped, fuming as he listened to Cody's words. Thunder roared in his ears and when he lifted his head and reached for his fork, his hand was shaking as he tightly clenched the piece of cutlery. He stabbed at a piece of turkey.

"Tanner, come on. It's . . ."

"The answer is no, Mia. Find someone else."

"She was already heading to Fiji on vacation and it was the only way to get her, so I organized for you to, well, join her. You'll be flying out together in a few weeks' time."

She stared at him and the rest of the table went quiet. He felt eyes on his burning hot skin, but no one said anything and Mia eventually smiled and changed the subject, striking up a conversation with her husband.

Lauren wasn't the only physical therapist around, and he'd rather suffer in pain for the rest of his life than ever see her again. There was no way in hell he was letting her touch him, let alone board a plane and spend weeks with her on a goddamn island in Fiji.

Lauren stretched out like a cat in a puddle of sunshine. Sleeping in was amazing. In fact, right now, it was her absolute favorite thing to do.

She'd been working twelve-hour days, seven days a week, for nine months straight, and she was still exhausted even a week after finishing up for the season. She flexed her toes and reluctantly pushed the covers back, dragging herself up and trying to decide if it was worth making her way to yoga, or if she'd be better off staying in bed and reading a book.

Then again, this was the only time in her life she had to go to yoga. There wasn't usually any time to make classes or hell, make any time for herself at all, if she was completely honest. Not when she was working. She sighed. And this was why she was waking up in a bed alone, again, after her last boyfriend had reminded her repeatedly about how little time he ever had with her because she was more interested in work than play.

Her phone buzzed on her bedside table and she reached for it, admiring her hot pink manicure—another thing she didn't get to indulge in very often. She smiled when she saw who it was from. Mia Ford had always been friendly, and whenever they'd run into each other over the years they'd always enjoyed catching up, but this time was different. She'd heard about Tanner's fall—hell, everyone had heard about what had happened to Texas's bull riding star at the World Finals—she just hadn't ever expected a personal invitation to work on his rehab. But Mia had been insistent, and she supposed that if Tanner was okay with seeing her again, then she could be too. She was a professional physical therapist. She worked on top athletes for a living and she'd perfected the friendly but professional relationship with all the men she saw on a regular basis. Why would Tanner be any different?

Her heart did a little flutter, but she ignored it. Tanner was in the past, period. This was a professional engagement, nothing more, nothing less. So what if she'd technically be vacationing with him on a beautiful island in Fiji? The fact her skin was on fire had nothing to do with Tanner, and she'd booked this trip months ago as a way to prove to herself and everyone else in her life that she was capable of relaxation. The irony that she'd now be working on her one vacation in almost a decade wasn't lost on her though.

She texted Mia back, her thumb flying fast over the screen of her iPhone.

All confirmed, available for the entire three weeks if needed. Send me through all the final details, including his latest scans and reports so I can review, and you should already have my itinerary so you can schedule his flights and room. Looking forward to it. Lauren.

She set her phone down and scooped her long dark hair up into a ponytail, slipping a tie from her wrist. She stripped down, put on tights and a t-shirt, then made her way into the adjoining bathroom. Lauren turned the faucet on and studied her face while she waited for the water to run hot. What would Tanner think after all this time? Would he think she'd aged? That she was different? Her face was a little slimmer than it had been back in high school and there were tiny lines feathering beside her eyes, but hell, that was twelve years ago. He'd probably changed since then, too.

She washed her face then dried it and rubbed in some tinted moisturizer before brushing her teeth and heading downstairs. She'd walk to yoga and grab a shake for breakfast on the way. Who knew, it might help her stop thinking about a handsome as hell, reckless, fun-loving cowboy who'd stolen her heart in high school and had never, ever truly given it back to her. Or if he had, it sure as heck wasn't in one piece.

She grabbed her phone off the counter and her keys, then let herself out and locked the door, smiling the second sunshine hit her face and a light breeze of wind tickled against her bare skin.

Lauren dialed her sister, Hannah, grinning to herself as she thought about her sister's reaction to what she was doing.

"Hey," Hannah answered. "Tell me something exciting. Did you go out last night?"

"Me, exciting?" Lauren laughed. "Come on, you know me, an exciting night is watching more than one show on Netflix and getting a big sleep."

"Seriously, when you're up to your elbows in diapers one day, with kids' television shows blaring, and you're operating on zero sleep and way too many coffees? You'll be wishing you'd made the most of your single years."

Lauren stifled a laugh. She didn't know whether Hannah was joking or whether it was a genuine plea for help. "You need me to come over and help out?" she asked. "Because seriously, I was just going to a class. I can jump in my car and be there in, like, an hour?"

"No." Hannah sighed. "I just, you know, I love my kids so much but sometimes I'd just like to hit pause for a day, a weekend, heck maybe even an entire week. It'd be nice to go to the toilet for once without having an audience of little people."

"I can't imagine being at home with kids. It must be . . ." she wasn't sure what the word was. *Boring? Repetitive?* "But I do totally get the operating on coffee and zero sleep thing, that's one thing I do understand."

"*Rewarding*," Hannah said for her. "It's all meant to be so rewarding, and I get it, I do. I love my kids so much my heart just about bursts sometimes, but I'm still the old me, too. I want to drink too much every once in a while and sleep in, or just talk to another adult for longer than thirty minutes without someone throwing up on me or pooping or needing to be fed."

"You realize you're totally putting me off ever having children, right?" Lauren teased. "You may never be an aunty if you keep being so honest with me about this whole child rearing business."

"You'd actually need to meet someone first, you do know that, don't you? And your last boyfriend doesn't count because he was a douche bag." Hannah said as crying erupted in the background. "You haven't started dating some gorgeous player, have you? Because if you have I want every juicy detail. Don't leave anything out!"

Lauren laughed. "Not a chance. You know I'm way too professional for that."

She heard it all the time from Hannah, and her mom, and just about every other woman in her life. She even received raised eyebrows from the player's wives and girlfriends early on, until they'd quickly realized they had nothing to worry about where she was concerned. She just didn't look at the guys she worked on like that. She took her job as physical therapist with the Texas Rangers seriously, and she would never, ever date a player or let anything happen to ruin her career. Or theirs.

"I was calling to say that my trip is next week," she said, talking louder as the crying intensified. "In case you'd forgotten."

"Ha!" Hannah scoffed. "Like I'd forget the exact hour you're flying to some magical island and leaving me in domestic bliss."

"I just, well, things have changed a little, so it's not exactly the vacation I planned."

"Don't tell me you're working in the off-season again? You need a proper break!"

"Well, it'll be part vacation, part work," Lauren told her. "Heavy on the vacation part though."

"I'd do *anything* to be going to Fiji right now, so I guess if you have to combine it with some work, so be it."

"The work's with, um, well, with Tanner. You remember Tanner Ford?"

There was silence down the line. She had no idea where the crying child had gone or if Hannah was even there still.

"*Tanner?*" Hannah suddenly hissed. "Tanner *Ford*? Quick, spill, I've locked myself outside for a minute."

Lauren smiled as she imagined Hannah on the other side of the door, with pudgy-faced, sticky-fingered little ones pressed to the glass, watching mommy from inside.

"It's a professional trip for him. He's injured and his sister called me to see if I'd work on him. He needs intensive rehab to get ready for the next season, and . . ."

"Is he okay with this? I mean, you kind of broke the guy's heart, Lauren."

And mine. Lauren had never, ever forgotten the deep burn in her chest and the pain that reverberated through every inch at her when she'd walked away from Tanner. It was heartbreak like she'd never known before, and she'd made sure to protect herself from it ever happening again, too.

"I guess I'll find out soon enough," she replied. "Honestly, he's probably forgotten all about me. He's a professional bull rider now and I doubt he'd have agreed to me treating him if he had a problem with it, and I said the only way I could work on him was if he met me in Fiji."

"Wow. Just, wow," Hannah sighed. "Sorry, the kids are staring at me through the glass like I've abandoned them. I'd better go."

"Okay, see you later."

Lauren hung up and smiled to herself as she walked, imagining Hannah with her kids. They were a handful, with twins who weren't yet two years old and a three-year-old too, but they were gorgeous. She was happy focusing on her career for now, but sometimes when she talked to Hannah or visited, it made her think about the future. She'd been so focused on work for so long that she needed to start making an effort with her social life, otherwise she'd probably wake up at 50, alone and wondering why the hell she'd never made an effort to go on any dates. And she knew she had a type—the guy who was fun for a little while but was never going to be anything serious, or someone nice who she had no intention of committing to. Deep down she knew she needed to put the effort into meeting the right guy, but . . .

There's always online dating, she thought, shuddering at the thought as she stopped outside her favorite café and headed in to order a juice. *Over my dead body.*

Chapter 2

"I feel like a kid being bossed around by his big sister," Tanner grumbled as he stood, propped against the fence, watching Mia ride. She was on her favorite mare, Indi, the only horse she was still exercising regularly now that she was six months pregnant.

"Except I'm your little sister," Mia called out, "and all I did was find the best PT in the state to work on you. You need to stop moaning and accept it."

"You do remember what it was like when Dad called in Sam, right? I recall you hearing he was the best horse trainer in Texas and still managing to act like a wild-cat." He wasn't going to let her get away with acting superior on this particular topic.

Mia pulled up in front of him, her horse blowing heavily. His sister was laughing. Why the hell did she find his plight so goddamn amusing?

"And look at me now," she said, gesturing to her stomach. "A belly full of baby and a cute-as-a-button kid inside the house. Maybe you'll rekindle things with Lauren? It could be good for you."

Tanner glared at her. If she wasn't pregnant, he'd have been tempted to climb through the railings and push her off her damn horse. He stretched his foot a little and grimaced, wishing his ankle wasn't feeling so tight. His whole body was sore still, and he was trying to ease off on the painkillers—the last thing he needed was to down pills to make him feel better instead of actually solving the issues. He needed his body strong, which was the only reason he was going along with Mia's plan.

"Look, she's the best, Tan. I'm not just trying to be a pain in the butt, I'm trying to do something meaningful to help you, okay?" She put one hand on her heart, holding her reins in the other. "I promise you that I looked at all options, but she was the only PT with such glowing references. She's amazing at what she does, and everyone sings her praises."

He grunted, still scowling. "Want any help with the horse?"

"Um, I'm pregnant, not disabled. Go get yourself ready for Lauren."

Tanner stared at her. Hard. "What? We don't leave for another week."

"Oops, sorry. Didn't I mention she was coming to check you over today? She wanted to make sure she understood your injuries so she could make a full plan for your recovery before your departure, and I mentioned you were staying here during your recuperation."

"And you're sure we have to go to Fiji? I don't see why you couldn't have just paid her more to—"

"It was Fiji or nothing, Tan. She'd already booked the vacation, and I sweetened the deal by upgrading her accommodation on this beautiful island and booking the jet. It's done, so all you need to do is go along with it.

Besides, where better to recuperate than a beautiful tropical island? It'll be magical."

Tanner scooped his hand around the crutch and squeezed the plastic so hard he hurt his good hand. Damn his sister! He watched as she smiled sweetly then rode off in the other direction—from behind she didn't even look pregnant, and if it were any other day he'd have laughed. Today he'd rather set her on fire. A week ago she'd broken the news to him, and now she'd set up an appointment without even telling him.

Lauren goddamn Lewis. He couldn't believe it. He'd thought about what he'd say to her if he ever saw her again, had even wondered what she looked like now. But he'd always resisted the urge to look her up on Facebook, and miraculously they'd never crossed paths. Until now.

He looked up as a swathe of dust billowed in the distance, a sure sign a car was approaching. It was early December and it had been a dry winter so far, which was lucky given his current state. It would have been hard getting around on crutches if the ground was wet and muddy.

Was this Lauren? He squinted as he stood, staring as a black Mercedes pulled up the drive and parked outside the ranch house. Tanner started to hobble, hating how dependent he was on the damn crutches. After all these years, the last thing he wanted was for her to see him looking useless and hunched over, but he didn't get his cast off until the day before they were due to fly.

And there she was. Lauren stood beside the car, her long dark hair pushed over her shoulders, glossy in the sunlight and looking no different than it had been a decade ago. The difference was that back then she'd have been wearing cut-off denim shorts and a tank top, whereas now she was in jeans, boots, and a sweater. He sucked in a breath when she turned, looking around, her chin held high, face so damn beautiful. He'd almost hoped she'd look different; that she'd have somehow aged terribly and not be anything like the beautiful girl he'd been head over heels in love with. But she hadn't.

Tanner leaned on his crutch and raised his hand in an awkward wave, before making his way over to her. He went slow, wondering what the hell he was going to say to her, and not wanting to slip and fall over and make an ass of himself.

"Hey," he called out when he was close enough for her to hear him.

"Hi, Tanner," she said, her voice warm in a professional kind of way. He felt her eyes sweep over him, up then down. "Good to see you up and about."

"As opposed to lying in bed feeling sorry for myself?"

"You'd be surprised. Anyway, where can we talk?"

He was tempted to be a smart-ass and tell her they were already talking, but instead he nodded toward the house. "We can head in there. I've been staying here since I was discharged from the hospital, so here's as good a place as anywhere." He was aching to go back to his own place, a small ranch he'd bought a couple of years earlier, but it made sense to be with his family until he was back up on his feet properly. He had a ranch hand employed full-time, so he only had to lend a hand when he felt like it, but he'd become used to his own space and his own house. It was nice having his own little piece of Texas paradise to retreat to.

Lauren stood back, gesturing for him to go first. He had to grind his teeth just to do it, his Texas manners getting the better of him at the whole not-letting-a-lady-go-first thing. But then again, she might have rolled her eyes at him and told him to get over himself if he'd insisted otherwise.

"So I've gone over your latest X-rays and all your doctors' notes, plus I took the liberty of talking to your orthopedic surgeon and viewing your ultrasounds," Lauren said, talking away as if they were just two professionals having a normal conversation about his injury, not two people with one hell of a history. "I'm confident that with the right plan and a solid three weeks or more of therapy, we'll have the building blocks in place to get you back to being the well-oiled athlete you've always been. But we're going to have to take it slow, and you'll still need regular, ongoing therapy once you're home."

"Is that right?" he muttered, pausing at the solid oak door and leaning into it to open it.

"Here, let me," she said, pushing past him.

"I don't need your goddamn help with the door!" he snapped. "You might have to pussyfoot around your baseball players, but I don't need a woman to take care of me. I'm a man, not a child."

She froze, staring back at him, her dark brown eyes so wide they reminded him of a puppy's. More accurately a puppy that had just been kicked by someone it trusted.

"I'm sorry," she stammered. "I was just trying to help."

"Yeah, well, you weren't." He felt like a dick but he couldn't help it. How the hell was she just standing there, pretending like nothing had ever happened between them? She was acting like they were friendly strangers, not enemy exes.

"Tanner, if me being here makes you uncomfortable—"

"You're damn right I'm uncomfortable," he shot back. "You walk away from me what, ten, twelve years ago, without so much as a goddamn explanation, and then you just arrive here and talk to me as if nothing ever happened. I call bullshit."

She didn't say anything, but he could see the rapid pulse at her neck, recognized the vein that rose in her forehead, the way her tongue darted out to moisten her dry lips. It was funny what you could remember about a person, even after so long apart. "If you don't want me here, Tanner, I'm happy to leave," she said quietly. "I can put together a few names of great physical therapists, and you'll receive great treatment either way." She sighed. "And it's *twelve* years. Trust me, I remember."

He sucked back a breath and calmed the hell down. Why was he behaving like a child while she was managing to behave like a perfectly professional adult?

"It's fine," he muttered. "I just didn't expect to ever see you again."

She smiled, her lips faintly turning up at the corners. "I know the feeling. But I'm good at what I do, Tanner, and I will get your body working again. I've made a career of keeping athletes in top shape and rehabilitating them when they need it, so you can trust me."

He nodded. So he could trust her with his body, just not with his heart. "Follow me then."

Tanner could smell her perfume; it filled his nostrils, and teased him, following him as he limped down the hall and into the living room. He flopped onto a sofa and dropped his crutches, staring at the woman standing in the center of the room. Dammit, she was beautiful. And when she sat down across from him, leaning forward so he got more than a glimpse of her creamy chest, he had to swallow a rock in his throat.

Lauren Lewis had been a gorgeous girl, but she'd turned into a devastatingly beautiful woman and it was going to drive Tanner nuts.

Lauren sat on her hands to stop them from shaking. She'd thought that after all these years, he wouldn't still have an effect on her, but how wrong she'd been. Tanner was a man now—all grown up and then some. His eyes were still the brightest blue, and she bet his skin crinkled more at the sides now when he smiled, but she hadn't seen him crack one yet. Instead she'd seen a coolness that she didn't recognize, as well as heavily stubbled cheeks, broad shoulders, and a chest that was all kinds of filled out. She glanced up and hated the way he was considering her, his gaze still cold. This wasn't the Tanner she'd known way back when, but he was even more gorgeous now, more sinewy and masculine than she cared to admit, despite the arrogant stare.

"I thought we'd start by reviewing your latest scans together," she said, clearing her throat and reluctantly releasing her hands.

"I'm all ears," he replied, leaning back into the sofa. She didn't miss the grimace as he lifted his foot to rest it on the table.

"When do you get your cast off?" she asked softly.

"Seven days and counting."

"Where is it hurting? The ankle still or elsewhere?"

Tanner's gaze met hers this time, warmer than before. "My thigh and my hip now. It's like there's no part of me that's been spared."

She smiled. "That's what happens when you lose a fight with a bull, huh?"

He laughed, but it sounded like more of a grunt. "Yeah, something like that."

"Honestly, I don't think there's anything that we're working with here that I can't help you with," she told him, relaxing more now that she was in work mode. If she stayed focused on her job, she'd be fine—working was what she did best. "You're sore because you've got a cast on that's making you move in an abnormal way to protect your ankle. That's putting pressure on other areas, and let's not forget that there are plenty of other parts of your body that were hurt during that accident."

"Sounds like you're on the right track, doc," Tanner muttered.

"Tanner, I know things are, well, awkward between us," she said, needing to get it out in the open, not wanting to leave it unsaid, "but I'm good at what I do. I love what I do and I love healing bodies and getting athletes back to work. With you, I've got time to heal you properly, but for that I need you to trust me."

He considered her, his eyes never leaving hers. She gulped, hating the feeling of being so thoroughly under inspection.

"Trust is something that's earned," he said slowly. "It's not something you can demand."

Lauren gulped. She got it. She'd been the one person he'd trusted outside of his family, and she'd ended their relationship with no warning and never looked back. Or at least that's what it would have felt like to him. At the time she'd broken her own heart as badly as she'd obviously ripped out his, but that was all in the past. There was no point in trying to make him understand why she'd done what she'd done. She had a job to do, and right now she needed him to trust that she was capable and prepared to do whatever she needed to get him back on a bull.

"I need you to trust me professionally, Tanner," she said, keeping her voice low and steady. "I can give you references and case studies so you can believe in my work, but I don't expect this to be anything more than a professional transaction, okay?"

He nodded. "Fine. Professional it is."

She let out a low, quiet breath. "So we're still leaving in a week?"

"Yup."

They sat awkwardly, Lauren looking at her boots and then back up at Tanner, wondering how the hell they were going to spend weeks together if they couldn't even get through a fifteen-minute conversation without struggling.

"Tanner, I know it's been a long time, but I don't have a problem keeping things strictly professional between us," she said. "There's no reason we can't work together, and we can both relax while we're away, too. It'll be an amazing place for you to recover, and I've been looking forward to this vacation for a long time. Like a seriously long time."

The look on his face surprised her. It was like a combination of hate and pain twisted into one for the briefest second, before a tight smile crossed his lips. "You're right. I need therapy and from what Mia keeps telling me, you're the best in the business."

Lauren hesitated, but curiosity got the better of her. "Can I just ask you one thing? Did Mia tell you before she contacted me?"

Tanner's laugh was deep and low. "You think you'd be sitting here right now if she had?"

The burn that spread up Lauren's neck and across her cheeks must have made her skin flare bright red. Of course. Tanner had had nothing to do with all this, it had all been Mia. She should have guessed.

"Well, if you change your mind about the trip, please let me know," she said, standing up and brushing her hands down her jeans for no good reason at all. But it gave her something to do and it meant she could avoid looking at Tanner for a short moment. "I'll let myself out."

He had one crutch extended like he was about to get up, but then he set it down and watched her, his mouth set in a grim line now. She wasn't sure if it was pain, discomfort, or just displeasure about the whole situation they were in.

"You don't want to examine me?" he asked.

Lauren shook her head. "We've got plenty of time for that in Fiji once you're out of your cast." She didn't want to get that close to him, not today. She didn't want to touch him or smell him or look up into eyes that she'd once imagined spending a lifetime looking into. "See you next week."

"Yeah, next week," Tanner replied.

Lauren walked quickly away, through the door to the living room, down the hall, and out the front to her car. When she got there, shoes crunching over the gravel, she leaned against the car and took a deep breath. It caught in her lungs, catching as she tried to exhale, and she pressed her palms to the metal.

Tanner Ford. She wanted to scream, to slam her

hands against the car, to march back in there and tell him to man the hell up and stop living in the past. But the trouble was, the past had just rushed back at her as fast as an oncoming freight train, and she was suddenly a head-over-heels eighteen-year-old again, walking away from the boy she loved.

Tanner stood in the kitchen, leaning on the counter and staring outside. Being inside and not doing something on the ranch felt like torture. He was a sun-on-his-face, hands-dirty, hard-work kind of guy. He glanced down at his fingernails and cracked up laughing at how clean they were—they looked like they belonged to another man. A city slicker. This must be what his brother's hands look like.

"How you doing there, son?"

Tanner turned and found his father standing a few paces away. He smiled and shrugged. "Honestly? I'm going stir crazy. I hate being stuck inside."

"Then go outside," his dad said. "Get one of the guys to bring up a quad bike and find a way to get out of the house."

He was right. He was miserable and driving himself crazy, but if he wanted to get out, he could be. "Yeah, you're right. I just hate being a burden on anyone, you know? I don't like asking for help."

"How'd it go with the physical therapist?" Walter asked, opening the fridge and pulling out a sandwich that had been prepared and left for him. He unwrapped it and put the plate on the counter dividing the kitchen, gesturing to Tanner to share it with him. "She sure left here in one hell of a hurry. Looked like she'd seen a ghost when she stood out there at her car. I thought she was going to burst into tears, but she just jumped in and off she went."

Tanner stifled a groan and reached for half the sandwich to avoid having to answer.

"I know you're pissed with the world right now, but there's no reason to treat a lady—"

"I didn't do anything," Tanner said, mouth full as he quickly chewed and swallowed. "We have history, that's all. Unpleasant history."

"Ah, I see." His father settled onto one of the kitchen stools, but Tanner stayed on the other side, propped up by his elbow as he leaned forward to take the weight off his foot. "Anything you want to talk about, son?"

Tanner grinned. "Nope." He could have told his dad that he was probably the only person on the planet who didn't know about his history with Lauren—he'd never been that interested in his kids' social lives back then—but he kept his mouth shut.

"Well, how about we finish this sandwich and then figure out a way to get you the hell out of this house," Walter said, chuckling as he spoke. "You're like a wild animal caged in here. The sooner we break you out, the better."

Tanner nodded. "Sounds like a plan. And I'll be out of your hair soon, I promise." It had been strange living at home again—he often stayed when he came to visit because his place was a couple hours' drive away, but being back for an extended period had been weird. Although it hadn't exactly been hard having the ground-floor bedroom and adjoining bathroom in his family home, with a housekeeper preparing his meals and a nurse coming by every couple of days to check on him.

"You know, it's nice having you home. It's a strange thing having grown-up kids."

Tanner grinned. "You love *not* having us around you mean," he joked.

His father shook his head. "It gets lonely rattling around in a house like this alone, trust me. I keep telling your sister that and she teases me about all the traveling I do and how often I eat out, but when you get older, the last thing you want to do is end up sitting alone, wearing slippers and watching television every night."

Tanner leaned over and slapped his father on the shoulder, meeting his gaze. "Well, how about we have a drink tonight and play cards, like old days," he suggested. "You might be able to teach me a thing or two."

Walter winked at Tanner. "You're on, son."

Tanner was about to open his mouth again, to tell his dad he was looking forward to it, when Walter stood up and took the plate to the sink. "While we're at it, you can tell me all about your plans for after this accident. You know I could do with you working on land acquisitions with me now that you're ready to give up bull riding and get a real job. What do you say?"

Tanner froze. Anger spread whip-fast up his body and he clenched his fists and stood upright. Why the hell did his family think they could goddamn tell him what to do? What was it about earning millions as one of the best professional bull riders since Ryder King had reigned supreme were they not getting? It wasn't some pathetic childhood hobby he'd plugged away at without succeeding in his own right.

"I'm not giving up my career, Dad," he said through gritted teeth. He was open to retirement one day, to looking forward, but he sure as hell wasn't about to think about it now. Or be pushed into it.

"We'll see," Walter replied, not even bothering to turn around. "We'll see, son. One day you're going to have to step up, and that day is coming sooner than we'd both like to admit, I can feel it."

Tanner stood still as a statue, trying to calm the hell down. If he opened his mouth, he'd only say something he'd live to regret. Was his father trying to tell him something, or had he just meant that he wasn't getting any younger? Either way, he had no intention of giving up his dreams and doing what he was told. Not until he was good and ready, and on his own terms at that.

"Surprise!"

What the hell? Lauren got such a fright, she felt her heart leap into her throat. Hannah was standing there, in her freaking living room, with her best friend from college beside her and a bottle of champagne in her hand.

"What . . . I mean . . ." Lauren stammered as Hannah came toward her and took her car keys from her hand. Her sister threw an arm around her.

"Happy birthday little sis," Hannah said with a laugh, smacking a kiss to Lauren's cheek.

"Happy birthday!" Casey grinned as she closed the distance between them, giving her a big hug and a squeeze.

"I don't even know what to say. My birthday isn't until next week!" Lauren could hardly get her words together. She was stammering away like she didn't have half a brain.

"Well, it just so happens you're away then, and we

didn't want you to miss out," Hannah said, holding the champagne bottle away from her and popping the cork. It flew skyward, hitting the ceiling. "Got any glasses?"

Lauren burst out laughing and hurried into her kitchen to find three champagne glasses. She gave them a quick glance over and hoped they weren't too dusty—they hadn't been used in a very, very long time. In fact, she wasn't entirely sure they'd been used at all since she'd moved into her house two years ago.

"I can't believe you're both here," she said, grinning ear to ear as she gave one glass to Casey and held the other two out for Hannah to fill. "Where are the kids? Why didn't you tell me you were planning to visit?"

Hannah filled up Casey's glass then set the bottle down. "I have fourteen hours of being child free. I seriously need to make the most of this. And sweetheart, it's not like you turn thirty every day, is it? And don't forget that *you're* the one who chose to disappear to *Fiji* for the big day."

Lauren gulped. *Thirty.* It was a scary number, the end of her twenties and the start of . . .

"Happy thirtieth!" Casey said, clinking their glasses.

"Happy birthday to the best little sister in the world," Hannah added.

Lauren happily touched her glass to theirs and took a sip. The bubbles tickled over her tongue and slid down her throat, and she took another sip before shaking her head at her sister.

"I can't believe you managed to keep this to yourself. It's a great surprise."

"Come on, you can get ready while we drink and chat," Hannah told her. "We have dinner reservations at eight, and I want to make the most of being able to sit in a bar and have a drink without worrying about getting home to a babysitter."

Lauren looked down at her jeans and T-shirt. She definitely needed to change. Her sister was wearing jeans with a pretty, floaty top underneath a jacket, and stilettos. Casey was in a dress and heels. Lauren was definitely the weak link, but then they'd dressed for going out and she'd just been with . . . *Tanner*. She pushed him out of her thoughts, refusing to think about the gorgeous cowboy and focus on her little party.

Her sister was right, it wasn't every day you got to celebrate turning thirty. It was one of the reasons she'd decided to splurge on a big vacation.

"We took the liberty of looking through your wardrobe while we were waiting for you," Hannah said. "You've got a lot of"—Lauren watched as her sister raised her eyebrows and exchanged glances with Casey—"*comfortable*-looking clothes."

Lauren burst out laughing. "I need to be comfortable for work!" she defended herself. "I don't exactly get out a lot unless it's work related."

Casey reached for the bottle and topped up their glasses, and Lauren was getting the feeling that it was going to be a very, very big night out.

"Well, it turns out you've got a very sexy little silk camisole in your wardrobe. We've decided on that with your skinny jeans and the only pair of super high heels we could find." They both laughed and Lauren felt her cheeks burn. "You seriously need to go shopping. It's embarrassing just looking at what you wear."

Lauren took a big gulp of her drink. She knew the cami—she'd bought it to wear on a hot date when she'd been set up earlier in the year, but something had come up with work and she'd never gotten around to going. It was also silky with lace around it, more like something she imagined sexier girls than her probably wore to bed, which meant she'd probably have chickened out of wearing it even if her date hadn't been cancelled.

"I don't know . . ." she started.

"You're wearing it," Hannah said firmly. "And while you're at it, we want all the details on Tanner Ford, don't we, Case?"

Casey and Hannah clinked glasses and laughed, and Lauren wished the carpet would open up and swallow her whole. She took a sip of champagne, then gulped down another.

"So?" Casey asked. "This is the guy you broke up with just before college started, right? The one you dated all through high school?"

She nodded. "Yup, that's the one." She'd met Casey at college, so she'd only heard about Tanner—she hadn't been there through the whole drama.

Lauren headed for her bedroom but they followed her, and she sighed when she saw the camisole, jeans, and heels on the bed, waiting for her. They'd clearly been busy while she was out. Her cheeks ignited when she saw the lacy underwear on her bedside table, in a tiny, open black box.

"We brought you a little birthday present," Hannah said. "Just in case you get lucky tonight."

"Or with the sexy cowboy in Fiji," Casey added with a giggle.

Lauren reluctantly moved closer to the open box and picked up the lacy, barely there bra and then the panties.

If they could even be called that. The scrap of black lace was a G-string, and it barely looked wearable.

"Oh my god," she whispered.

"We'll leave you to get ready," Hannah said. "Then we want to know everything about Tanner *McSexy* Ford."

Chapter 3

One Week Later

LAUREN stared out the tinted windows of the car that had been sent to get her, as they drove slowly toward the private jet waiting on the tarmac. There was another car parked close to it, the brake lights on, indicating to her that it might have just pulled up. She'd been booked to fly coach on the long-haul flight, but as soon as Mia Ford had been in contact, her journey had been upgraded every step of the way.

She gulped. Part of her had thought it would never really happen, that she would never end up on a private jet with Tanner heading to a tropical island. She'd expected him to cancel, which would mean she could legitimately say she'd behaved professionally and he hadn't, and she'd simply go back to having the holiday she'd planned all along. Instead, his family's private plane was all fueled up and waiting for its two passengers, and there was no getting out of what she'd agreed to now.

When the car stopped and her driver smiled at her in the rearview mirror, she smiled back, gripping the door handle before finally pushing it open. She knew the drill. The driver would usually open the door and pass her bags to her, but today she couldn't wait. She needed to gulp in the fresh air and fill her lungs for a moment. This was the kind of thing she did often, traveling with the team and being ferried around in nice cars and private jets. Only the jet was usually filled with the entire team and some of the support crew, not with a single handsome cowboy who was driving her crazy just thinking about him.

Lauren fixed her smile and put on her game face. *I am a professional. I am great at my job. I can do this.* She'd landed one of the most coveted jobs in her industry as physical therapist for the Texas Rangers—she needed to hold her head high and treat Tanner the same way she'd treat any of the players she worked on.

Shit. There he was.

The door of the other car opened and she watched as Tanner stepped out. His cast was gone and she saw big boots, tapered jeans, and a plaid shirt with the sleeves rolled up. Followed by big shoulders, brown hair that was just a touch too long, and when he turned, eyes that made every part of her turn to liquid.

"Hey," he called out, eyes traveling up and down her body, making her blush. Her cheeks ignited and she was certain even her scalp was flaming red in response. Her only saving grace was that he might not be close enough to notice.

"Morning," she said, pleased that her voice sounded clear. She'd expected her greeting to sound as shaky as she felt.

"Your luggage," a voice from behind said.

Lauren turned and took the suitcase on wheels from the driver along with her smaller duffel bag. "Thanks."

She stood and waited as Tanner opened the trunk of his car himself, waving the driver away. He was limping slightly, still favoring his bad leg, and even though it was only natural, she could see that he was trying hard to stay upright and not show it. His shoulders were straight and his back was even straighter as he turned, suitcase on the ground.

"Ready?"

Lauren nodded. "Ready."

She wheeled her suitcase to the stairs that lead up to the door, and when a pretty young woman dressed in uniform appeared and waved at the top of the stairs, the lump in Lauren's throat slowly disappeared. She was going to be fine. This was just a work trip, nothing more, nothing less. This was no different than the trips she took with her team, only on this one she would have a whole lot of time for herself.

"Leave your bags there and I'll take care of them," the attendant called out politely.

Lauren left her case on the tarmac but carried her duffel bag with her. She had her Kindle in there, and her phone, and other bits and pieces she might want on the flight.

"Welcome, Ms. Lewis," the attendant said, her smile warm as she touched her arm and gestured inside the plane. "It's a pleasure to have you flying with us today."

She smiled her thanks and chose a seat, putting her bag down and then dropping into the big, cream-leather chair. Flying coach would be awful now that she was used to private jets. She stifled a laugh. She got how stupid that sounded and would never say it out loud, because she wasn't the type to ever have the chance to fly private if it wasn't for work. Her sister would smack her around the back of her head if she ever confessed her thoughts to her, and she'd deserve it.

Tanner was on board now, she could feel his presence even though she was looking out the window. His body moved past her and she heard him settle into the seat across from her. She took a breath and turned her head, saw that he'd extended his left leg out straight, the denim stretched tight across his thigh.

"Not sure if you were sent an itinerary, but we've got a one-hour layover in Hawaii to refuel," Tanner said, his eyes meeting hers briefly before looking away. "We'll be in here for the better part of fourteen hours."

"Hope you've got a good book," she mumbled, not sure what else to say.

"I'm more of a movie man myself."

Her face went red again. She should have known that. When they were at school she was always trying to get him to study more, but he was more interested in kicking back and watching *her* study, his slow smile teasing her whenever she looked up at him. And when they had a night alone, they'd always start out watching a movie, before Tanner would make a move and they'd end up making out on the sofa. Or his bed.

The door closed and the engine noise increased. Lauren looked up when the attendant reappeared, holding a silver tray with two glasses of champagne perched on top.

"Would either of you care for a drink?"

Lauren eyed the bubbles, knowing she should decline and ask for an orange juice instead, but right now she was tempted to say yes. *To hell with it.* She nodded and extended her hand. "Thank you," she said, holding the stem of the tall glass and watching as Tanner shook his head and asked for a beer instead. She never usually drank when she was on the clock, but right now she needed something to settle her nerves. Besides, it reminded her of the fun night she'd had on Friday with her sister and Casey, and she'd made it clear to Mia that she'd work on Tanner *during* her vacation. She was technically on holiday whenever she wasn't engaged in Tanner's rehabilitation.

Happy birthday to me, she thought, raising her glass and taking a sip. The bubbles were cool and delicious on her tongue, and she sighed as she closed her eyes for a moment and leaned back in her seat. Today was the day she turned thirty, so if she didn't deserve a drink now, then when?

She was on a private jet about to fly to one of the world's most beautiful countries. There was going to be white sand and vivid blue ocean greeting her every day, the sun was going to be on her shoulders as she worked, and she was going to come back feeling amazing.

Lauren glanced at the hulking cowboy drinking his beer across from her and took another sip of champagne. She just had to stop feeling like a teenager again in his presence and show him the woman she'd grown into. Why was it that merely being near him was making her feel like a girl? She listened to him thank the attendant for his drink when she returned, and politely tell her that they'd ask if they needed anything, so she was welcome to relax during the flight.

Typical. He could be the world's biggest idiot and behave recklessly over and over again, but he was unfailingly polite and never acted like he came from wealth the size of Texas.

It was one of the things she'd always loved about him. *And still did.*

Tanner slowly swallowed his beer and stretched out his ankle. If he was honest, it hurt like hell when he flexed it, and it was the one reason he was trying so damn hard to be polite to Lauren. He needed her help, more than he wanted to admit, and when he'd asked around over the past week, everyone had sung her praises. Then when his cast had come off, he'd known there was no way he could cancel their trip. He needed her.

The truth was, he was desperate to get back on a bull. He missed the adrenaline, missed being on the circuit, and his greatest fear was that when the season started again, he'd be sitting on the sidelines—and that was *not* a place he wanted to be.

"I requested your latest ankle scans this morning," Lauren said, her soft voice jolting him from his thoughts.

"What did you think?"

She smiled when she eventually looked at him, and he liked it. He'd hated her for so many years—or more correctly hated what she'd done to him and how she'd made him feel—but looking into her eyes and seeing her warm smile, it made it damn hard to hate her now.

"I think you have more soft tissue damage and ligament issues than I'd hoped for, but it's only to be expected." She chuckled. "I'm used to plenty of soft tissue problems, just not ones that occur from crushing. None of my players have come into contact with a fifteen-hundred-pound opponent, thank goodness."

Tanner cracked up and took another pull of his beer.

"I've been damn lucky to go this long with so few injuries. Guess my lucky streak couldn't go on forever."

"Anything else that's been niggling you? Any other pain that you've been putting up with since before the accident?" she asked. "Aside from the general aches and pains we discussed the other day?"

Tanner looked down at his wrist and gripped the beer bottle a little tighter, feeling the pinch of pain that he'd become used to living with. He couldn't pretend that it wasn't a big problem, because it was.

"My wrist," he admitted. "I hurt it damn bad that day, but before then the joint had felt, well, a bit sticky I guess. It just never felt quite right and it still doesn't."

"Hmm," she made a low mumbling sound in her throat. "I know this sounds crazy, but you don't have any footage of you riding, do you? It'd actually help me if I could see the way you hold yourself and get a better understanding of your sport. I like to visualize what I'm trying to achieve for my clients so I can see where they want to be, what they need to be doing."

He raised a brow. "You're serious?"

She nodded. "Deadly. Is that a problem?"

Tanner shrugged. "No problem." He put his beer down on the table and opened up the small bag beside him, pulling out an iPad. "You want to see the fall, too?"

He heard her sharp inhale and it surprised him. Did she not want to watch the moment he got hurt? He'd seen it and it was brutal—there was no sugarcoating that the accident could easily have killed him—but surely it was something she needed to see?

"Yeah," she murmured. "Please."

Tanner clicked on the video clip and passed it over to her, extending his arm out. When her fingers closed over the device, her eyes darted upward and met his and he couldn't help staring at her. How was she so damn beautiful? How had she managed to get better looking with age? Her skin was creamy, a result of the winter weather and her probably not getting outside as much as he did on a daily basis, but he knew that after a few days in Fiji she'd be lightly golden and tanning darker. Years ago they'd spent hours horseback riding under the sun, lying in grassy fields on long summer days, and her legs had been tanned as dark as his arms. She'd always be in cut-off shorts, even out riding, and he still remembered the feel of her soft skin beneath his fingertips.

Tanner sucked in a breath and let go, pushing back into his chair and looking away. He reached for his beer and drained half the bottle.

Lauren was out of bounds. She'd broken his heart once and he was never, ever going to let her or anyone else do that to him ever again.

He shut his eyes as the video started, knowing which one it was. She was watching him take the title the year previous, the crowd erupting into cheers as he rode to victory in Las Vegas. The year before he'd placed second, but that was his year, the day he'd beaten out every other competitor and taken home the biggest prize. He finished his beer as that video ended and another started. He counted down, waited for it, that moment when the crowd went silent. When everything changed. This video was the one that gave him nightmares.

Thump. He could feel himself hitting the ground all over again, his back making contact with the hard surface. *Crunch*—his ankle making that sickening sound. *Rip*—his skin tearing open as the horn of the bull had slipped straight through him.

The inside of the jet went silent then and he listened to Lauren put the iPad down. The jet fired to life then and started down the runway, and Tanner shut his eyes again, refusing to look over at Lauren even though he could feel her watching him.

"You having nightmares about this?" she asked in a low voice as she glanced over at him.

He could have lied and said no, but it wasn't like he was trying to impress her. "Yeah, you could say that."

"And does it put you off getting back out there?" she asked. "Because I'm guessing, and please tell me if I'm wrong, that the reason I'm here is to get you back up on a bull again?"

He nodded. "Right again." He paused, looked at her, and tried to read the expression on her face. "You going to give me a lecture about how I should give up and do something safer?"

Lauren held up her hands. "Hey, I'm not your girlfriend and I'm not your mother. You want to make a living climbing onto a bull and having your teeth rattled out of your head? Go for it. This is all about you, Tanner. That's why I'm here."

His girlfriend. He winced and finished his beer. "So, talking about being my girlfriend, what have you been doing this past decade? Aside from landing a job in pro sports?" He should have changed the subject, but she was the one who'd brought it up.

"Tanner, look," she said as he watched her slim fingers clench around the stem of her champagne flute. "What I did to you, the way I ended things, I've always regretted how it happened. I think we need to get all that out in the air now instead of letting it fester anymore."

He shook his head. "Seriously? You think now is the time to take a walk down memory lane?"

Her sigh was loud, and she shook her head. "Maybe we should get everything out now so we don't have to deal with it again."

Tanner grunted. "Look, far as I can see, you decided I wasn't good enough for you or something better came up and you ran for the hills. Some warning would have been nice, but hey, we were teenagers. I don't know why I expected any different, but I did."

The look she gave him was pain mixed with shock. Maybe he'd overstepped.

"You know what, how about we start with what you've been up to since college," he said, when a minute later she was still silent. "That might keep things a little more civil."

Her stare was cool now, and when her eyebrows arched high and her eyes narrowed, he knew he'd struck a nerve. "You want to know what I did after college?"

"Sure. Seems like as good a place as any to start." Tanner stared down at his bottle and wished he hadn't drunk it so fast. The attendant wouldn't be able to get him a new one until they'd finished their ascent, so he should have made it last. "While I was starting out on bulls and trying to heal my broken heart, how were you doing?"

Her laugh was low, and he watched as she sat back and drained her champagne glass until there wasn't a drop left. "You know what, Tanner? I put on my big girl panties, I worked hard, and I never looked back."

Chapter 4

LAUREN dug her nails hard into her palm as she fisted her hand. Dammit! Why did she have to let him get to her like that? And why had she snapped back such a snarky reply?

"Maybe we should find a new subject then," Tanner said, his voice softer than she'd expected. "I know I was a jerk the other day, but right now I'm actually just trying to make conversation."

She took a deep breath, eyes shut, before facing him. "Yeah, I know. I don't know where that came from."

His laugh took her by surprise. "It was pretty darn funny though, I'll give you that. I'm guessing those kind of pithy statements are how you manage to hold your own with a team of jocks."

The atmosphere in the plane changed as quickly as it had soured. "You really think it was pithy?"

He grinned. "Don't go getting a big head, but yeah, maybe I did. Now what do you say about another drink?"

"I'd say it'll be my last, otherwise I'll be drunk and

then hungover all on the same flight, and that wouldn't be pretty."

Lauren pushed her shoulders down and wondered what the warm, slow feeling spreading through her was. She stared out the window into fluffy white clouds, already imaging how good her second glass of champagne would make her feel.

Relaxed. That's what the unusual feeling was. She was relaxed! She would have laughed out loud if Tanner hadn't been seated so close, but she didn't want to have to explain herself. Instead she just smiled to herself and enjoyed the feeling as the clouds drifted by.

"Ms. Lewis? Would you like another glass?"

She turned when she heard her name and gratefully held out her glass. "Absolutely."

Lauren took a little sip, wanting to take this one slow. It was easy to drink fast instead of trying to make conversation, but she wasn't going to fall into that trap again.

"So tell me how it all happened. I'd actually like to know how you ended up with the Rangers."

She settled back, deciding not to make direct eye contact with him again. What was it about this man that affected her still, after so many years? But she knew what it was: She'd never wanted to end things in the first place, and part of her had always wondered *what if.* What if they'd stayed together? What if she'd turned her back on her family instead of her boyfriend? What if she'd told him the truth about why she'd had to call it off? She wasn't unhappy with how her life had turned out. She'd landed her dream job and she'd worked hard for everything she'd achieved, but there would always be that little niggle, wondering what could have been.

"I suppose my college years were fairly uneventful," she said, smiling as she remembered Casey dragging her to parties and insisting she wasn't allowed to stay in their dorm room on her own on weekends. To start with, it had taken all her willpower not to call Tanner, to beg his forgiveness and apologize for what she'd done. Then she'd look around and remember why college was so important to her, why she wanted to have control of her future and do the work she'd always imagined herself doing. She'd never wanted to have to rely on a man, she'd wanted to create her own future and her own financial independence, and nothing had changed. "I wasn't exactly the life of the party there, but I knuckled down and worked hard. When I graduated, I started working in the sports medicine industry, at a private practice, and eventually I had the chance of a lifetime."

His chuckle made her pause and she chanced a quick peek at him, diverting her eyes the moment she saw his were trained on her face.

"Let me guess, you charmed your way in there?"

Lauren bristled. She hated anyone thinking that she used her looks or charm or anything else "female" to get where she'd gotten to. "You know, I've never had to charm anyone," she said, taking a sip of bubbly and refusing to give him a reaction. "My work speaks for itself and it always has."

"Hey, no offense," he said, holding up a hand. "You're a beautiful woman working in a man's world, that's all. I bet you charmed the hell out of them without even realizing."

"You really want to know what I did?" she asked, not giving him the opportunity to say anything else. "I found out their therapist was retiring at the end of the season, and I gave up my job and worked for them for free so I could learn from the best and prove myself. I had to live off my savings and move into a tiny place that I could barely afford, but I was determined to land the top job."

"Sounds like the girl I used to know. You never did change your mind once you'd decided on something."

Like them breaking up. They were the words that hung unsaid between them. But he was right, that was something about her that definitely hadn't changed.

"When the season finished, I was sweating big time. I didn't know if I'd done enough to impress them or if they were interviewing other candidates, and I was down to my last few hundred dollars. There was no way I could keep paying my rent, and I was terrified I was going to have to tell my parents I was back bartending. I mean, it was fine when I was at college working part-time slinging beers at night, but their little girl all grown up and graduated working a bar would have killed them. They didn't put aside all their savings for me to get a Doctor of Physical Therapy degree and then walk away from a paying job in the first place!"

Tanner's laugh echoed around them, warmed her like a cashmere sweater being wrapped around her shoulders. How could he still do that to her? How could the soft, deep timbre of his laugh take her back years, reminding her of being in his arms and listening to that same laugh with her cheek pressed to his chest?

"But you got the job," he said.

"Yeah, I got the job. Turns out they were just letting me sweat, but the players had all gotten together and requested me. I was able to make my rent check, and soon after I was able to put a down payment on my own place." She smiled, thinking how much life had changed, and how proud she'd been inviting her parents over to see the house she'd brought with no help from anyone. "I've been with them for two years now and my contract has been renewed."

"You did good, Lol. I'm proud of you."

She froze. The warm feeling that had engulfed her had fallen away, replaced by a shudder of goose bumps that coursed rapidly across her skin. She hadn't heard a man use that nickname since ... *since Tanner.* Her sister was the only other person who ever called her that, and it had been years since she'd heard it even from her. It was a silly name that Tanner had started, because everyone always joked that she was always laughing out loud.

"It was an uphill battle for a while there, but life's good now. I'm happy, the work is rewarding, and I don't have a lot of downtime so it pays to enjoy my work."

They sat in silence awhile as Lauren sipped her drink. The seat was so comfortable and she tucked her legs up beneath her as she went back to staring out the window. She'd never been to a tropical island, and Fiji sounded like heaven. The only part of the equation she didn't like was not knowing what she was going to say to Tanner for the next three weeks.

"So while you were being a nerd studying at college, I was pretty busy too," Tanner told her. She listened but she didn't look. "I studied, my dad wouldn't have it any other way and I agreed with him, but I only lasted long enough at Baylor University to get my undergrad degree, and even then it took me forever to get it. I rode bulls between semesters, and eventually I took up riding full-time." He laughed. "I've secretly always wanted to do an MBA, maybe once I've retired, but it'll probably never happen."

Lauren was pleased she wasn't watching him, because then he'd have seen the surprise written all over her face. He'd impressed her, but then wasn't that why he was telling her? Or maybe he just wanted to make it clear that he hadn't been moping around with a broken heart.

"You'd probably be the only rider on the circuit with an MBA if you did it," she said. "You could do it online."

"Haha, I probably would be. It's not something I ever bothered to ask when we were shooting the breeze, waiting to climb aboard some asshole of a bull." He sat back as she watched him. "Maybe I *should* look at doing it online—it'd be easier than having to turn up on campus somewhere. I'll think about it."

Lauren stroked her fingers up and down the stem of the glass. How were they just doing this? Suddenly talking like old friends catching up when earlier there had been such an overwhelming sense of animosity? And if talking to him was like this, what was it going to be like touching him? She was going to have to put her hands on him, she was going to have to breathe in the air around him and place her skin against his.

"Dammit," he softly swore, his mutter commanding her attention.

"What is it?" she asked, pushing her glass away and turning in her seat. She could see the pain etched on his face, even though he was clearly trying not to let it show. She was used to men trying to be tough guys, and she was just as used to seeing right through any façade they tried to put up.

"Nothin'. I just—" He sucked back a breath. "Mother

f—." Tanner glanced at her, not finishing his curse. "I'm fine."

She stifled her laugh. It was cute he'd stopped himself from swearing around her, and she remembered how polite and charming he'd always been. A true Southern gentleman, even when he'd been sneaking into her room late at night or roaring off down the road on his motorcycle with her hanging on from behind.

"Let me help," she said, getting up from her seat. She held onto the armrest for a moment, the champagne hitting her faster than she'd expected it to. *No more drinks for you, missy.*

"No, just sit down," he ordered. "It'll pass."

She watched as Tanner stretched his leg out, wincing as he shifted his weight.

"Where does it hurt?" she asked, taking the step to his chair and dropping to her knees. She watched his face and saw him hiss in a breath of air as he lengthened his leg.

"Just sitting here, it's . . ." He shook his head. "I don't know. Maybe it's being stiff because I'm not moving here but, hell, nothing feels right. Shouldn't I be feeling better than this after being in a cast?"

She shrugged. "Honestly, I don't know that you *should* be feeling better yet. You've just had your cast off and you've been through one hell of a trauma, and all that's happened is that the *bone* has healed, not everything around it." She dropped to her knees and touched her hand to his leg, glancing up at him to catch his eye before she went any further. "May I?"

He grunted and she took that as a yes. Lauren pressed more firmly, the softness of the worn denim at odds with the tight, solid muscle beneath it. His calf was bunched up, and she knew that the only bit of relief she could give him now was a massage of sorts. She leaned in, head bent as she ran her fingers up and down his leg, pushing into his muscles to try to help him, even though what she really needed was to be touching skin not denim.

Lauren startled when he exhaled, the noise taking her by surprise, and when she looked up at him, her eyes fixed on his, she saw so much there. The pain of what they'd once had, longing and dammit, she'd be lying if she didn't see desire matched by the heat coursing the length of her own body right now.

"Lauren . . ."

"Oh, I'm so sorry!"

Lauren's head snapped up, her skin ignited as if she'd been set on fire. The poor attendant was standing there, face as red as Lauren's felt, backing up so she could disappear into where she'd just emerged from. She looked at Tanner, at her hand on his leg, at the way she was bent forward . . .

"I'm a physical therapist," she choked out. "I . . ."

"It's none of my business. Excuse me," the attendant said. "Please let me know if there's anything you need."

Lauren pushed up, palm to Tanner's leg.

"Shit, you trying to hurt me or heal me?" he muttered.

She quickly pulled her hand back, wrapping both arms around herself. "She thought I was giving you a *blow job*," she whispered. "Oh my god, she thought I was . . . shit! What if she knows someone from my team? What if . . ."

Tanner looked amused. A smile played across his lips as she glowered at him.

"If you'd spent your entire career trying to prove to

everyone around you that you were beyond professional in your role, you'd be pissed too," she fumed. "You have no idea how hard I've had to work to get the trust of the players' wives and girlfriends!"

"Hey, I wasn't the one who told you to drop to your knees, sweetheart."

She opened her mouth to say something back but bit down on her lip instead. *Asshole.* Just when she'd been wondering if walking away from Tanner all those years ago had been a mistake, he went and acted like a total jerk.

Lauren sat back in her seat, downed the last of her champagne, and pulled out her headphones and iPad. It was going to be a long flight, and she intended on watching a movie or two and not looking up until they'd landed.

She certainly wasn't going to give Tanner the satisfaction of showing him how much he'd hurt her. Not now, not ever.

Tanner looked up from his device and watched Lauren. She'd been ignoring him for almost two hours, and he was starting to realize just how much his joking around had hurt her. The attendant had been brave enough to come back out, offering Lauren a cashmere blanket and bringing her bottled water, but other than seeing her shy smile and watching her mouth move as she'd spoken to the attendant, that was it. She hadn't looked at him, hadn't spoken to him, and she sure as hell hadn't smiled at him.

The girl he'd known way back when had liked to joke around and hadn't stopped laughing. She'd spent more time with her lips stretched wide into a smile, head back, laughing the hell out of whatever dumb thing he said. Her eyes had danced when she'd spoken, lighting up whenever she was happy. But Lauren was every inch a woman now, no longer just a fun-loving girl, and from her reaction before? One who had worked her tail feathers off to get where she was today. And defying others' expectations and walking your own path were two things that Tanner respected.

He tried to stretch his leg out but his ankle was stuck and everything felt rigid. He needed Lauren's help, and he needed it badly. Her nightmare might be someone thinking she wasn't behaving in a professional manner toward one of her clients, but his was never climbing aboard a bull again. And right now she was the one thing standing between his retirement and his comeback.

I'm sorry. They were the words he needed to say. He just had to find a way to actually get them off his chest, which wouldn't have been so hard if they weren't the two words he'd been waiting twelve years for her to say to him.

"Mr. Ford, would you like me to serve lunch now?"

He looked up into the warm, pretty-as-a-picture blue eyes of the attendant, but suddenly all the pretty blue eyes in the world didn't appeal to him. The only eyes he wanted up close and looking back into his were a different color.

"Thanks, that'd be great," he said.

"I have turkey and Swiss cheese sandwiches, or I can fix you something different," she said, her smile fixed as she spoke. "We are well stocked with fresh fruit, cheese and crackers—"

"The sandwich is fine," he interrupted. "And an OJ please."

She nodded and then moved on to Lauren. His view was obscured, but he watched the way Lauren looked up, the polite way she said thank you and enquired about the attendant's plans for Christmas.

Lauren was familiar enough to make him yearn for what they'd had in the past, yet at the same time she was a complete stranger. He just wasn't sure whether he wanted to keep things that way, or whether he wanted to know every damn thing there was to know about the woman who'd made him shut off his heart to the world from the day she'd walked away.

It's not you, it's me," Lauren said, arms wrapped tightly around herself as she pulled her shoulders forward, hunched over, stomach concaved. "We're too young, Tanner, and I'm off to college. Everything's changing."

He stared at her, feeling like he'd been sucker punched. "What?"

One minute they'd been making out, her back against the wall, one leg curled around his butt as he pushed hard up against her. He was still catching his breath from kissing her, from having her body warm to his and her fingers clenched in his hair. And now she was breaking up with him?

"Where the hell did this come from? Did your parents put you up to this?"

She shook her head, but he watched the way she sucked in her lower lip, catching it beneath her teeth as she stumbled backwards.

"Tanner, it's for the best. We've been way too serious and we're too young."

He clenched his fists. They were Tan and Lol. They were supposed to stay together, they were going to be the couple who kept it together no matter what. "Lauren, come on. You're not thinking straight. What the hell is up with you?"

She moved back toward him and pressed her hands to his chest, leaning in. Her mouth touched his, warm and soft, as tears fell to her mouth, salty as he kissed her back.

"Goodbye, Tanner," she said, stepping away so he could see her tear-stained cheeks before she turned and ran.

He'd stood there, waiting for her to come back, to tell him it was some kind of sick joke. But Lauren had never come back, and no matter how many times he'd slammed his fist into the wall, the pain in his knuckles never caught up to the aching, grinding pain in his chest that almost split him in half.

Chapter 5

LAUREN shut her eyes and dug her fingers into the leather armrests as the jet landed on the tarmac. She never got particularly nervous flying, but there was something about the descent that always made her stomach flip a little. When she opened her eyes, she knew it was time to put on her game face—and those big girl panties she'd talked about before.

"Now *that* was a long flight," Tanner said with a groan.

She slowly released her fingers and wiggled them, stretching out her legs and flexing her feet at the same time. "Yeah, you can say that again."

Trying to ignore Tanner and keep herself occupied for so long had felt like the most tedious task she'd ever faced, but she wasn't about to confess that to him. She reached for her bag, put her Kindle, iPad, and ear buds into it, and took out her makeup. She hastily glanced in the little mirror, dabbing some concealer beneath her eyes, dusting bronzer over her cheeks and then dabbing on some lip gloss. Her eyes were red and she was ready to find her bed and sleep off the jet lag for at least ten hours.

"We'll be ready to disembark shortly," the attendant informed them, appearing from behind the privacy curtain. "Don't forget to take some bottles of water with you. The humidity here is insane."

Lauren took the half-empty water bottle, opened the lid, and guzzled it down. She knew better than to get dehydrated leaving a plane—it was one of the key things she always reminded the players to help keep their bodies in good shape. Water, water, and more water.

She looked out the window one last time, then stood. She was about to turn, about to look at Tanner and swallow the lump in her throat and say something, when his hand closed around her wrist.

Lauren looked down at his skin against hers and fought the urge to rip her arm away.

"I'm sorry about before," he said, his voice gruff.

"It's fine."

"No, it's not fine. If it was fine, we wouldn't have spent the last fifteen hours in silence."

He had her there. "How about we agree to forget about the plane ride?" she suggested. "New country, fresh start."

His deep chuckle sent a trill down her spine as his fingers left her wrist. "How about I request a different attendant for the flight home, huh?"

They both laughed, although Lauren knew her cheeks were pink. She'd always been the straitlaced one and Tanner had been the daredevil—it was why her parents had found their relationship so hard to deal with. He might have grown up and mellowed out a lot, but underneath the stubble and the more weathered appearance she knew he was still the same risk-taking, fun-loving boy he'd always been.

"Come on, help a guy out of his seat, would you?"

Lauren held out a hand and helped haul Tanner up. She had to clasp her other hand over his arm as she pulled him up, and given how much effort she had to put into it, she knew how stiff and sore he must be.

"This Fiji weather better help my aching bones," he muttered.

Lauren's breath caught in her throat as he looked down at her. *One step.* One step was all it would take to have his body rammed hard against hers, her fingers clenched in his hair, her lips dancing with his.

He cleared his throat and she took a step back.

The trouble was that she didn't sleep with clients. She didn't kiss clients. She didn't even joke around inappropriately with clients. Which meant that Tanner Ford was more than off-limits—he was forbidden.

Tanner raised an eyebrow, looking down at her, like he was waiting for her to do something or say something.

"You ready for some tropical sunshine, Lol?"

"How about you stop calling me Lol?" she replied. "In case you hadn't noticed, I'm a grown-ass woman now."

"Oh, I've noticed." Tanner laughed. "How about you stop staring at my mouth and just hurry up and kiss me?"

Lauren's skin burned hot and she glared at Tanner, opening her mouth to say something smart back. Only words failed her. She balled her fist, aching to open her palm and slap him straight across the cheek as punishment, but she didn't. She wasn't a little girl lashing out, she was a woman who wanted respect—and it looked like she was going to have to earn it.

"Come on, sweetheart, let's go," Tanner said, grinning like he'd never said anything in the first place.

Tanner let Lauren go first, not wanting her to see what a struggle it would be for him to go down the stairs. As sore and stiff as he'd been before the flight, he felt like an old man now, his joints so tight and sticky he could hardly make his leg do what he expected of it.

He felt the thick, humid air as he walked off the jet, and by the time his feet hit the ground he wished he'd worn flip-flops instead of boots. What kind of idiot wears boots to arrive in Fiji anyway? He pushed up his shirtsleeves a little more, then locked eyes with a big man, easily as tall as him, with the widest smile he'd ever encountered.

"*Bula!*" the man announced. "*Bula!* Welcome to Nadi!"

Tanner grinned back at him. "*Bula,*" he replied, bending his head to allow some sort of shell necklace to be placed around his neck as he said hello. He looked over at Lauren, waiting for him, hand raised to shield her face from the sun. She was wearing the same necklace as him, and there was a Fijian man standing beside her, too, happily chatting away like they were old friends. How the hell could she chat so easily to a stranger, yet when *they* talked it was either painfully hard or they ended up rubbing each other up the wrong way.

"Come, Mr. Ford. Come with me," his man said.

Tanner waved to Lauren and she joined him. There was a golf cart waiting to take them to the terminal, and he raised his eyebrows at Lauren.

"You told them I was a cripple?" he asked.

She shook her head. "Not me. But see over there?"

He looked and noticed some more men getting around in the same type of vehicle.

"I wouldn't take it so personally, I think it's a popular way of transport here."

Tanner sat back, one arm stretched out behind Lauren. She might have won that round, but the way she was all fluttery beside him the second his arm brushed her back? He definitely took points for that.

They were processed at customs and then escorted to a helicopter. The sleek, black machine was all prepped and ready to go, the rotors already whipping around.

"Enjoy your stay in Fiji!"

Tanner's gaze passed over Lauren and settled on the man speaking to him. His smile was wide, his face glowing with perspiration as he leaned forward from the driver's seat. As the other man was collecting their bags from the back and running them over to the chopper, Tanner realized how much he hated that someone else had to carry his luggage for him. Any other day, any other time, he'd have never let someone heft his bags.

"Do you have a family?" Tanner asked, speaking louder against the aviation noise.

"Five children," the man said proudly. "Four girls and a son."

Tanner took out his wallet from his back pocket, awkwardly leaning forward and trying not to put too much weight on his leg. "And your colleague over there? He has children too?"

"Oh yes. He has just had his first baby. A boy."

Tanner took out some hundred-dollar bills and passed

half over to tip him. "Something for your family. Sorry it's American currency."

The man's face rose, then fell. "I can't take so much. No sir . . ."

"Do something nice for your kids, it's fine." Tanner pushed up and got out, holding out his hand for Lauren. She didn't take it, getting out the opposite side and walking around.

"Congratulations on your new baby," he told the other man, holding out his hand and then pressing the rest of the bills into his palm.

"Oh, *vinaka! Vinaka!*" he said, thanking him in the local language.

Tanner grinned and held up his hand, taking his sunglasses from where he'd hooked them over his front pocket and pushing them on. He stood back as Lauren ducked her head low and hurried to the helicopter, then did the same and climbed aboard beside her. His thigh brushed hers and neither did anything to stop it.

"That was really kind of you," she said, leaning in a little.

He could smell her perfume, her shampoo, the lovely scent of her that was doing its best to tease him.

"It's nice to help out," he said. And it was. Generous tipping was an easy way for him to help others and he did it whenever he could. "For all I know they're probably paid a few dollars an hour in their local currency. I'm sure it's damn hard to feed kids and keep a roof over their heads, so me giving them a few hundred dollars each means a lot to them and doesn't dent my pocket. It's a win-win situation."

Her eyes were warm now, the grit from earlier nowhere to be seen. "Well, it was a nice thing to do."

While Tanner hadn't done it to impress her, seeing the change in the way she was looking at him wasn't half bad. "There's not much point being wealthy if you can't give others a hand up." His mother had instilled that in all of them when they were kids. They'd had a swear jar at home when he was younger, and it had been emptied and given to charity regularly. His mother had also made them take twenty percent of their pocket money as a "tax" and put it away. They were allowed to choose their own charities to be recipients of their tax money, or even give it to specific homeless people, so long as they gave it to someone in need.

He smiled to himself as he thought about that damn jar. His mom had died when he was only a teenager, but if she hadn't passed away, she'd have a swear jar full every few days from him and Cody alone. They'd watched their language around her, but once she was gone and they'd all grown up a bit more, the swear jar had been long forgotten and their expletives had gotten a whole lot worse.

"What's so funny?" Lauren asked.

"Nothing," Tanner replied.

He passed Lauren her headset and put his on just as the rotors began to speed up and the pilot spoke to them.

"We're looking at a flight time of approximately fifteen minutes from Nadi to Vomo Island," he informed them. "So buckle up, sit back, and enjoy the sparkling blue waters of paradise."

Tanner sat back as instructed, unbuttoning his shirt and pushing his sleeves up some more. He was sweating like he'd just run a marathon and then some.

"I don't think I got the memo on dressing appropriately," Tanner said. "Seriously, I'm dying here."

"What kind of fool needs a memo on how hot a tropical island is going to be?" Lauren asked, looking amused. "And how can a Texan not be used to the heat?"

"You feel this humidity?" he asked. He looked at her jeans, flip-flops, and pretty little top. Her jumper was long gone, and he envied how cool she looked. "I don't think anyone could be used to this."

"Come on, cowboy, toughen up," she said, patting him on the thigh and making him feel everything but tough and cool.

Tanner gazed out the window as they lifted off the ground, steadying for a moment before flying across the sky. It took only minutes for them to reach the ocean, and he admired the twinkling, bright blue waters and imagined how good it would feel.

"Swimming's good for my recovery, right, doc?"

"Absolutely."

Tanner stared at the water some more, realizing how quickly he'd warmed up to Lauren and hating how rapidly he'd betrayed himself. When Mia had first told him the physical therapist was Lauren, he'd have rather submerged himself in a pit of snakes than have to spend time with her. Maybe she was his weakness, or perhaps he was finally starting to realize that her leaving him might not have been all her fault. And even if it had been, what sensible man over thirty would still blame his high school sweetheart for screwing him up when it came to women?

His brother had always said Lauren was a good excuse. Tanner had cursed her when he'd drunk himself stupid, when he'd slept with way too many women and refused to get involved in anything more than a one-night, or few-night, stand. But seeing her seated beside him, long dark hair tucked behind one air and the sweetest goddamn smile on her face as she surveyed the island, he knew he'd been the villain, not her. Whatever her reasons had been for ending things, she wasn't responsible for his bad behavior over the years.

It didn't mean he had to forgive her or even like her, but he did need to grow up and stop blaming her for ending things all those years ago.

"Welcome to Vomo Island," the pilot said. "Enjoy your stay in paradise."

"You okay?" he asked Lauren. He watched as she removed her headset and he did the same.

"Yeah, I'm great," she said, and he could see the light in her eyes, the almost childlike excitement as she kept glancing out the window. "It's been a long time since I had a vacation, so this truly does look like paradise to me."

He had to agree. "Me too. Sometimes we spend so long working and trying to prove ourselves that we forget to just enjoy life."

"Easy to do when you can afford to stay somewhere like this." Lauren sighed. "And I don't believe for a second that you haven't been enjoying life." He watched as she stared out at the big white letters on the grass spelling out VOMO and the tropical trees dotted all around. She'd originally booked somewhere nice but within her budget, but this place looked incredible.

Tanner shrugged as the door beside him opened. "What can I say? The ladies like their bull riders."

Lauren was in shock. This place . . . it was jaw dropping. She'd stayed in plenty of beautiful hotels and always been given a nice room, but this was something else. This was the kind of luxury she looked at online and drooled over—how on earth could this be her home for the next three weeks?

"So what do you think? Is it up to scratch?"

"Put it this way: I don't think I'll ever want to go back to my place after vacationing here." She tried not to laugh at the sight of him. He was every inch the cowboy—still in his boots, jeans, and plaid shirt. The only thing missing was the hat. And maybe the horse. Compared to the friendly locals in their leather sandals and breathable cotton tops and skirts, he stuck out like a sore thumb.

Their bags were brought in, and she watched as Tanner turned and passed the concierge a few bills. "Sorry, they're American, I need to get some local currency."

The concierge's smile turned from big to bigger. "*Vinaka*, sir. *Vinaka*."

Lauren walked away from Tanner to explore the place some more. They were staying in the Beach House, which was away from the other villas and faced out to the bluest stretch of ocean Lauren had ever seen. She opened the big sliding door and stepped out onto the timber deck, flanked with six outdoor loungers facing their own private pool. She slipped off her flip-flops and dipped a toe in—it felt heavenly—and when she studied the pool, she realized it was actually the perfect size for Tanner to train in. She would definitely get him swimming laps to help strengthen his body and ease him back into cardio again.

A gentle breeze brushed against her skin as she moved to the edge of the deck, looking down at the beach and admiring the white sand and the way the ocean lapped rhythmically so close to where she was standing, the waves so gentle. It was paradise here, no doubt about it. When Mia had promised her a luxury working vacation, she hadn't been kidding—it was possibly the most beautiful, tranquil place she'd ever been to, and they hadn't even explored the island yet.

"What do you think?" Tanner asked.

Lauren turned, looking Tanner up and down and trying not to laugh. Why was the man still dressed like he was about to attend a rodeo? She would have changed the minute she'd arrived if she was dressed like him. "I think it's time you got your pants off, put that shirt away for good, and changed into something more appropriate."

Tanner raised one brow, looking mightily unimpressed. "You don't think I'm dressed appropriately?"

She put her hands on her hips and studied him. He sure was doing a good poker face. "Please tell me you didn't pack that bag of yours with more plaid shirts and jeans? You do realize we're on an island, not a ranch, right? Or were you not kidding about getting the how-to-dress memo."

The slow smile that spread across his lips was sinfully seductive. She was pleased she wasn't standing any closer to him, because the way he was looking at her—like she was a mouse caught under his paw—was sending shivers through her that even the Fiji sun couldn't halt.

"I got the memo, darlin'. I'm still capable of wearing summer clothes."

She didn't recall seeing him in anything other than jeans and a shirt or T-shirt, other than when he'd been naked. Lauren frantically pushed the thoughts away, not wanting to remember being between the sheets with him, or out in a field, under a tree . . . *stop!*

She stood still, watching Tanner as he gave her one last look then limped away. *Limped*, she reminded herself. There was a reason she was here, and it was to stop him from moving like that. From now on, there was to be no more imagining her patient naked or thinking about how incredible his body had felt against hers. She was here to do a job and that was all.

Once Tanner had disappeared back into the house, she went in and collected her bag. It had been left in the main living space, and as much as she wanted to flop down on the big sofa and sleep off her jet lag, she didn't. Instead she went to explore the bedrooms, peering into the first one and deciding to claim it. The big king-sized bed was made up with white linen strewn with tropical petals, and the windows faced out to the beach—the perfect place for her to hide away from Tanner. She set her case down, opened up the sliding door that led out to the deck, and then took a look in the en suite bathroom tucked away behind the bed. She returned to the bed, quickly stripped off her clothes, and pulled out a pretty summer dress. They'd arrived just in time for dinner and she wasn't about to miss whatever gourmet feast was on offer at a resort she'd never, ever have the kind of funds to visit again.

Chapter 6

TANNER grunted as he sat down on the bed. Damn, he hurt. Every part of him was sore, achy, or thumping with a deep pain. It had been only seven weeks since the accident, but he was struggling to remember what it was like to be pain free. The doctors had given him a huge supply of pain medication, but other than when he was struggling to get comfortable enough to get to sleep at night, he wasn't taking them. The last thing he wanted was to be popping pills—he wanted to make his body strong again, not mask the pain and pretend like he was okay when he wasn't.

"You coming for dinner?"

Lauren's voice was muffled as she called out from the other side of his door. He was sitting in his boxers, on the perfectly made white bed, with barely enough energy or strength to change into a fresh set of clothes.

"Just give me a minute," he called back, pushing his palms down into the bed and rising. His wrist screamed out at him to stop, but it was better than putting all his weight onto his bad leg.

He unzipped his bag, grabbed a pair of shorts and a T-shirt, and leaned against the wall to get the shorts on. Thank god he didn't need to wear shoes—his boots had just about killed him. Instead he slowly bent to collect a pair of flip-flops he hoped weren't going to be too hard to wear, deciding to walk barefoot and put them on just before they arrived at the restaurant.

Tanner found Lauren sitting outside on one of the loungers, legs stretched out in front of her as she stared out at the water. The sun was slowly disappearing and he wondered how early it got dark in Fiji. He'd never been before, usually vacationing closer to home whenever he got away.

"It's beautiful, isn't it?" he asked.

"It certainly is. I feel like I've spent my entire working career rushing, and I can't remember the last time I even sat on a beach."

"Remember Hawaii?" Tanner asked, moving to sit beside her.

Her eyes met his, just for the briefest of seconds, before she turned her gaze back to the ocean or whatever else she was staring at.

"Yeah, I remember."

Tanner turned when movement caught his eye and he watched as two men ran down the sand, lighting the big torches that dotted the beach. Once night fell, the effect would be beautiful, just like everything else about the island so far.

Lauren touched his arm and he smiled down at her, his thoughts still on Hawaii. They'd gone on a family vacation there, and his father had let him bring someone, since his older brother was taking his girlfriend. It was only a short time after that they'd parted ways, but it had been a magical vacation and he'd often wondered if he'd done something wrong while they were away, if something had happened that he hadn't realized, because it was when they got home that things had slowly started to change between them.

"We'd better go. Are you staying barefoot?" Lauren asked.

He nodded. "Yes, ma'am. Unless you think I've breached the dress code again?"

Her laugh caught him by surprise. "You look great, Tan. And I want you barefoot as much as possible here. It'll be good for you."

He saluted at her as she walked away, following her out and then securing the door. He couldn't decide if he was starting to enjoy her company, or whether it was just the balmy island air that was making him forget just how badly she'd hurt him in the past.

"Bula!" A resort worker waved out as he walked past.

"Bula," Tanner called back. "Hey, we could have gotten a ride down. Didn't they say something about coming to get you if—"

"Out of the question," she said. "I knew you'd be sore and stiff after the flight, but a slow barefoot walk is just what you need to loosen your joints up. Tomorrow we start getting you back in shape."

Tomorrow? "I thought I'd have a few days relaxing on the beach first." There was no way his body was ready for anything other than some sun and relaxation yet. He'd only just had his cast taken off.

Lauren looked effortless in her short dress, her shoulders bare and her arms surprisingly golden. Maybe she'd been for a spray tan, because he bet she didn't get much time sitting out in the sun, and it wasn't exactly balmy weather this time of year back home.

"You know, walking along here with you now, I can almost forget what happened," he said. "It's like we knew each other a lifetime ago, but we're two different people. It's hard to explain."

"I know the feeling." Lauren was staying more than an arm's length away, but he caught her sideways glance. "Does that mean you forgive me?"

Tanner cleared his throat. "Not a chance. But I don't feel like I'd rather die than be stuck on an island with you now, so I guess that's progress."

Her laugh was soft, almost timid, and he hoped he hadn't made her uncomfortable. But he didn't want her thinking she was off the hook where their shared past was concerned. Something had happened arriving here—maybe it was the weather, or maybe he was just so desperate to feel like himself again, or maybe he'd never truly fallen out of love with Lauren.

Only that last thought was for him alone, because he'd never admit that to her for as long as he lived.

"You know, I was surprised when Mia said you'd come here with me at Christmas. I kind of expected you'd have someone to spend the holidays with," Lauren said. "Sorry, I hope that's not overstepping, I just . . ." Her voice trailed off and she wished she hadn't spoken at all.

Tanner looked up at her from across the table. They'd set it for the two of them on the beach, maybe guessing they were honeymooners or on a romantic getaway— maybe word would start to spread among the resort staff when they found both king beds were being used at the Beach House.

"Do you think I'd be here with you if I had a girl-friend or significant other back home? Seriously, any woman would be mad to let me come here with you."

Lauren almost choked on her wine. "Excuse me?"

Tanner sat back in his chair, slowly putting his beer bottle to his lips. She watched as he slowly sipped it, like he was purposely drawing the conversation out. "Look, we have history and you're a beautiful woman. I doubt there'd be many men who'd be allowed to spend time with you without their other half keeping an eye on them."

"Meaning their *other half* couldn't trust me?"

He frowned and shook his head. "No, meaning you're beautiful and intelligent and I can imagine most women being jealous of you."

She sighed. "I'll take the compliment. I guess I'm just a little touchy when it comes to being around men. You know, I've had to spend most of my career proving to players' wives and girlfriends that they don't have to worry about my presence by never, ever dating a player."

"I get it," he said softly.

"Your salmon," the waiter announced, and Lauren looked up to see him standing beside her. She'd been so focused on Tanner she hadn't even noticed.

"Thank you." She sat back and let him place it on the table in front of her.

"The braised pork belly."

Lauren looked down at her food, the awkwardness of their conversation killing her appetite. But the salmon sitting on a bed of rice with Asian greens on the side was so beautifully presented and she didn't want to offend the chef by not eating it. She reluctantly picked up her knife and fork.

"So you've actually never dated a player before? I'd have thought those guys would have been lining up to ask a beautiful woman like you out on a date."

Lauren took a mouthful of salmon, enjoying the flavor and eating it slowly. It gave her time to consider her answer. "I've been asked out plenty, but when you say no every time, it starts to become clear that it's never going to happen. And it's never going to happen, not while I'm working with the team in a professional capacity."

Tanner was eating now too, and Lauren focused on her food and stopped thinking about him. Or tried to. A little voice in her head kept telling her he was only asking these questions to find out if she had a man in her life or not, but surely he'd realize she hadn't. How many women in relationships booked overseas beach vacations without their partner?

"How about you tell me about your family? Mia sounds like she's in a happy place," Lauren said, trying to change the subject so that they could at least enjoy dinner.

Tanner's face changed when she mentioned Mia, and she knew she'd finally found a safe topic. "Mia's great. Sam is perfect for her, and they're both nuts about horses, so I'm guessing their offspring will all be horse mad. They'll have all of them riding before they can walk."

Lauren laughed. "I can just imagine their babies strapped to horses and being carted around the ranch."

"Mia's still riding. She gets a hard time about it, but riding is what she loves. She might be pregnant, but I'm not about to tell her to give it up."

She took another mouthful. Tanner and Mia had always been close, and they'd always seemed completely different compared to their older siblings, but she was seeing now that it was more than just being similar. They stuck up for each other, and they were both doing things they loved—hearing him defend his sister for still doing what she was passionate about proved that.

"And does Mia feel the same about you? Does she support you doing what you love or does she secretly want you to give up bull riding?"

Tanner gave her what she could only guess was a surprised look. "If she wants me to give it up, then it's definitely a secret she's holding close." He paused and she watched him closely, saw that maybe he hadn't actually considered that possibility. "She found you and sent me here though, didn't she? I don't think she'd have done that if she didn't want me back on a bull."

Lauren finished her dinner and set her utensils down. One thing she'd done before boarding the plane had been to look up all Tanner's stats—she liked to have a feel for her athletes; what made them tick, what their strengths and weaknesses were, and why they were committed to their sport. She had to admit that Tanner was hard to get a read on, because he was so unlike the athletes she usually worked with. Hardly any of the professional athletes she knew came from big money, in fact it was usually the opposite, and money was often the key motivator—other than playing the sport they loved. For Tanner, she couldn't figure out what his motivator was, other than perhaps the adrenaline fix, which was the very reason her parents had wanted her to steer well clear of him.

"Tanner, as far as I can tell, you've achieved what most riders can't or haven't during their careers," she said, smiling when the waiter took their plates. She reached for the wine glass and stroked the stem to help distract her from her own nerves. "You've been riding professionally for ten years. You've earned a staggering, what was it, seven million dollars during that time? And this is your first catastrophic injury. Am I correct on those stats?"

Tanner held up his bottle and touched it to her glass. "Damn right. I just don't know why you're boosting my ego by telling me what I already know. Or are you just trying to show me that you can do your research?"

"I'm trying to get in your head, Tan. I need to know—"

"Honey, you were in my head once, and you're not getting back in there again any time soon."

She bit back a frustrated sigh, trying to ignore his reference to her past. "I'm trying to figure out what makes you tick, that's all. The money? The thrill? The fans? I want to know more about your career."

He drained his beer, and she studied his face when he turned to the ocean. The gentle lap was soothing, the torches burning along the beach magical in the dark, and Lauren wished they'd just sat in silence and admired the beauty around them. But she wasn't here for fun; this wasn't a date. This was work, and come tomorrow she had a lot of damn work to do on the man seated across from her.

"Tanner, what I'm asking is, when is enough enough? What do you have left to prove when you've already won every competition? Correct me if I'm wrong, but you could leave your sport now and go down in history as one of the highest-earning pro riders of all time."

His gaze was cold when he finally faced her again.

"You're my PT, Lauren, not my shrink. All you need to know is that you're here to fix me and get me back in the game again. You don't want to do that? Then get on the next goddamn helicopter out of here in the morning and send someone back who will do the job without interrogating me about my motives."

Lauren sat back, trying not to react, to maintain some degree of professionalism, but it wasn't easy. Without trying, she'd hit a nerve, and Tanner didn't look like he was about to warm up to her again anytime soon.

"I just want you to be honest with me, that's all," she said softly. "If we're going to work together, I want to know your goals. Your professional aspirations. I like to see the whole picture." She took a deep breath. "And please don't forget that you joined *me* on *my* vacation, not the other way around."

Their dessert arrived, but Tanner never even looked down at the decadent white chocolate cheesecake. He didn't miss a beat and he sure as hell didn't acknowledge what she'd just said.

"My goal is to be back on top again. When I retire is my business and no one else's, but I can tell you that it's not on my current agenda and I'm more motivated about making a successful comeback than I've ever been. Are we clear?"

"We're clear," she agreed.

He pushed back his chair and stood, an imposing figure standing over her. "I'm going to head back."

She swallowed, feeling her face flush as she watched him study her face. His blue eyes were troubled, there was so much there that she wished she could find out, but tonight wasn't the night to ask more questions.

"Get a good sleep. We'll start with a massage and training session after breakfast."

Tanner gave her a tight smile and walked away, leaving her with her dessert and an almost-finished glass of wine. Lauren took a deep, shuddering breath and turned her chair slightly to face the beach, not wanting to see if the other couples around them were giving her sympathetic looks. She wanted to call out that she was fine, that he wasn't her partner and he hadn't just walked out on her and left her alone at the table. Instead she stayed silent, eating every last bit of the cheesecake and smiling as she heard the squeals of young children. Soon they were running past, racing from torch to torch along the beach, and before long a woman came running too, chasing after them.

Lauren looked at Tanner's dessert and decided to eat that, too. It wasn't every day she was staying on a five-star resort with a world-class chef. And besides, she intended on spending her days here being active, swimming and paddleboarding and running. An extra slice of cake seemed like the least of her worries compared to the man she was charged with rehabilitating.

"Is everything okay here, ma'am?"

Lauren smiled at the waiter, thanked him for a lovely evening, then took off her sandals and decided to walk down the beach. The children were playing ahead, probably being naughty for their nanny, but she liked their idea. So long as a crab didn't nip at her toes, it was the perfect way to spend the evening, with the sand beneath her feet and the sound of the water reminding her just how fortunate she was to be in Fiji. The brochures hadn't been wrong—the island was blissful—it was her companion who was proving problematic. And the fact that she couldn't get their past out of her head.

"Daddy, I love him." Lauren had pleaded. She'd held her father's hand and looked into his eyes, but by then, he'd already made his mind up.

"He's not right for you, sweetheart. When you look back on this decision, you'll know we were only looking out for you."

"Mom?" Lauren turned, looking for support from her mother, but she'd received the same kind of blank stare there too. They'd conspired together, made a decision, and neither one of them was going to go back on it.

"Lauren, you're at a crossroads here, and Tanner Ford is only going to hold you back. What does your future look like with him?"

"He's from a good family," she choked out. "And he loves me. We're meant to be together."

"You're not even eighteen yet. What do you know about love?" her dad had insisted. "What happens when he leaves you for someone else, when everything falls apart, and you've got no college degree or career to fall back on? That's not what you want and deep down you know it."

Tears streamed down Lauren's cheeks. "He wants me to go to college!"

"No, darling, he wants you on the back of his motorcycle to show off to his friends. He wants to drag you around to bull-riding competitions and rodeos, he wants to drink beer and get high. He doesn't have any motivation to succeed."

They were wrong. They were so wrong.

"*You have until the end of summer, Lauren. We'll pay your tuition fees, we'll do whatever we can to support you into the career you're dreaming of, but not if you're still with the Ford boy. We've been patient, but enough's enough.*"

Lauren stood, wiping at her cheeks, knowing there was nothing left to say. She'd find a way. She'd finance her own college education. She'd do it without her parents. She wasn't walking away from the boy she loved just because they told her to.

"*The end of summer?*" *she asked. "You promise you won't stop me seeing him until then?*"

Her mom and dad exchanged looks before her mom answered. "Your normal curfew applies still, but yes, until the end of summer."

Lauren nodded and walked away, slowly trudging up the stairs into her bedroom. She collapsed onto her bed, pillow stuffed against her face as she sobbed, her chest full of so much emotion she thought she was going to choke, to suffocate on her own tears.

There was no way she was giving up Tanner Ford without a fight. He was the love of her life, and she wouldn't let anyone tell her what she could and couldn't do, not even her parents.

Chapter 7

"RISE and shine," Lauren said, knocking on Tanner's door. She waited a few seconds before knocking again. Nothing. "Tanner?" She nudged the door, reluctantly peering into the room. It was identical to hers, except for the rumpled sheets and different suitcase. And it smelled different; there was that distinct smell of male in the room. She was used to it, she worked and traveled with men all the time, but the difference was that she wasn't used to having a man in her bed.

Lauren went back through the house, into the open plan kitchen and living area, but there was no sign of Tanner. Was he working out? Swimming? She looked in the pool but there was no sign of him. The sun was already up, shining brightly and bathing the beach, as she opened the door and let herself out onto the deck. *There he was.*

Tanner was lying beneath a coconut tree, legs stretched out in front of him, wearing shorts and a T-shirt. She walked over, shielding her eyes with her hand when she finally reached him.

"Mornin'," he said without looking up.

"Good morning. I've been looking for you."

"I couldn't sleep. The time zone thing is a bitch."

She couldn't say she felt the same. She'd been so tired that by the time she'd returned to her room, she'd fallen into a deep slumber and hadn't woken until sunlight streamed through her open blinds.

"You want a moment to get ready before we start for the day? I want to begin with a deep tissue massage, then we can relax for a bit and do some more work this afternoon."

Tanner didn't move.

"Tanner?"

"I think I'll just stay here a bit longer."

What the hell? "Look, you're the one footing the bill, so it's up to you if we stay here three weeks or five. But last night you were all fired up about climbing aboard a bull again. You want a wrist strong enough to hold the rigging? You want to be able to walk without a limp?"

Tanner pushed up, his eyes meeting hers. "I think coming here was a mistake. The island is great, but I could have recuperated just fine at home."

"What the hell is going on here?" Lauren asked. "Tanner, come on!"

He went to settle back down, but she kicked him, her toes butting into him. He grunted and she planted her hands on her hips, ready to scream. Athletes were often frustrating, but Tanner was beyond annoying! Why was he behaving like a child?

"You want to be a thirty-year-old man with the arthritic, grinding joints of a ninety-year-old? Then be my guest. But don't act like you didn't have the chance to heal, not on my watch."

Lauren spun around and marched back to the house. Screw him! They'd been civil, things had been going just fine, and then he'd flared up the night before and dared to treat her like she was dirt? As if she was just some girl he could act cool with, and not a highly trained professional hired to assist his recovery? He was more stubborn than she'd realized.

"Lauren, wait up."

She stopped, fists bunched, still seething. She didn't bother turning.

"Sorry. I was being a jerk. You're in charge. I'm just pissed with the world I guess and you're an easy target right now. I'm sorry."

That got her. She understood "pissed with the world." She understood giving up. She didn't understand acting like a jerk.

"I'm in charge?" she asked, watching as he limped around in front of her. The guy was seriously sore, and part of her worried that she wouldn't be able to heal him. Maybe that was one of the reasons he was acting so moody—pain did weird things to a person.

"Yeah," he said softly. "You're in charge, Lauren."

"Then get your ass back to the beach and wait for me," she said. "It's time for a deep tissue massage, and you'd better be prepared for some pain."

He saluted her, but she refused to crack a smile.

"No pain, no gain. I get it."

"Good. I'll be back down soon."

Lauren walked past him, up to the house, stopping in the kitchen for a glass of water. Her hands shook as she reached into the fridge for one of the small bottles and stood, guzzling it down. She prided herself on having nerves of steel and being able to take all kinds to crap from her players, but Tanner was different. Because Tanner put her on edge just by looking at her, and nothing about that was ever going to change.

"You weren't joking about the pain part." Tanner grimaced, gritting his teeth as Lauren pushed hard into his muscle, her table set out on the sand. "I recall massages being pleasant, not excruciating."

She didn't look up, her concentration absolute. "It's not meant to feel good, it's meant to help."

Tanner suffered in silence, resisting the urge to groan or push her the hell away from his body.

"We've got a lot to work through," Lauren said matter-of-factly. "Just to make sure I get this right, you had an ankle fracture, broken ribs, crushed knee ligaments, horn piercings, wrist damage, a bad concussion, but no spinal damage, correct?"

He gasped as she pushed into a sore spot. *Motherfucker!* "Yeah, I don't think you missed anything." His breath was wheezing in and out as he tried to cope with the pain.

"Do you like swimming?"

Why the hell was she asking him that when she already knew the answer? Lauren paused and looked up, and he stared straight back at her until her neck and cheeks turned deep red.

"Ah, sorry. I forgot who I was working on. Forget it."

They'd swum together in Hawaii, they'd swum in the river on the ranch, splashing each other and fooling around in the water when the temperature had driven any sane person crazy. He had plenty of memories of her skin, her slick and wet body dripping all over his.

"I'll finish up soon. I don't want to do too much on

day one." Lauren pushed harder, and he thought his thigh was going to explode. "You're doing great. After this you can rest a bit, then before lunch we can take a nice long swim. It'll be good cardio for you and gentle on your joints and muscles."

"Are you swimming with me?" he grunted.

"Ha, you mean to make sure you don't drown?"

"Yeah, something like that."

She pushed again, the pressure far from enjoyable still, but if it was good for him, then he wasn't going to complain. He leaned back, pleased that he was at least lying by the ocean instead of being treated in a medical environment. He needed to focus on the water, imagine the feeling of the cool liquid on his skin once she was done.

"Sorry, I need to go a little higher here before I finish," Lauren said.

Tanner fought the urge to stiffen as her warm, soft hands moved up his leg, skimming his inside thigh as she refocused on his muscle and started to push deep, in circles then holding her pressure.

Holy hell. He stared up at the sky, wishing she wouldn't touch him there. Nerve endings seemed to find their way to the surface of his skin and he moved, trying not to squirm. What the heck was she trying to do to him?

"I don't think—"

Her hands went higher, closer to his hip, which is what he guessed she was actually working on, but her long ponytail came closer too as she bent her head, her hair brushing against his skin. Tanner tried to think about his granny, then he focused on horses, then he . . . *dammit*. Blood was flowing into the wrong part of his goddamn body.

"I think we need to call it a day," he said, muttering as he tried unsuccessfully to push Lauren's hand away.

"What? No, I'm just getting . . ."

Tanner didn't bother saying anything else. Lauren could see exactly what she'd so expertly stimulated through his shorts.

"Oh."

He grunted. "Yeah. *Oh*."

"Maybe we could resume this later or you could roll onto your stomach," she suggested. "It's only natural and to be honest with you, it's not really that unusual."

"So it's not unusual for your clients to get hard-ons, is that what you're saying?" Talk about embarrassed— his body was behaving like a teenager's!

Lauren looked mortified, her face like she'd seen a ghost, but when he cracked up she did too. "Tanner! I'm just saying that sometimes when my hand is on a man's skin . . ."

"He gets a goddamn erection," Tanner finished for her. "Yeah, I don't need it spelled out for me, it's bad enough experiencing it."

Lauren surprised him by slapping his leg and pointing at him sternly. "Turn over and flatten it, or lie on your side—just don't point it at me."

Tanner couldn't help his laughter as he turned over, happy to comply if it meant she'd leave his upper thigh and groin area the hell alone.

"Funny, I remember you liking when I pointed it at you." He couldn't resist the taunt, not when she was torturing him so expertly.

"Shut up and lie still," she replied. "Or I'll make this massage even deeper and you'll be begging for mercy."

Tanner shut the hell up and did what he was told,

not wanting to know how much worse it could get. The sooner this damn massage was over, the better, because he couldn't decide what was worse—her hands or the pain.

Lauren had had men get stimulated when she was working on them before. Not often, but over the course of her career it had happened enough that she knew how to ignore it and brush it off. It was just blood flow. It was a natural reaction to having a woman's hands rubbing and pushing against their skin. It didn't mean anything and she was always careful to either ignore it or suggest the patient roll over or take a break or something. But with Tanner? Oh, with Tanner it was an entirely different ball game. Because she'd seen Tanner naked. She'd *felt* Tanner naked. She'd dreamed for years about Tanner naked. And now here he was, in his briefs, with a white towel over him, and all she could think about was how much she'd like to explore that body of his in completely unprofessional ways.

She remembered their songs, what they'd listened to out in the open lying under the big oak tree near the river; she could shut her eyes and feel and see and remember what it had been like. Just like she could remember what his hands had felt like on her and how warm and soft his mouth had been against hers. Those feelings were indented in her memory and she'd never forget them, because no one else had ever made her feel quite the same as Tanner had. Now he was all grown up, and probably a whole lot more experienced, and she couldn't help but wonder what it would be like between the sheets with him now.

She gulped, trying to focus on the job at hand.

"I'm, ah, going to have to tape you up," she said. "But I think we'll wait until after your swim."

"That's not exactly going to help my full body tan," Tanner replied.

Lauren swatted at him playfully before she could stop herself. "Stop teasing, this is serious."

"Says the woman teasing me with every damn touch."

Lauren's hands hovered—she almost stopped, but she pushed on. She was doing her job, she just needed to forget that the man whose strong, hard skin she was touching was Tanner.

She worked in silence a bit longer, holding the pressure and knowing it was hurting him. But when he finally spoke there was nothing to suggest he was in pain.

"I know it's ancient history, and it's not going to change anything, but can I ask you why?" Tanner's voice was low. "I've never believed you that you wanted some space, that you were too young. I guess I've just always wondered what made you call time on us."

She released the pressure but left her hand on his leg. "You're right, Tanner, it is ancient history. There's no point going back in time."

He half turned and she could see how stormy his eyes were, how different they looked from the always-dancing ones she remembered. "Because you can't remember? Or because I'm right, that it was something else?"

She fixed her smile, refused to crack even under his scrutiny. "Because there's no point going back. Simple as that." Lauren sucked in a breath. "Now how about we have that swim?"

Tanner kept watching her, before dropping the towel

and standing up. "Christ! I'm worse now than before you started."

She stood alongside him and reached out a hand to touch his arm, but he pulled away before she had a chance to do more than brush her fingers against his skin. Funny, before she'd been touching him repeatedly, but now, as she reached for him, it felt like she hadn't touched him in a lifetime.

"It's supposed to be sore. We have a long road ahead of us."

Tanner made a noise deep in his throat that she couldn't decipher before hobbling into the house, leaving her standing there. What was she supposed to do? Was she supposed to put her feelings aside and pretend like calling time on their relationship hadn't ripped her heart out and left her gasping for air for weeks, months, longer? Because she wasn't sure if she'd gotten over Tanner yet, even more than ten years later, so what the hell was she supposed to say to him when he acted like she hadn't given a damn? She might have acted like a prize bitch at the time, but her hand had been forced. She'd had to make a choice, and she'd made the only one she could.

Tanner appeared again, but he didn't give her a second glance. Instead he pushed off from the side of the pool and dived straight in, sending an arc of water at her, splashing her toes. His big body pushed through the water, slicing across it as he swam powerfully to the other end.

Lauren clapped when his head emerged, hair slicked and looking even longer than it had before. "Impressive. Maybe your body's not as damaged as I thought."

It was only then that she saw the ripple of pain pass through his face as he reached for the edge of the pool, gasping, before slipping back down below the surface again.

"Tanner!" she screamed, running the few steps between the deck and the edge of the pool and leaping in, swimming quickly to where he was. "Tanner!"

"Fuck, my leg, it's . . ."

She hooked an arm under his and started to tread water as she reached for the edge. "Just take it easy."

"I'm not going to drown," he ground out. "I'm just goddamn sore. The side of my leg just exploded in heat, like it was on fire. And the cramp in my calf is—dammit!"

Lauren took a breath and ducked under the surface, pushing down as far as she could, and reached for his leg. She pushed his heel down, holding on to his toes, and rubbing his tight muscles. She stayed below as long as she could, and just as she was about to come up for air a strong arm wrapped around her and hauled her up to the surface.

She gasped when she came up, sucking back air and blinking water from her lashes. She pushed her wet hair off her face, and when she went to open her mouth she realized she was less than an inch from Tanner, and that he was staring down at her, his eyes on hers. She touched a hand to his chest.

"Are you okay now? How are you feeling?"

"No, I'm not okay. I'm so far from fucking okay that it's ridiculous."

She stared back at him. She needed to push away. Her hand was still on his chest. She just needed to push back.

Tanner grabbed her wrist, his gaze dropping to her mouth.

"Is it your leg? I can—"

"This doesn't mean I've forgiven you," he growled out.

"What—"

Tanner's mouth closed over hers in a searing kiss before she had time to react, his hand letting go of her wrist and moving around her, pressed to the small of her back and pulling her straight into that rock solid chest of his.

What the hell was he doing? Tanner stroked his hand possessively down Lauren's back, pressing against her so she moved closer to him. Her lips were wet and soft as he kissed her, and he tangled one hand in her wet hair as he kissed her again. Pain shot up his leg but he didn't stop, put up with it so he could keep moving his mouth against hers. Maybe it had been the touching before or the heat or the—hell, he didn't know why, all he knew was that it felt so damn good.

"Stop," she whispered, her hand rising between them, fingertips settling just below his collarbone.

"Why?" He leaned forward to touch his lips to hers again, needing his mouth against hers, craving the taste of her, the feel of her against him.

"You just need to stop," she said, softly this time but not quite a whisper. "We can't do this."

Tanner pulled back, clearing his throat and dropping his hand from her back. His leg hurt like crazy again all of a sudden, although maybe it was because he'd been good at ignoring it when he was distracted.

"You should get out and rest that leg," she told him, treading water as she moved away. "Or we could do a few laps together. Just take it slow."

Tanner dragged his eyes from her, thinking how much he'd like to swim to her, wrap his arms around her, and show her exactly what she'd been missing all these years. But since he couldn't do that, then maybe swimming was a good distraction.

"Yeah, let's swim," he grunted out.

Lauren moved into place beside him and started to do the breaststroke. "Just move through the water however feels best for you. I want to keep everything very low impact today, we have plenty of time to build up slowly."

Build up slowly? Maybe there was hope for him after all. Because if that kiss was a sign of things to come, then perhaps his time away with Lauren wouldn't be tedious after all.

Chapter 8

"TANNER, can we talk about what happened before?"

Tanner opened his eyes. He was lying beneath a coconut tree on the grass between the beach and their house, and until that moment his only concern was whether a coconut might fall on his head. But this kind of conversation was worse. He decided to keep his eyes shut and pretend he was asleep.

"Tanner?"

He groaned and rolled to his side. "How about we forget it ever happened?"

"It's not that easy."

Yeah, he was well aware of that. The only thing he'd thought of since was how damn good her lips had felt, all pillowy and melted into his. Her skin was so soft, her fingertips so light when they'd pressed into his skin. For the past few hours, he'd tried to relax, tried to ignore the aches in his body, and attempt to put Lauren out of his head. All he'd succeeded in doing was thinking about every inch of her instead.

"It's complicated between us," she said, moving closer. He looked sideways and saw her shuffling over, toes buried into the perfect white sand as she stared at him. "I don't know why I thought we'd be able to do this."

"You want out?" he asked, finally pushing himself up so he could look at her properly.

"Honestly? I don't know. I mean I want to help you, but even after all this time, it's just . . ."

"Complicated," he said. "I know."

They sat there a bit longer, him looking at her and her looking out at the ocean. He studied her profile, admiring her features. She was beautiful sitting beside him without makeup on, her face a slightly lighter shade than her arms. She was wearing sunglasses so he couldn't see her eyes, but the way she had her long dark hair scooped up into a ponytail, bottom lip sucked in beneath her top teeth, it made her look like the schoolgirl he'd known. She was more mature and she was a successful, grown-ass woman now, of course, but he could still see the girl she'd once been lingering close to the surface.

"We never were good at keeping our hands off each other," he said, laughing at the memory. She'd always been in his lap, arms around his neck; when they walked side by side her hand was always slipped into his back pocket. They'd been joined at the hip since their first date—until the day she'd abruptly ended it.

"So this is just, what, a chemical reaction? We're programmed to, I don't know, behave a certain way around each other?" she asked, turning back to him.

Tanner shrugged. "Hell if I know," he admitted. "The only thing I know for sure is that I never wanted to see you again for as long as I lived, and now that we're here, I'm starting to think that was pretty goddamn immature."

Her laugh was soft, uncertain almost. "You do realize that I had only just turned eighteen when I broke up with you, right? We were kids."

"We didn't behave like kids and you know it." He bristled just thinking about it, remembering how she'd blindsided him. They'd spent so many long hours, bodies intertwined, talking about spending the rest of their lives together. There hadn't been a cheerleader in sight who'd ever tempted him to stray from Lauren, not once. "But yeah, I know it's childish to hold on to a grudge this long." Only it wasn't a grudge. He'd gone from opening up to someone for the first time in his life to having his heart ripped out. No one he'd met since, not all the women he'd been with and met over so many years, had come close to Lauren, or to the memory he had of her. Maybe that was his fault for not dealing with his shit and keeping her on a pedestal.

"Can we try not to let anything intimate happen again?" she asked. "I mean, we're obviously attracted to each other, it's not like a lot has changed physically over the years."

"Except for my ninety-year-old body?" he teased as a smile crept across his lips.

"I said *if* you didn't do what I told you to, then that's what you'd end up with, stupid. Not that you've got one now!"

Her gaze drop lower, he could feel it even though her eyes were hard to make out through her sunglasses. Then he watched her swallow and he reached out a hand to touch her arm. He shouldn't have, but there was some sand clinging to her skin and he carefully brushed it away.

"Tell me again that you don't want anything to happen between us," he said. "Because I'm not sure I believe you."

She pulled her arm away and crossed it over her stomach. He watched as her tongue darted out to moisten her lips.

"We need to keep things professional between us," she said, her voice low and husky. "That's it, Tanner, no more contact."

He lay back down and shut his eyes. "Until my next massage, that is."

He bet she would have slapped him if she could have. But when she lay back down, her book back in her hand, he forced himself to man the hell up and stop joking around.

"Lauren, look, I know I'm not the easiest guy to be around, and I shouldn't have been such a jerk to you before we came here."

She was holding her book steady and she didn't turn, but he knew she was listening.

"Whatever your reason was back then, you made it. I've made you out to be the villain all these years, but it was *your* decision, and the past is the past."

"Thanks."

"It's not quite me forgiving you, but it's probably the best my ego can deal with."

She smiled—he could just make out the way her mouth curved at the side. "Right now, I'll take whatever I can get."

Tanner lay back, wishing that Lauren would take that pretty mouth and find her way to him. Or even better, climb aboard and show him exactly why he'd missed her so much.

Later that day, Lauren was watching Tanner from her bed. She was stretched out, still in her bikini from sunbathing earlier, lying on the crisp white sheets. She'd advised him to take a nice long, slow walk along the beach, barefoot, to help his muscles and build up strength, and she'd decided not to go with him. Strolling with him, listening to the waves, the sun on their skin, and the temptation of his body so close to hers . . . she knew right 'from wrong, but the moment he was up in her space, she didn't exactly trust herself.

Her phone vibrated and she reached for it, smiling when she saw it was her sister. She'd been texting back and forth earlier with Casey, but now her sister had probably found out and would be demanding her own updates about what was happening. She could just imagine the two of them gossiping on the phone or firing off text messages about her. Lauren grinned when she read the message: *So how's beauty and the beast?*

Instead of messaging her back, Lauren decided to FaceTime Hannah as she stared out the glass, still focused on Tanner. He'd already walked past twice, but he'd stopped and was stretching now, just like she'd told him too.

"He's hardly the beast," she said when her sister picked up, her face appearing on the screen as she grinned back at her.

"Oh my god, you've already slept with him, haven't you?" Hannah sighed. "I knew you two wouldn't be able to keep your hands off each other. How long did it take? Two seconds or two minutes?"

"Definitely longer than two minutes," she teased, lying back on the bed.

Lauren laughed. Maybe he *was* a bit of a beast. He pulled his T-shirt over his head, and she watched as he moved to the edge of the pool. His golden skin was tinged darker, especially over his shoulders, but she knew that he'd just turn a darker shade of tanned and would never even look burnt throughout the entire vacation.

His back was muscled, same as his chest, and she longed to explore that chiseled skin with her fingers. She guessed his abs had been even more defined before the accident, but for a guy who'd had the better part of two months in a hospital bed or in a cast, he looked damn fine. She turned the screen so Hannah could get a glimpse of him.

"He's a gorgeous specimen of man, I'll give you that," she said.

"Yeah, I know. Definitely no beast here, except for his attitude sometimes."

"That's what Mom used to call him, you know," Hannah said. "She'd watch the two of you roar off on his motorcycle, you clinging to him as he gunned it down the road, and she'd mutter *beauty and the goddamn beast.*"

"How have I never heard this?" she asked, standing and moving closer to the glass when Tanner slid into the pool and disappeared into the water, her screen facing her again. She touched her palm to the cool surface and tracked him with her eyes for a second before turning her focus back to her sister.

"Don't know why I didn't tell you back then, but after it ended you made us all promise to never mention his name again. What's it like over there? Is the island amazing?"

"It's incredible," Lauren said, giving Hannah a tour of the room as she spoke, then pushing the door open and holding the screen outside. "The house we have is incredible, it even has a private pool that faces the beach, and once I have Tan back up and moving properly again, we'll be able to explore the island better."

" 'Tan'?" Hannah repeated. "We're back to calling him *Tan* now?"

Lauren quickly retreated back into her bedroom, not wanting Tanner to hear. "It's just a name. Old habits die hard."

"All old habits or just the name?"

Lauren laughed. "Don't be silly. You know how I am with my work. I haven't slept with him and I have no intentions of going there." If only saying it was as easy as doing it—or *not* doing it.

"I know, I know. You're possibly the only woman on the planet who refuses to date hot, single ballplayers."

"Hey, if you were trying to get the respect of their wives *and* your bosses, you'd do the same."

"Sweetheart, after all the time you've been working there, I think it would be okay to date just *one* of the single guys. You know, no one will ask you out again if you keep on turning them down."

Lauren stood again, finding it hard to settle. "How are the kids?"

"Great. They're messy and loud and fun, same as always. But it's you I want to hear about!"

Lauren could hear them in the background, but Hannah was in the kitchen so the kids weren't in sight. She stood at the door again, watching the water ripple and smiled when Tanner rose out of the water. He saw her there but didn't smile or hold up his hand. He just shook the water off, droplets falling from every part of him. He was so gorgeous. He might be arrogant and he might still hate her for what she did, but right now she was certain she'd never wanted something, or someone, so badly in her whole life.

She filled her sister in on Vomo, telling her more about the island, the gorgeous food, and everything else— except getting up close and personal with Tanner.

"Bula!"

Lauren put her finger to her lips and listened. Tanner had obviously come inside, because he was talking to a man and she couldn't make out what they were saying. She opened the door.

"What's going on?" her sister muttered.

"Sorry, I just heard someone arrive." Lauren's eyebrows shot up when she realized what was going on. "It seems we have a butler and he's just arrived with champagne."

Her sister burst out laughing. "Shoot me now! You're on a luxury island and you have a freaking butler, too?"

"Seems like it," Lauren said, gratefully holding out her hand as Tanner came toward her with the champagne, shrugging his shoulders as if to say "Well, why the hell wouldn't we?"

"I'll call you another day," Lauren said. "Miss you."

"Go drink champagne and have fun," Hannah replied with a laugh. "Bye!"

Tanner passed Lauren the glass of champagne and wondered what she was thinking. She'd become very good at guarding her expression, and that wasn't something he was used to, not from her. When they'd been younger, it had seemed like every thought that had passed through her head he'd been able to read on her face.

"He's left us some canapés too," Tanner said. "The only thing he forgot to leave was the bottle."

He sipped the champagne. Not usually his drink of choice, but he wasn't going to complain.

"Cheers," Lauren said, holding up her glass and clinking it to his before taking a sip. He watched as she swallowed it down.

"You know," Lauren said, "I was going to tell you tonight that we should skip the alcohol while we're here, to help with your recovery, but I'm thinking that maybe my rules were a little strict."

Tanner grinned. "Yeah, I think we should focus on the whole relaxation part of the trip." He could think of some other great ways to relax too, but given her reaction after the kiss, he was going to keep those thoughts to himself. For now.

"Want to go sit outside?" he asked. "Seems a shame not to soak up the last rays of sunshine."

She moved in front of him and he followed her out, squinting as his eyes adjusted to the change in light.

"Who were you talking to before?" he asked, before realizing his question hadn't come out quite right. "I mean, you sounded like you were having a laugh. I don't actually need to know if—"

"Cue the jealous ex-boyfriend?" she asked, before laughing and shaking her head. "It's fine. It was Hannah actually. She was just recounting some things from the past that Mom and Dad used to say about you."

He cringed. "Do I even want to know? Damn, your

dad used to give me this look, like he'd pull out a shotgun and shoot me right there on the spot if he could."

Lauren's grimace matched his. "Yeah, I remember."

"And your mom?" He downed some more champagne. "Lord, did she want me dead! I could tell from the way she looked at me, like she wished she could just scream at me not to put my filthy paws on her baby girl."

Lauren looked unsure, almost awkward as she clutched the champagne flute and dropped into the lounger by the pool.

"What? Don't tell me that's what she actually used to say to you about me?"

"You really want to know what she used to call us?" Lauren asked, looking guilty. "Hannah just told me, I swear I never knew until now."

"Hit me with it."

"Beauty and the beast," Lauren said, hand over her mouth like she couldn't believe she'd told him. "I just about died."

"Geez, what a cruel mother, calling her own daughter a beast."

Lauren's eyes widened. "Tanner! I'm pretty sure I wasn't the beast in the story."

Tanner laughed so hard his sides hurt, pain rippling between his ribs as tears streamed down his cheeks. Lauren was laughing hard too, wiping at her cheeks and splashing her champagne over her pretty top.

"I guess I would have felt the same if my daughter had come home with a motorcycle-riding seventeen-year-old."

"Yeah, I know, but still," Lauren said.

"Still what?"

Her cheeks flushed pink, but she didn't elaborate. Instead she changed the subject. "You know, I could get used to having a butler. This is definitely the life."

Tanner didn't push her, but he did walk back inside and dial their butler. When he came back out and took up residence on the lounger beside her, Lauren gave him a quizzical look.

"What were you just doing?"

"Telling our butler to bring the bottle this time, and arranging for dinner to be brought up for us. I thought we'd stay in tonight."

"Because you want to keep me prisoner in this exquisite house?"

"Maybe," he replied. "Or maybe my body hurts like a goddamn freight train just ploughed headfirst into me, and I can't face the idea of walking to the restaurant."

Her look was one of sympathy, but in all honesty he wasn't sure which part of his response had been truthful. Maybe he did want to keep her all to himself. It was strange how being away from his normal life had made him more accepting of being around his former flame.

"Tanner," Lauren said as she stretched out, leg flexing as she pointed her toes. He noticed that her skin was already looking more golden than when they'd first arrived. "What was your reaction when Mia suggested we work together?"

He finished his drink and set it down on the low table between their loungers. "Trust me, you don't want to know."

"I do." He watched as she took a way more delicate sip, not the big gulp that he'd just done to finish his champagne. "Because I can tell you for sure that it took a bit of convincing to get me to say yes, and I wasn't the one who'd . . ."

"Had their heart broken?" he asked, chuckling. "I looked her in the eye and said 'Lauren *goddamn* Lewis.' Or something like that. Anyway, I flat out said no, and she told me to check my bullshit because I needed to work with the best, and the best was you."

She was quiet a long moment, and when their butler arrived and called out, bringing them their champagne and telling them that their food would be coming soon, Tanner thanked him and poured more Veuve Clicquot into their glasses.

"So we still have a bit of catching up to do," he said, settling back down. He tried to position himself so that it didn't hurt, but no matter how he moved, some part of him ached.

"We need to strap you up before I have too many drinks," Lauren said.

"Once we finish the bottle," he teased. "Then your elbows poking into my muscles won't feel so torturous!"

"Like I use my elbows," she muttered, but he could see her smiling behind her glass.

"Seriously though, what's been happening? Have you been married? Divorced? Any kids?"

She gave him a withering look. "I wouldn't be chilling on an island with you right now if I'd had kids in the past ten years. As for the other two questions? No and no. You?"

"Nope. I've been keeping my options open, you know, practicing while I try to find the right girl." Only he'd had the right girl and she'd managed to get away. Did he tell her that no one had ever been able to live up to the memory he had of her?

"That's gross."

"Bet you haven't exactly been a saint."

"Um, compared to you? I'd to be lucky to have made my way through an entire box of condoms since I met you, but I'm guessing you've been keeping Durex in business."

"How long have you been working on that one-liner?"

Lauren held up her glass. "Oh, I've been working on that one for hours."

They sat in silence awhile longer, polishing off the bottle before Lauren set down her glass and rose.

"I need to work some magic on you before I get too drunk."

Tanner looked up into her eyes. "Hmm, not sure if I trust you. I think you're buzzed already."

She rolled her eyes and walked into the house, coming back with a bag that he guessed contained her strapping and supplies. She pointed to her table, which was still set up.

"Lie down and stay still," she ordered.

Tanner did as he was told, more relaxed than he'd been the first time around when she'd massaged him. This time she focused on slightly different parts of his body, rubbing into his muscles and pushing deep, and then strapping him up and making him look like she was trying to cover up as much of his skin as possible.

When she'd finished his lower half, she paused at his wrist. "Is it okay if I do a little work on this now? I'm worried about how badly you might have damaged all the ligaments and soft tissue here and it could end up being the most problematic of all your injuries."

He turned his wrist over, palm open and facing the sky. "Do your worst, doc."

Her fingers were warm and firm as she pressed into him, working his forearm and then down to his hand.

When she looked up at him, bent down beside his lounger, her hair falling forward over her shoulder, eyes so big and brown as she gazed up, he felt something instead of him fall apart. All these years he'd tried to hate her, thought he *had* hated her—but hate wasn't the thing he was full of right now, far from it.

She broke their connection, her fingers moving again when before they'd paused, softly against his skin. She cut and pressed the strapping firmly, supporting his wrist as he stayed still, not moving a muscle.

When she'd finished, her fingers hit pause again, not leaving him. And when she looked up, even more wide-eyed than before, he still didn't move. Lauren slowly rose, only halfway, and her hand hovered before moving to his shoulder. Tanner swallowed and waited, until she slowly, slowly bent down. Her hair fell against one of his cheeks as she pushed her palm into his shoulder with more force. For a second he wondered if he'd read the situation wrong, thought perhaps she was just leaning in to massage his shoulder, until her mouth finally found its way to his and she kissed him. Her lips gently brushed against his in a barely there touch, moving back and forth, tasting him, teasing him so bad. Tanner fought the urge to raise his hands and touch her hips, wishing he could coax her down to sit astride him, his fingers itching to wind around her long locks and anchor her in place. But she was the one who'd made the move, and he wasn't going to push his luck. If she wanted to be in control, then dammit, she could be. And he didn't know if the table could take it.

Just as he expected the kiss to deepen, for her to lean into him and dip her tongue into his mouth, she pulled back, fingertips stroking down his cheek. With her other hand she tucked her long hair behind one ear.

There was a gentle knock at the door followed by an enthusiastic *"Bula!"* from their butler.

"Dinner is served," she whispered, leaving him lying there as she rose and disappeared.

Chapter 9

LAUREN watched Tanner rise and head off to bed. It had been a strange day. She'd thought their time together would be tense; that they'd fight or have such a weird animosity between them that it'd be hard to know what to say and how to behave around him. But oddly enough they'd fallen back into step, and she was finding it hard to piece together the fact they'd gone so long without seeing each other.

The truth was, she knew why they weren't fighting, and it was because of what hadn't changed between them. They'd had chemistry like she'd never imagined possible when they'd dated, and it hadn't disappeared. It was the same reason she'd never had any other relationships, because she'd just never felt that same physical connection with any other guy. Life had been good to her, it simply hadn't given her mind-blowing sex or the rush of adrenaline from a man that she'd experienced before with Tanner.

She thought about heading to the beach for a walk in the dark, with the lit torches to guide her, but decided against it. She considered going outside and lying in a lounger for a bit, to enjoy the gentle sound of lapping waves, to maybe pour the last of the champagne—their second bottle—into her glass and curl up on the sofa with her book. But there was only one thing she truly wanted to do, and now that it was in her head . . .

Lauren emptied the rest of the bottle and drank slowly as she tried to muster some courage. Was he stripping off his clothes right now in his room? Was he naked beneath the sheets? She gulped, shutting her eyes and remembering the feel of his skin beneath hers when she'd been massaging him, or the soft, sensual push and pull of his lips against hers when they'd kissed.

She knocked back the rest of her glass, stood and steadied herself, and then headed for the bedrooms. She was barefoot and her feet made the softest padding noise on the timber floor as she walked to his door. She breathed deep and held up her hand. She paused, balling it into a fist, preparing to knock.

Stop.

She hesitated, her hand hovering. If she did this, there was no going back. There was no acting professional and maintaining the high road. Her head spun and she knew she'd had too much to drink. She'd prided herself her entire career on being professional, on *not* getting personal with her clients. Tanner was different, but it was still work, and she wondered whether she would regret it?

Lauren leaned against the door, a more-relaxed palm against it now—and her forehead too. She could almost feel him on the other side. Her fingertips ached, knowing that he was in there and how badly she wanted to touch him.

She took a few silent, deep breaths, then quietly pushed back and headed for her room, closing the door behind her and falling onto her bed. It was better this way, and even though it didn't feel like the right decision now, she knew it would in the morning.

Tanner listened, ears straining to hear what Lauren was doing. He'd heard her moving, even though she was barefoot, and listened to the light switches being flicked in the living room, then the soft pad of her feet as she walked and then stopped. He'd waited, certain she was going to knock, and when he'd looked down and seen the darkness of a shadow outside his bedroom door, he'd been positive she was about to either knock or push his door open. But she hadn't done either.

He shifted in his bed, his head too full of thoughts of Lauren to have any chance of sleeping. He was tempted to go to her room, but if she'd wanted him, she'd have damn well knocked, and he wasn't going to push her.

Instead he reached for his iPhone and decided to do a quick check-in on social media. He never posted anything—the last thing he wanted was the world knowing what he was doing or where he was all the time, but he thought he'd see what the rest of his family was up to. They all loved the side of social media that he hated so vehemently. His dad was the only other family member who wasn't addicted to Facebook—and that was hardly surprising, considering he was in his late seventies.

A message pinged through from Mia then, asking how the vacation was going. He sent her a quick reply saying everything was great, then noticed a link his brother had shared. Tanner clicked and realized it was a weather warning for the South Pacific. He'd also missed five calls from his brother, one from his other sister, and three from his agent, but he'd chosen to ignore them all. He didn't want to deal with questions and demands and more questions, but he did appreciate the weather warning.

"Chance of Gnarly Weather Hitting the Islands." He read the headline twice and groaned. Seriously? Why the hell did he have to be on an island in the middle of goddamn nowhere when the weather turned bad? He scrolled through the rest of the article and saw that this time of year was the rainy season in Fiji, but he wasn't about to let that ruin his time there. The weather had been picture perfect so far, and he wasn't about to jinx it by worrying. He wasn't afraid of a little rain.

He turned his device off and lay down, his head cocooned by a fluffy hotel pillow and his thoughts consumed with the beautiful, leggy brunette lying on her own bed just down the hall. So damn close, but so, so far away.

Lauren woke early, put her hair in a high ponytail and dressed in her running gear. She doubted Tanner would be up, and when she opened her bedroom door the house was silent. She slipped out and couldn't believe how warm it was already—the temperature seemed to be balmy no matter what the time of day. Lauren stretched and limbered up, then settled into a slow jog, smiling as she felt the familiar pull of her muscles. Running was her happy place—it made her brain stop and her senses come to life. She set her sights on the mountain in front of her, moving onto the track and staying slow and steady. She could sprint on the way down if she had the energy, but she didn't know how far it was and she didn't want to have to walk back down if she'd used up all her energy.

She'd come out without her music, and after admiring the scenery and finding her pace, listening to the familiar thud of her shoes hitting the track, her mind started to wander. *Go away*, she said, as if she were speaking to someone in her mind. But the little voice in there wasn't leaving her alone. *What about Tanner?*

She decided to ignore the voice and her own reasoning and run faster. She pushed harder, trying to block it out, but she couldn't. Dammit! She'd made the right choice, the only choice she'd had, so why was she living in her past and even thinking *What if?* What-ifs were dangerous, she knew that, and Tanner seemed happy. They'd both done well, doing what they'd always wanted to do. The only difference was that they hadn't done it together.

"I won't do it," she said defiantly, standing with her hands on her hips and staring at her mother. *"You can't force me to do it!"*

"Lauren, trust me, you have your whole life ahead of you. I remember how appealing the bad boy was. When I was your age I would have felt the same as you do right now, but we know what's right for you."

She'd looked pleadingly at her sister, but there was nothing Hannah could do to help her. She'd already tried talking to Mom for her, but now that they'd made their minds up and given her an ultimatum, they weren't going to back down, no matter what anyone tried to say to get them to change their minds.

"What if I quit then?" she'd asked. "What if I get a job and don't ever go to college?"

Her mom had smiled. "Sweetheart, you're a smart girl. You wouldn't be flipping burgers for long before you'd be begging us to pay for your college tuition."

She laughed then, shaking her head. "And what if Tanner pays for my college education? What if I don't even need you to help me?"

Her father had risen from the table then and come to stand at the foot of the stairs. Lauren was standing halfway up, refusing to give in. She was down to her last days now—summer was almost over and she was going to have to break up with Tanner tomorrow or the day after if she was actually going to do it.

"Quit arguing with your mother, Lauren. You can ask him to pay if you like, be my guest—it'll save me six figures and I'd be eternally grateful—but I think you'll find it's his father who's wealthy, darling, not him. You really think Walter Ford is going to so generously pay for the college education of his son's teenage girlfriend?"

She refused to back down, kept her face fixed even though she was falling to pieces inside.

"His son is a rebel, and from what I've heard his grades are terrible. He might be fun now, but there's no future in fun."

"He's dyslexic, Dad, not dumb!" Lauren could feel her blood boiling but she clamped a hand over her mouth. Why had she said that? Tanner hadn't wanted anyone else to know.

"Dyslexic or not, he's a motorcycle-riding, cigarette-smoking, beer-guzzling bad influence on you, and I will not have him sucking away all your potential. A whole new world opens up when you leave high school, and mark my word, a boy like him is not going to be faithful to a sweet girl like you. It's my job to protect you,

*and if you want me to invest my hard-earned money into
your education, to finish college without debt, then you
will do as we've asked."*

*Lauren's eyes filled with burning hot tears. There
was no way she could ever afford to attend the college
she wanted to go to if she had to pay for it herself. And
if she did manage to get a loan, she'd spend the rest of
her life paying it off. She wanted her own career, to
stand on her own two feet. She'd always dreamed of
turning her love of sports into a career, and if she
couldn't be a sports doctor or a physical therapist, then
what was she going to do?*

*She loved Tanner fiercely, but she wasn't about to be
his plus-one for the rest of her life. She wanted her own
identity, and if her family would never accept him, then
what hope did they have? They might be driving her
crazy, but she loved her mom and dad, and their dis-
like of Tanner had grown rather than faded.*

"Lauren?"

*"Fine," she said. "But if I look back when I'm thirty
and regret what you made me do, then I know who I
have to blame."*

Lauren ran faster, sprinting up the hill until her calves
burned and her throat ached from sucking back so much
humid air. When she reached the top she almost dou-
bled over, leaning forward and trying not to be sick. It
wasn't until she finally stood up that she realized what a
magic spot she was standing on, with 360-degree views
of the islands.

She paced around slowly, needing a moment to catch
her breath and let her heart rest to stop it from explod-
ing. The trouble was, it wasn't the run that her heart was

in danger from, it was Tanner. Because she'd never truly gotten over him, no matter how hard she'd tried, and the words she'd so angrily spat at her parents as a teenager, yelling at them from the family staircase, had come true. She did know who to blame for her heartache, for the fact she'd never met another man who'd even come close to Tanner, but now that she was thirty, she could understand why they'd pushed her to end things.

She and Tanner had been consumed by each other, and if they'd stayed together he would have ended up holding her back. Not because he'd have ever intended on doing it, but because they were like that. They were always joined at the hip, so she would never have taken a job that would have meant extended periods of time away from him. And she would definitely have resented being the plus-one in his life rather than growing on her own. The older she got, the more her financial independence meant to her.

And that was assuming they'd stayed together. That Tanner wouldn't have strayed or wished he'd had the chance to be with other women instead of committing to the girl he'd lost his virginity to. And maybe he wouldn't have been so fearless in the ring. Or maybe she would have tried to stop him from doing something so dangerous.

There were so many what-ifs, it made her head spin.

Lauren turned around and admired the view one last time before heading back down Mount Vomo. In the end, it didn't matter. Shit happened, and her life had been good. She had an amazing career, a home she was proud of, and her family was her rock. She'd long ago forgiven them for their decision about Tanner, but it didn't mean it didn't still hurt like hell, because it damn well did.

But now she was at a crossroads. She was running back to the Beach House, headfirst into Tanner, the former love of her life, and the only man she'd ever truly loved. And maybe the only man she ever would.

"I thought you'd caught the first helicopter out of here."

Tanner watched as Lauren collapsed onto the sofa. Her face was red, hair that had escaped her ponytail was stuck to her skin, and her eyes were shut the second she hit the cushions.

"Been running," she said, slightly out of breath.

Tanner picked up the phone and waited until someone answered.

"Room service."

"Can I have orange juice, fresh fruit, and pancakes for two please?" he asked. "And a couple of strong coffees."

He waited for the order to be repeated to him, thanked the woman on the other end of the line, and turned his attention back to Lauren.

"How was it?"

"It just about killed me but it was amazing."

Tanner stretched out, wishing he didn't feel like an old man and jealous of her workout. He was itching to exercise, to run and sweat and push himself. Instead he was facing a day of painful massage, some light training, and maybe a swim or two. Hardly anything to moan about—he got how lucky he was—but he wasn't great at doing nothing. After a ride around the ranch back home or a big run or working with cattle all day? Hell yeah, he liked to laze about and do nothing. Trouble was that doing nothing had been his life for the better part of two months now.

"I need to run that mountain," Tanner said. "I want to run to the top and beat you."

Lauren groaned and sat up. "You want to race me?"

"Damn straight."

Her laughter made him scowl. "You don't think I can beat you?"

"I don't think you could have beaten me before your accident, let alone now," she said, her face less flushed and her breathing noticeably less rapid. "But we can definitely start with a slow hike and build up to a jog."

Tanner didn't want a slow jog, he wanted a damn-fast, lungs-screaming, arms-pumping kind of sprint.

"I don't want to take a gentleman's jog, Lauren. I want to kick your butt."

This time she didn't laugh. Maybe she'd seen the determination within him, or maybe she just didn't want to burst his bubble.

"Okay, well, you'd better behave and do whatever I tell you to do then," she said. "Call me when breakfast is ready, I'm going for a quick swim."

Tanner expected her to change into a bikini and dive into the pool, but instead she kicked off her shoes, socks, and running top, and ran barefoot out onto the patio and down to the beach in her teeny running shorts and sports bra. He moved to the big open glass doors to watch her cross the beach and run into the water, diving into the aqua-blue ocean. He was tempted to join her, but he decided to leave her be. They were here for work, not pleasure, and that meant letting her do her own thing.

He watched her a bit longer, squinting to see her in the water, and then there was a knock at the door. Breakfast was served.

The butler laid out their food and drinks at the kitchen

table, refusing to let Tanner help, so he grabbed a towel and went out to find Lauren. She was walking up the beach when he made it back outside, and he crossed the deck, opening the towel for her.

She looked radiant—her hair was slicked back off her face, the tie around her wrist and her hair loose down her back. Her skin was still wet, droplets clung to her lashes, and he fought not to look down her body at the sports bra and soaking wet shorts.

"Hungry?"

Lauren grinned. "I could eat a horse."

Tanner let her go first, and she disappeared for a bit as he sat down. He stretched his leg out, happy that it didn't hurt quite as bad today. Maybe all the strapping was working, or perhaps she'd been right about the root of the problem being elsewhere in his body. She'd sure worked hard on his hip and upper leg the day before.

When she returned, she was wearing cut-off denim shorts and a T-shirt and he coughed, almost choking on his juice. Well, damn. It was like someone had wound back the clock and sent him straight back to high school.

"Is there a problem?" she asked, sinking into the chair across from him and instantly picking up her fork and stabbing a piece of pineapple.

"Nope, no problem," he replied, collecting his own fork and starting to eat the fruit platter.

It was filled with sliced banana, melons, pineapple, and strawberries.

"I didn't pick you for a fruit kind of guy," she said. "I thought you'd be all about the bacon and eggs, something fried maybe."

"Something like Mama would make down on the ranch?" he laughed at himself. "In all honesty, I usually do cook my breakfast, but I was trying to impress you. And the fruit is actually damn good."

"We are what we eat," she said, devouring her food. "I always eat fruit and muesli, or if I'm in a hurry it'll be a smoothie on the go, filled with fruit and some protein powder. I can't exactly talk the talk to the players and not follow through myself."

He finished most of his fruit and reached for the pancakes. He'd expected maple syrup when he'd made the order, but instead they'd been served with a side of double cream and strawberries. He raised his eyes and smiled at Lauren. "This negates all that healthy fruit, but damn."

"Hey, I ran to the top of a mountain," she said, pushing her fruit aside. "I can eat pancakes with not a trace of guilt."

"You know, I'm starting to see a pattern with you," Tanner said, setting his fork down and reaching for the coffee. It had been served in a pot, and he poured Lauren a cup first, then himself. "You set your mind to something; you have a pretty gutsy kind of determination."

She shrugged, but he could tell that he'd hit the nail on the head.

"I suppose."

"It's weird, knowing someone so well for a short period in their life, then realizing you actually know nothing about the person they've become." It was becoming abundantly clear that he didn't know a lot about Lauren, not about the woman she'd become. "I feel like you're so familiar to me, but you're a complete stranger too."

"Yeah, same here," she said. "When I look at you, I don't know, it's like walking down memory lane, but

I don't know what makes you tick now. I mean, we were kids back then, right?"

Kids who'd loved the hell out of each other, he thought. Not that it mattered now, but when you'd spent most of your adult life with a chip on your shoulder about the girl you loved ditching you? It was hard to shake it off all in one go. He'd never trust her again, not with his heart, but he kind of liked the woman she'd become. Hell, he admired what she'd done. She'd followed her dreams, and she hadn't stopped until she'd achieved what she'd set out to do.

"Can I ask you something, just for old times' sake?"

"Shoot," she said, smiling at him as she ate another big piece of pancake smeared with cream.

"Do you ever think about what would have happened if we'd stayed together? How different our lives might have turned out?"

She laughed. "Well, I sometimes wonder if I would have been barefoot and pregnant with child number four by now, but . . ."

He shook his head. "I shouldn't have asked."

"It's fine. And to be honest"—he watched as she sat back in her chair, abandoning her food—"I actually used to think about it a lot. I'd wonder what you were doing, whether we'd have been able to make the distance work, whether we'd still be together."

They sat in silence after she said that. It didn't matter what they thought, what *might* have happened. They hadn't stayed together, and that part of their lives was long over.

"Maybe we'd have held each other back," she said. "I often wonder if I'd have been able to do my job and hold down the kind of relationship we had."

"You mean the not-being-able-to-keep-our-hands-off-each-other or spend-a-night-apart aspects?"

The color in her face told him she remembered their time together exactly as he did. He would never forget the intensity of what they'd shared—they'd had their share of fights, often fueled by jealousy or stupid teen-age insecurities—but whenever they were together it was incredible. Every touch, every whisper, everything about them being connected had sent him wild. The thought of being alone with Lauren was enough to fill him with as much anticipation and adrenaline as riding a bull in the ring.

Tanner reached his hand across the table, wanting to touch her but not convinced it was the right thing to do. No wonder he'd hated her so passionately—everything about them was extreme. The love, the hate, the passion.

"My job's demanding and I travel a lot. And so do you," she said. "Would you have been happy doing another job or—"

"Maybe you would have followed me around." He'd meant it as a joke but she clearly didn't find it funny.

"You know, maybe my parents were right about you," she said, taking a swipe at the cream on her plate and licking it from her finger before giving him a stern look. "They told me I'd never be happy being your girl, following you around and having no career or passion of my own. It's funny how you can see that so clearly as a grown-up, but it's so hard to wrap your head around as an eighteen-year-old."

Tanner finished his coffee, eyes leveled on her as he pushed the cup away. "Your parents never did approve of me, did they? I was never good enough for their little girl."

She shook her head. "Would *you* have approved of you? You might have been rich, but you were a bad boy to the core."

"If I had a daughter, I'd be letting her set her own ground rules. You weren't a precious little princess then, you had enough sass to tell me what you wanted or didn't want." He laughed. "I recall you being very vocal about what I was allowed to do, and I never made you do anything you didn't want to do."

Lauren slammed her palm on the table and stood up. She hovered, staring at him, opening her mouth like she was about to say something, then shutting it.

"Am I wrong?" he asked, not backing down and not breaking their stare.

He watched as she gripped the edge of the table, knuckles white like she was grappling with something. Tanner's pulse started to race when he saw a familiar challenge in her gaze.

"Screw what my daddy thought," she murmured, marching around the table to him and placing a hand to his chest to push him back in his seat.

Tanner leaned back as she straddled him, both palms to his chest now, her dark eyes fixed on his. She shifted one hand to his face, staring at his mouth, her own lips parted.

"What are we doing?" he whispered.

She leaned in so close, her lips hovering over his. "Going back to where it all began," she said softly, her breath warm and sweet. "*That's* what we're doing."

Chapter 10

LAUREN refused to listen to the little voice in her head telling her to stop. Why would she stop something that felt so, so good? To hell with being the good girl and doing what was right all the time, because Tanner's mouth against hers felt so damn good, and why couldn't that be the right thing to do? This was just fun. This wasn't serious, this wasn't changing her future or compromising what she wanted. This was something that felt good *for now*.

She shut her eyes and lost herself in the sensation of her lips brushing back and forth against his, her fingers tangled in his hair, pulling his head back so it was at just the perfect angle. She touched his cheek, felt the rough stubble beneath her fingertips—so at odds with the softness of his mouth, with the gentle way he was kissing her.

Lauren pushed harder into him, her thighs pressing to his, tightening around him as she opened her mouth wider, kissed him more fiercely, losing herself to the taste and feel of him. Ohhh, how she'd missed this man!

"Lauren," he murmured, groaning a little and pushing her back.

Her eyes popped open and she saw the strain on his face. Was he not into it? What was—

"This goes against everything I want, but I need you to stop."

She froze.

"You've got a damn tight grip, girl, it's killing me."

Oh shit! "Ohmygod, Tan." She leapt up, realizing that she'd been putting all her weight into him and she'd been squeezing her thighs against him, right into his sore hip, and probably putting way too much pressure on his chest, too. "I'm so sorry. I didn't mean to hurt you."

He laughed and held out a hand to her. She took it, palm to his, looking down at him and wondering how she could be so conflicted when it came to this gorgeous, frustrating man.

"Trust me, I'd normally love that little body of yours all over mine. You're a damn featherweight." He chuckled. "But I'm not exactly in peak condition right now."

She swallowed, seeing the way he was looking at her, knowing what that look meant. He wanted this as badly as she did. Lauren tucked her fingers around his hand, still palm to palm, not wanting him to pull his hand away. The connection made her feel alive, the buzz of anticipation coursing through her body made every nerve ending tingle, every tiny hair on her body stand on end.

"You want to do this?" she asked, sounding braver than she felt about initiating physical contact between them.

"That depends on what *this* is," he replied, the corners of his mouth tugging up into the most irresistible of smiles.

"Me and you," she said. "But just while we're here."

He laughed, deep and throaty and sexy as hell. "You want me for sex and nothing else? Or am I not understanding you correctly?"

She let out a shuddery breath that she hadn't even realized she was holding. "I just want us to"—she paused—"to just *be* while we're here. We can get your body in top shape again and we can enjoy whatever happens between us here, too. A fling."

Tanner looked smug, like the cat that had just swiped all the cream. "I'm not saying no."

She dropped to her knees then saw the surprised look on his face. Lauren laughed. "Easy, tiger, it's not what you think."

She started to rub his leg, massaging it again, kneading deep into his skin. "I might have hurt you before, but my number-one priority while we're here is healing you."

"I know a better way you could heal me," Tanner said, hissing when she pressed hard into his thigh. "That damn bull broke my body, but you were the one who broke my heart."

"Shut up with the broken heart stuff," she said, not wanting to dwell on the past. She already felt guilty enough about what she'd done back then, even though she'd also hurt herself in the process, not just him. It was why she was never going to put herself in that position again—her future husband or long-term partner was going to be a sensible choice, someone who fit the little list she'd made for her potential mate. Steady, reliable, loving. Not someone who made her blood run boiling hot one minute and ice cold the next—that kind of attraction was too explosive, and it made a breakup almost impossible to recover from. Or to survive.

"Or what?" he asked. "What exactly are you going to do to me if I don't shut up?"

She pressed harder into him, making him squirm. "Maybe I'll mount you again and squeeze so hard with my thighs I'll make you scream."

Tanner laughed then, but he was soon howling when she upped the pressure. She was so focused on treating him, trying to keep her own raging libido in check, that she didn't realize he'd leaned forward. His hand suddenly closed around her hair, pulling her up.

"Ouch!" she complained, having to move to relieve the pain. "Stop that!"

"Come here then," he demanded.

Lauren glared up at him, but he'd caught her and she couldn't extract herself without it hurting even more. She clambered forward and ended up leaning over him, his smug smile telling her everything she needed to know. He was a patient man, but he wasn't *that* patient.

"You don't tease me like that, offer me up sex on a platter, and then just switch to work mode."

"I thought I was the one calling the shots?" she asked, her breathing shallow as her heart beat overtime.

"Just because I'm injured doesn't mean you're the boss," he said. "I'm the man, and I say get that pretty little ass over here, sweetheart." He patted his knee.

Lauren wanted to swipe the smile straight off his face, but there was something exciting about his back talk. She was never going to be a girl who was told what to do, but in a fantasy world where she could trust the guy? Right now it was sounding kind of fun, especially when the guy doing the demanding was the man who teased and taunted her over and over in her dreams. And that made it even more obvious to her that this was just a fun thing, it being so far outside her comfort zone of what she'd ever normally engage in.

"Don't you think we should work on you before we . . ." she said, playing with her almost-dry hair and pulling it over one shoulder.

Tanner looked her up and down, and she knew she'd be blushing from her roots to her toes. But this was Tanner. It was the weirdest blend of excitement at being with someone for the first time and anticipation because she'd already been with him and knew exactly how good it would be.

"Sure," he said, as if waiting wasn't difficult, as if he didn't give a damn when he bedded her.

Lauren squirmed on the spot, swallowing and wishing she could just body-slam into him, taking what she wanted. But Tanner was injured, which meant she couldn't treat him as her plaything.

"You want me to massage you? Do you want to take a walk and go for a swim? Maybe we should start practicing for that run you want to do?"

He nodded, clearly trying to act nonchalant when in actual fact she'd bet he was as desperate for her as she was for him.

"You told me you don't like to mix business with pleasure, right? So maybe we should be strictly professional during the day."

Lauren felt like her insides were about to explode. He was repeating her own thoughts to her, and she wished to God he hadn't been listening to her when she'd proudly announced that she'd never been involved with a client. He was toying with her, and she didn't want to take the bait.

"Works for me," she said, trying so hard to stay calm while praying he couldn't detect the rapid beat of her pulse.

"So it's a deal then? We work hard then play harder?" he asked, one eyebrow arched.

She balled her fists, defying the itch of her fingers as they begged to stretch forward. They wanted to touch him, to explore him; just like her mouth did. "Come on then, Tan, let's put you to work."

He opened his mouth to say something but she lunged forward and gripped his hair, her fingers too fast for the hand that grabbed at her wrist to stop her. Just like he'd done to her, she locked him in place, tilting his head back and bending to claim his mouth. She kissed him so hard and so long that it stole the breath from her, left her panting as she slowly released her fingers.

"You can be the boss after dark," she murmured, leaning back in for one more quick kiss, reassuring herself that it was the right thing to do when her stomach erupted into flips. "But when the sun is shining, I'm the boss, and you do as I damn well say."

Tanner's eye glinted, the challenge undeniable. She was in big trouble now—and she couldn't wait.

Her phone rang, breaking the tension and the silence. Lauren waited a beat, not wanting to be the first to look away, but when he didn't back down she just laughed and jumped up to grab it. She didn't recognize the number, and within a second of her missing the call it started again.

"This is Lauren," she answered, presuming it would be work related.

The male voice on the other end was unfamiliar, and extremely quick to get to the point.

"Where the hell are you two and how's his recovery coming along?"

Lauren held the phone away from her ear a little, not liking the tone or the volume. "Ah, and you would be?"

"Tanner's agent. The one he didn't bother filling in on his recuperation plans. I need to know when he's good to go again."

She sighed, looking over at Tanner. He had his eyebrows raised in question. "I don't know how you got my number or why you think I'd breach patient confidentiality, but if you want to speak to your client, I suggest you call your *goddamn client*." Lauren clicked end and then switched her phone off.

"Please don't tell me that was my agent checking up on me?" Tanner said with a groan. "He must be sick of me not answering my phone."

She shrugged. "Come on, we have work to do. You want to talk to him?

"Hell no!" Tanner said. "I'm sick of being asked questions, being told what to do, all of it. I don't want to answer to anyone while I'm here."

"Well, good," she said, meaning it. "If he calls me again, he'll wish he hadn't."

Tanner felt like he'd had an erection all day, and he knew how impressive that was given how damn rough she'd worked him. He was getting punished and he knew it, but whatever she gave him, he grit his teeth and took it, because he was hating not being strong enough to do the things he wanted to do. *Like scoop Lauren up and carry her back to his bedroom like a goddamn caveman.* The fact he'd had to call an end to their fun at the kitchen table this morning had almost killed him, but it had also reminded him of just how hard he had to work to get his body back.

Without his strength, he felt useless. He craved the feeling of his calves burning from a run instead of every muscle, bone, and ligament in his leg feeling like they were going to collapse. And he wanted to feel the same kind of burn in his lungs from fighting for air after a workout rather than the piercing stab he still grappled with from where he'd been gouged.

"How you feeling, cowboy?" Lauren asked.

He could feel sweat on his brow, knew he was glistening, while she looked cool as a cucumber.

They'd been walking, they'd stretched and stretched some more, then gone for a light swim. Now he was lying on his stomach while she performed another deep massage, focusing on his upper body this time, and he was more strapped up than he'd been the day before. He was seriously getting used to living on Fiji time, and he seriously liked that she'd let him lie on the sand for this massage.

"I'm feeling like by the time it's my turn to be the boss, I won't have any skin left to show. You'll be naked and I'll look like a mummy all bandaged up."

Her laugh was sweet. "Sorry. It got pretty intense there, but you're in a bad way."

"So you keep telling me." He groaned as he rolled over.

"So what are our plans for the rest of the day?" he

asked, looking up into her big brown eyes and wishing she'd been giving him an entirely different kind of massage. He reached for her hair, coaxing his fingers beneath the tie that held it up off her face. It didn't take long for it come free, and her hair tumbled down her shoulders. That's the way he liked it—her dark mane wild and loose.

"Well, you know Fiji," she mused, sucking in her bottom lip and giving him the cutest damn look. "It gets dark here pretty early."

He inhaled, sharply, biting down on his fist to stop from touching her. "So I'm officially yours until sunset. Do I get to rest now?"

She slowly bent to him, her lips hovering into a smile. "Uh-huh," she murmured, her lips so close to his he could feel the heat of her breath, could sense the hum of her skin as she paused.

Finally she kissed him, so softly it was barely even a touch. "I'm going in to take a shower. I'll see you at dinner."

"Dinner?" He'd been thinking they'd head straight to bed.

"A girl needs her strength," she said as she rose and winked at him, laughing as she walked off.

"When you said *shower* . . ." he called out after her.

"I meant me, in the shower, alone," she confirmed, holding onto the big glass door as she looked back at him. "See you at dinner, Tanner. And I'll leave out some turmeric supplements for you to take."

"Turmeric?"

"It's a wonder food, trust me. A week of taking that twice daily and my expert care, and you'll be feeling like a fine-tuned athlete." She gave him a look that he couldn't decipher. "If you're game, I'll even switch your coffee to a turmeric latte. It's surprisingly good."

He raised a brow and shook his head. "Sweetheart, I'll swallow the pills, but try to get me drinking turmeric coffee and that'll be the end of me following orders. Period."

Tanner stayed propped up on his elbow watching her go before collapsing back down onto the lounger. His body was sore still, but he was getting used to that—it was the fatigue he was finding hard to deal with. The recovery post-accident wasn't something he'd expected to be so hard, but then his recovery was turning out like nothing he could ever have expected.

When Mia had suggested he work with Lauren, it had been like he was the bull and someone was wildly waving a red flag in his line of sight. He'd snapped at his sister and been like a bear with a thorn in his paw in the days and weeks leading up to their departure for Fiji. And now? Now he was salivating over the one woman who'd stopped him trusting any female he'd ever been intimate with.

He knew he'd never trust her like that again, but sex was sex. The fact he hated what she'd done to him way back when didn't mean he'd ever stopped being attracted to her. Hell, he'd woken up slick with sweat, the sheets tangled around him, plenty of times, with naked Lauren images filling his head. The dreams he'd had about her, the fantasies of having his wicked way with her one more time, had never left him. Which is why he'd probably never forgiven her, because a part of her had always stayed with him.

Now he had the chance to get her out of his system

once and for all, and it was him calling the shots. He was the one who'd decide when they caught their private jet back to Texas, meaning he was the one deciding when their summer fling would end. There would be no broken hearts, just two satisfied adults who made the most of the dark hours on an island in the middle of the Pacific.

Tanner was all about the no-strings-attached affair; hell, it had been his motto his entire adult life. He closed his eyes and decided to rest awhile, needing the downtime to recover from the deep tissue massage, but behind his lids all he saw was Lauren.

His fingers clenched around her hair, tipping her head back so he could see the soft, creamy skin of her throat. He grazed his teeth across her, his other hand finding its way to her butt, indenting into her skin as he felt her rock against him. That had always been the fantasy, opening his eyes to find her mounted on him, riding him, her beautiful, shapely body filling his hands and his senses. Until she'd open her eyes and look down at him, as if she was seeing him for the first time, realizing who she was with.

Stop. He opened his eyes, no longer wanting to rest. That wasn't how it was going to end tonight. Tonight, he wouldn't wake up at that same moment. Tonight, he would look into Lauren's eyes and she'd know exactly who she was climbing into bed with. And the only thing he'd see was the same desire reflected in his own gaze. Lauren wanted him and he wanted her.

He was in for one hell of a ride, that was for damn sure.

His phone started to vibrate and he groaned, reaching for it. So much for ignoring it for the next week. He stared at the screen, annoyed the number was showing as private.

"Hello," he growled down the line.

"Tanner, what the hell do you think you're doing just leaving without—"

"Shut up," he said. "Just shut the hell up and leave me alone. I left a message for you stating that I was to be contacted only in an emergency."

His agent was relentless, which Tanner had always liked—until recently. Now it was driving him nuts. "This *is* an emergency! I have media wanting big interviews, and we need to convince Wrangler that you're going to be making a comeback or they won't exactly be receptive next week when I'm trying to renew your sponsorship contract."

"Marty, that's *not* an emergency," Tanner said, surprised by how calm he was being. "Call me again in the next fortnight, and I'll be ending *our* contract and looking for a new agent. Are we clear?"

He ended the call and checked his text messages before holding down the side button, turning off the phone. He stared at the blank screen and grinned. Now *that* was more like it. He'd turn it on again later, but for now he was going to enjoy the silence.

Chapter 11

LAUREN could barely sit still. She was seated across from Tanner at what was possibly the most beautiful place she'd ever eaten dinner. They had a private table on the beach, away from the other guests, with tropical flowers set in the middle of the wooden tabletop and lines of torches burning to either side of them. It was perfect.

And so was the man seated across from her. Not "perfect" in a forever kind of way, but "perfect" for now. This was her chance to get him out of her system, to relax and play like she'd never done in college, to just be herself and to hell with the consequences. Because when they got home, they'd walk away from each other and step straight back into their old lives.

The look he was giving her was smoldering, his eyes never leaving hers, the hint of a smile playing constantly over his lips. Tanner reached for the champagne, within arm's reach in a bucket of ice, and poured both of them a second glass.

"Have you noticed that the sun has gone down?" he asked.

The dark pink sky had slowly turned to inky black, and Lauren swallowed as she stared back at him, holding her champagne flute so tightly she feared the stem might snap.

"I have."

His wink was slow and purposeful and she felt her stomach quiver, flip-flopping and full of nerves. This was torturous, knowing what was going to happen between them, knowing how badly they each wanted a rematch. But she had a feeling he was enjoying every second of drawing their evening out.

"Lobster linguine," the waiter said, placing their second course on the table in front of them.

Lauren inhaled the smell of butter and garlic, her mouth salivating. "This looks incredible," she said. "It's just lucky we're eating the same food. Our garlic breath is going to be terrible!"

Tanner laughed and picked up his fork, and she watched as he twirled his first mouthful of linguine. What surprised her was that with his left hand he reached for her, fingers stroking gently across the inside of her wrist before settling over her own fingers.

Her pulse ignited and she stayed still, listening to her own breath as he looked at her. "It's been twelve years since I held your hand."

She knew exactly how long it had been. "And twelve years since we lay in the back of your pickup and stared up at the stars."

That had been the side of him that she'd wished her parents had known—the young man who wasn't trying to show off, who shared his dreams and his thoughts with her. She'd loved both sides of him, because the show-off Tanner had been so much fun, but what she'd missed was the moments they'd spent alone. Two kids in love, just being real. At school he'd tried to act out and cover up his learning issues, never telling anyone else and swearing her to secrecy when he found out he was dyslexic, so when they were alone it was the real him. Or at least that's how it had always felt.

"Twelve years since we made out by the river."

"Made out?" she laughed. "I think we did more than just make out and you know it."

Tanner slowly released his fingers from hers and she stared down at her dinner, no longer wanting food. Anticipation fueled her, made her want to just tell him to shut the hell up with the reminiscing and make some new damn memories.

"Not in the mood for lobster?" he asked.

Lauren reluctantly picked up her fork and eyed the succulent, big pieces of lobster among the linguine and garlic. Dinner looked delicious, she was just hungry for something else.

"So are you serious about making a comeback in the ring?" she asked, deciding to change the subject. "Or are you just all talk, not wanting to admit defeat yet?"

"Hell yes," he said, looking surprised by her question. "I thought I'd made that clear? It's the reason we're here. I'll be making my comeback, you can be damn sure of that."

Lauren finished her mouthful. "I just, I don't know—don't take this the wrong way—but I've been wondering if you were just pushing back at your family, because they wanted you to stop."

"I'm a grown man now, Lol, in case you haven't

noticed. I don't need my father's permission when it comes to my work *or* my personal life." He gave her a long look. "Can you say the same?"

She coughed as she looked up at him, garlic catching in her throat. "You know, there's a difference between needing permission and showing respect," she said, choosing her words carefully. "I make my own decisions about my life, but would I be with a man my parents or even my sister didn't approve of? I can unashamedly say I wouldn't be, because our family time together is too precious to me. I love spending holidays together, my family means so much to me, and if I have a husband one day I want him to be a true member of my family."

Tanner turned his attention back to his dinner, and she wished she knew what he was thinking. Had he changed his mind about wanting to be with her? Had she offended him?

"Is that why you ended things with me? Or was I just not good enough for you?"

Lauren groaned. For a moment she turned her attention to her food, eating a mouthful and then another, trying to figure out what to say. Was she supposed to be honest, after all this time, or did she keep her secret? Maybe Tanner deserved to know, but then what use was it confessing the truth to him?

"I thought we were just going to enjoy being together while we were here?" she asked. "But whatever my reasons were, they had nothing to do with you not being good enough for me. That's the stupidest thing I've ever heard." He was from one of the wealthiest, most well-known families this side of Texas—how the hell could he think for a second that she somehow didn't think he was good enough for her?

"We are just in this for fun," he said, his voice low as he reached for her hand again. This time his touch felt stronger, more determined. "But I've never forgotten that look on your face, and I've wondered all these years whether it was your decision or not. It was the one thing that drove me crazy, not knowing why."

"You've got to be kidding me," she said, trying to throw him off the trail, not wanting to go down this path. "All the beautiful women you've bedded, all the groupies who salivate over you when you're on tour, haven't been enough to get your mind off that moment? You've seriously thought about the why?"

His laugh was deep. "I've been well distracted, I'm not gonna lie, but something about you has always stuck with me. Tell me you didn't feel the same and I'll call you a liar."

She shrugged. "Maybe I did think about that moment," she said, confessing that much at least. In reality she'd played the moment over and over in her mind every single night, sometimes multiple times a day, remembering the hurt in his eyes, the pain she'd caused them both when she'd broken things off. "But it was a long time ago."

"Tell me the why, Lauren," he asked, and she knew she couldn't keep putting him off without giving him an answer. "I just need to know if it was your parents. After all this time, surely it doesn't matter if I find out?"

She sighed and took a long, cool sip of champagne. "It's true. They gave me an ultimatum, and I gave in."

"Just like that?"

She slammed her glass down on the table harder than she meant to. "No, Tanner, not *just like that*. I fought and kicked and screamed, but in the end I had to make the choice I made. And it was the right damn choice."

"What was it?" His voice was low, his stare was impossible to avoid. "What was more important than us?"

"My college tuition," she confessed, her voice low as she finally told him what she'd held close all these years. "They paid my college tuition in full and I came out debt free and able to focus on the future I wanted to build for myself. The career I'd been dreaming of became possible because they helped me, because I traded us for my education. You happy now?"

He was silent for a long time, still holding her hand. She'd expected him to pull it away, but he didn't.

"They say the truth sets you free," he finally replied, "but now all I'm thinking is why the hell didn't you just ask me for the money? Were you too proud? Why wouldn't you have tried to find another way?" He laughed. "I could have paid whatever tuition you needed from my trust fund if you couldn't have gotten your own loan."

She blinked away tears as they slowly filled her eyes. It wasn't often she felt the raw burn of emotion like that, not wanting to cry over anything ever, but this was Tanner, and talking about all this had plunged her straight back into the past. The decision she'd had to make, the things she'd considered to avoid having to end things, and why she knew she'd made the right choice.

"I did try to get a loan. I went to three different banks, I worked out my options, but seven years of studying was just . . ." She blew out a breath. "Working part-time covered my living costs, but my folks paid for the best education money could buy and I couldn't match it. And I sure as hell wasn't going to ask my boyfriend for the cash. What would your dad have thought if you'd told him you needed money for some floozy to go to college? I could never have asked that of you, and my pride wouldn't have let you pay my way for me anyway." She shook her head sadly. "I wanted to make my own way in the world, and my parents helping their daughter achieve her dreams is different than a boyfriend doing it."

"You were hardly some floozy, Lauren."

"To you, maybe not. But to Walter Ford? I'd have looked like some money-hungry gold-digger, and I could never have lived with anyone thinking I was with you because I wanted something other than just plain old you."

They both stayed silent, and then it was Lauren who pulled away. She went back to eating, not wanting to waste what was one of the most beautiful dinners she'd ever had. She shouldn't have told him, because Tanner would only see how he could have fixed the situation. And it hadn't been something she'd wanted him to fix.

"Can we just forget about the past?" she asked. "Our breakup ripped my own heart out as much as it ripped out yours, and I don't want to go back."

His smile was tight now, his expression more melancholy than she'd seen since they'd arrived in Fiji.

"All this time, that's been the one thing I've wanted to know. I should have asked you a decade ago why you'd ended things, and maybe I wouldn't have become so damn bitter and twisted."

"Yeah, well, water under the bridge now, right?"

"Water under the bridge," he repeated, but she knew they were just words. Neither of them would ever forget their heartache as teenagers, the pain of having your first love ended so abruptly.

"Do you think less of me now?" she asked. "Now that you know I gave you up for college?"

"No." His answer was fast. "It changes everything, actually."

"How?" Lauren was confused. Why did he not hate her even more now that knew the truth?

"Because all this time, I thought you'd been a heartless bitch who'd somehow managed to string me along when you had no intention of staying together," Tanner told her, the huskiness of his voice telling her that he was finding this whole conversation as emotional as she was. "But following your dreams is one thing I do understand. My family has tried to push me in other directions, tried to bully me into doing something different with all kinds of the threats and tactics, but I stayed true to what I wanted. Bull riding was my passion and I wouldn't give that up for anyone or anything, although I've always promised myself that if I need to step in to our family business, if anything ever happens to Dad, I'll do it in a heartbeat. I won't be pressured into it or told what to do, but when that day comes, my allegiance will be clear."

"So you get it?"

"I more than get it, I goddamn admire it," he said. "I just wish you'd been able to give your parents the two-finger salute and get the guy at the same time."

She met his gaze then smiled back at him, his grin contagious. "Maybe having a fling with the guy twelve years later is enough."

"Damn right," he repeated. "Now finish eating, we've

got dessert to go and then I'm throwing you over my shoulder and taking you to bed."

His phone buzzed then and Tanner reached for it, his eyes not leaving hers, making her squirm in her seat. When he glanced at the screen he groaned.

"Why did I even bring this damn thing with me?"

"Your agent again?" She'd noticed that he'd switched his phone to silent after the first day of calls—everyone seemed to want a piece of him, even while he was away.

He nodded. "I thought I couldn't get my family off my back, but this guy is . . ." He refused the call, and she watched as he held his finger on the button to turn the phone off. "They all want me to recover? They can leave me the hell alone to do it. And they can stop asking me when, what, how . . ." Tanner groaned. "I told him I'd fire him if he called me again, so I guess he's called my bluff."

She laughed. "I wholeheartedly agree." His agent wanted to know when he'd be making his comeback, his sister wanted to know how everything was going, and the rest of his family . . . well, she guessed they were wanting to talk him into retirement. Whatever they were all hassling him about, he didn't seem to want to engage with them.

Tanner grinned back and pushed his phone away, and Lauren suddenly couldn't take her eyes off him.

Tanner stretched out in his chair, staring at Lauren and realizing there had been so much going on in her head that he hadn't known about. Why the hell hadn't he guessed what had happened all those years ago? He'd hated her for something that had hurt her as much as it had hurt him, and all this time he'd hated her for what she'd done.

He watched as she tossed her long hair back over her shoulder, leaning back in her seat now that she'd finished her linguine. She was so effortlessly beautiful, and he wondered if she knew just how attractive she was. In a world full of bottle blondes, too-white teeth, and fake everything, she was a classic brunette beauty, and he liked the fact that she'd been so open about her ambitions. It might have ended their relationship, but she was driven and that's what he liked about her. He could have found a way to help her pay for college, he was sure of it, but it would have been him taking charge, him pulling the strings instead of her parents. And he would have also caused a divide between her and the family she loved more than anything.

He poured the last of their champagne and held up his glass. Lauren had an air of uncertainty about her, and he wanted to quell any fears she had about her confession.

"To fresh starts and new beginnings," he said, clinking his glass to hers.

She smiled, lighting up her entire face. "To fresh starts," she echoed.

Tanner sipped his drink and watched her do the same, not breaking their connection even when dessert arrived.

"Chocolate torte with almond brittle ice cream," the waiter announced, setting the plates in front of them.

"Sounds delicious," Tanner murmured.

And even in the dim light, he was certain he could see Lauren's cheeks flush a deep, cute-as-hell pink.

"Stop looking at me like that," she whispered when they were alone again.

"Like what?"

"Like you're about to eat me alive."

He laughed, not bothering to respond. She clearly knew him too well.

They ate in silence, her stealing glances at him that he couldn't help but notice as he downed his dessert and patiently waited for her. She devoured every last bite and then slowly, almost shyly, met his gaze.

"How's your body feeling?" she asked.

"My body?" he laughed. "My *body* is feeling great right now."

"I mean how are you feeling post-treatment? I'm really hoping the turmeric will help with your recovery and combined with—"

Tanner stood and held out a hand, pulling Lauren up to her feet and then placing a finger across her lips. "Stop talking."

She kissed his finger and he shook his head, not expecting her to flirt with him so unashamedly when before she'd been blushing.

"Come with me," he said, taking her hand and linking their fingers. Tanner nodded his thanks to the waiter and led Lauren away, down the beach heading for the Beach House. She dropped her head to his shoulder and it took him back in time, back to the woman who'd driven him crazy with lust.

When they were almost there, Tanner stopped walking and turned into Lauren. It was completely dark out, but the flaming torches provided enough light to illuminate the sand they were walking on and for Tanner to make out the features of Lauren's face. There was something about relaxing into a routine with her, their days full of nothing other than sunshine, rehabilitation, and . . . whatever the hell was going on between them.

He cupped her cheeks, looking into her eyes as he dipped his mouth to hers. Her arms encircled his neck and her mouth met his, lips hungrily searching out his as they kissed. Tanner rubbed the pads of his thumbs across her skin, then slowly released his hands and let them skim down her shoulders and to her waist. When his hands stopped, she leaned into him, drawing him closer, fusing their bodies together, chest to chest, hip to hip, thigh to thigh.

Tanner knew they should start walking again but he didn't want to stop. Her lips, her butt as he ran his fingers further down and stopped at the delicious curve, her soft moan against his mouth. It was already shaping up to be one hell of a rematch and they hadn't even started taking their clothes off yet.

It was Lauren who finally pulled back, her hands slipping between them and resting against his chest. Tanner's heart was beating rapidly beneath her palms, and when she tilted back to look up at him, he could see a desperation in her eyes that he recognized only too well.

"Take me to bed, cowboy," she whispered.

"Honey, I'd sweep you up into my arms if I could, but tonight you'll have to settle for an arm around you."

Lauren nestled under the crook of his arm, her hand slipping into his back pocket as she settled in snug to his body. He dropped a kiss into her hair and walked as quickly as his awkward limp would let them.

Chapter 12

LAUREN stood in the bathroom, trying not to double over. She stared at herself in the mirror, knowing that if she didn't give herself a damn good pep talk soon, she'd end up chickening out of this entire . . . she didn't even know what it was. *Sex*. That's what it was.

"Sex," she whispered to herself, looking into her own eyes in the reflection and wishing they looked more confident and less scared little mouse. "You don't forget how to do it, girl. It's like riding a horse."

It hadn't been that long, had it? She thought back to the last guy she'd been with and shuddered. Oh yeah, it had been that long. It seemed like only recently they'd ended things but . . . she gulped. But this was Tanner. If she'd needed a boost to her libido, then he'd already done it, but actually walking out that door and into his naked arms? Her pulse started to race again. She should have drunk more at dinner, and then maybe she wouldn't be having such a panic attack.

Knock, knock. "Everything okay in there?"

Holy shit. She needed a paper bag to breathe into or a big glass of whisky or . . .

"Lauren?"

She sucked back a breath. "Everything's fine," she said, hearing the hesitation in her own voice.

"Can I come in?"

She didn't answer, just kept staring at herself for as long as she could until Tanner appeared and she turned around.

"Hey," he said. "You look—"

"Scared?" she whispered, knowing how pathetic it was that she'd talked the talk but was now holed up inside his bathroom. She inhaled the smell of his cologne, still clinging to the bathroom from when he'd showered and gotten ready to go out for dinner. As he stepped closer, she could smell it all over again, only this time it was mixed with the masculine smell that was all Tanner.

"Why are you scared?" he asked, stopping a foot or so in front of her. He held out a hand and she raised her own shaky one to his. "If you've changed your mind, it's okay. All that talk about me being the boss after dark, it was just talk." His smile was sweet, just like she remembered, and when he opened his mouth to say something else, she rushed the distance between them and pressed her lips to his. Tanner didn't miss a beat, his arms encircling her, pressed to her lower back as she lost herself in the feel of him kissing her.

Lauren tasted him, her tongue touching his, hands running down his back and exploring the firmness of his body. To hell with doubting herself and feeling scared, she was a single woman and if she wanted to reunite with her ex for a steamy couple of weeks, then why the hell couldn't she?

"It's like riding a horse," she whispered against his mouth.

Tanner pulled back a little. "What?" he murmured.

"Nothing. Just shut up and keep kissing me."

A noise deep in his throat might have been laughter, but it also sounded a whole lot like a moan as her fingers skimmed the hem of his T-shirt and lifted, breaking their kiss to tug it up. Tanner lifted his arms as she pulled it over his head, dropping the soft fabric straightaway so she could explore his chest. It was smooth and hard, his shoulders and biceps bigger now, broader and more muscled than she remembered them being. She traced her fingers through the light smattering of hair on his chest and then over his shoulders down his back. When she curved them back around she gasped, realizing she'd just traced over the scars from where the bull had caught him.

"Sorry," she murmured.

Tanner ignored her and tilted her chin up, fingers locked beneath it, his mouth crushing down on hers and not giving her a chance to gasp for air. He walked her backward, her butt connecting with the vanity, and he grunted as he boosted her up, hands cupped beneath her.

She wondered if his wrist hurt, if he was sore, but Tanner wasn't giving her time to worry about the state of his body. She kept her hands on his bare skin, wanting to touch every inch of him, loving the feel of his hard, male body against hers. But Tanner wasn't going to let her have all the fun. His mouth dropped to her neck and he kissed down her chest, lips touching the top of her breasts, making her gasp.

Lauren's dress was riding high and Tanner pushed into her, forcing her legs to part even wider as he stepped into her space, lips still teasing her. The moan she heard in the distance must have come from her, the sounds of pleasure she couldn't keep quiet as Tanner slowly pushed one strap of her dress off her shoulder and then skimmed across her skin to the other side.

With a little coaxing, her dress fell down to her waist, exposing her breasts, and Tanner's mouth moved lower, kissing her, plucking at her skin, before passing slowly, softly over her nipples.

"Tanner," she whispered, wriggling into him, trying to push his head up so she could claim his mouth and kiss him again. She wanted her lips to his, wanted to taste him more, to feel his tongue teasing her mouth.

He ignored her and went back to her breasts, but she flicked her fingers around his jaw and forced his head up, quickly moving her mouth against his and pressing her breasts to his chest. The warmth of him was in contrast to the cool of the vanity against her butt, and she wrapped her arms around him.

As a senior in high school, her favorite thing to do had been kissing Tanner. She'd liked everything with him, but his full lips had driven her crazy, that lazy way he could kiss her—as if he had all the time in world—had driven her crazy. And he still kissed the same—as if there was no reason to hurry, like he could do it all day.

But Lauren had been waiting a long time and she wasn't going to settle just for kisses. She reached down and fumbled with his buttons, trying to keep her lips to his as she worked on ridding him of his clothes. When she'd succeeded she tucked her fingers beneath the waistband of his boxers and pushed them down.

"What's the hurry?" he asked, sounding amused as

he murmured against her skin, stepping out of his underwear.

She looked him up then down, seeing exactly how much he wanted her. Tanner's smile told her he knew exactly how impressive his package was, and when he slipped his hand under her dress and slid her panties down, she didn't try to stop him.

A ripple of pleasure surged through her and she knew how silly she'd been to worry. She might not have been intimate with a man for a while, but her body knew exactly what to do and everything about Tanner was pushing her to the edge. She wanted him and she wanted him now!

"Do you have any protection?" she asked.

"Shit, no," he swore, looking panicked when he stared down at her. "But I'm clear. I had an STD test when I was in the hospital."

"I'm on the pill." She hesitated, not about to elaborate and tell him that pregnancy wasn't actually something that was likely to happen anyway. "We've got nothing to worry about."

His fingers dug into her thigh as he tugged her forward, his mouth finding hers again, and Lauren sucked on his bottom lip as she wriggled all the way forward, one hand on Tanner's shoulder and the other bracing herself from behind. She slid down onto him, making him groan, neck arching back in ecstasy.

"Geez, Lauren," he whispered, "you want this to be over in two seconds?"

She laughed and matched his thrust, loving the feel of him, wrapping her legs tight around him. "We've got all night, don't we?"

Tanner made a low growl in his throat and thrust

harder, making her moan as she clung on to him. If she was hurting him he never said, although maybe he couldn't feel the pain through the pleasure.

"Lauren," he murmured, and she dug her fingers into his butt, forcing him forward, pleasuring herself against him as he thrust forward.

Tanner grit his teeth, trying to hold back. Damn her! The little vixen had taken him by surprise, and he would have put an end to it, would have insisted on slowing things down, but the pleasure on her face was abundantly clear. He refused the urge to shut his eyes as waves of pleasure pulsed through him—he wanted to see her. Who would have thought he'd be butt naked in a bathroom in Fiji with Lauren goddamn Lewis.

"Harder," she mumbled, biting into his shoulder as she tightened her grip around him, legs wrapped tight around his torso.

"No," he ground out, refusing to give in when he was so close to climaxing. He pulled back and sucked in deep breaths, wishing to hell they'd put the air-conditioning on before they'd gone out to combat the humid air. "Bedroom, now," he ordered, pointing to his bed through the open door. His ankle protested when he turned and stretched, but not before Lauren noticed that something was wrong.

"Crap, did I hurt you?"

"You haven't broken me yet, sweetheart," he said, slapping her on the backside and laughing as she ran ahead and flopped down on the bed. He stalked after her, not giving a damn about any pain in his body as he looked at naked Lauren lying so invitingly on the bed. Her hair was all around her as she lay on her back, full breasts sending him wild, but with her knees still together. She parted them, only just, and he roughly pushed one leg down and dropped to his knees.

His hip hurt then, grinding as he bent to kiss Lauren, and he rolled to his side instead, arms wrapped around her and taking her with him.

"I *did* break you," she whispered, looking worried.

"I'm not broken," he replied, reaching up and stroking her long hair as it fell forward, toward him. "I just need you to do all the work for a bit."

She leaned down and kissed him, slowly, teasing him with her tongue. "Sounds good to me."

Tanner placed his hands on Lauren's lips as she eased down onto him and rocked back and forth, her long hair teasing across his chest, like a feather tickling his skin. She threw her head back and her hair went over her shoulders, brushing his thighs when she leaned back.

She moved faster and he lifted one hand to cup her breast, loving the heaviness in his palm as she leaned forward a little, her eyes opening and fixing on his. Lauren stared at him as she pleasured herself, and he smiled up at her, wondering how he'd ended up with her in charge when the nights were supposed to be his. But he wasn't about to complain, because this was turning out to be the perfect kind of night, regardless of who was in charge. And best of all it wasn't making his injuries flare up—he could enjoy every second of it.

"Tanner," she whispered, stopping and moving down, her hands landing on either side of his head as she skimmed her lips to his. He kissed her back, not noticing the wet of her lashes against his cheek immediately. It wasn't until she sat back up that he realized there were tears in her eyes.

The moment passed and Lauren was arched back again. He ran his hands down her back, fingers pressed to her butt to make her move faster, and the more he watched her, the more he fixed his eyes on this gorgeous creature sitting astride him, the closer he got to the edge.

"Lauren," he cautioned, about to tell her to stop, that he wanted to last longer.

Her smile was wicked as she placed a hand flat to his chest and refused to slow down. She pushed him to the edge and he gave in, as likely to stop his climax from shuddering through him as he would have been able to stop a storm from swirling through the sky.

She stayed on top of him, rocking more slowly, eyes still shut as she basked in what he hoped was the same level of pleasure that he'd just experienced.

"That was amazing," she whispered as she collapsed down on top of him, elbows bracing her as she stared down into his eyes then rolled over.

Tanner propped himself up on one elbow and looked down at her; at her flushed cheeks and the relaxed way she had one arm flung above her head, hair all mussed up and covering the pillow.

"I've waited a long time for that," he said, grinning when she play-punched his arm.

"I'm exhausted," she mumbled, rolling over and snuggling into him. "Can I lie here for a minute? I just . . ." Her voice trailed off and Tanner lay back down, letting her tuck in against his chest. He shut his eyes and wondered what the hell he was doing, in bed with the woman who'd caused him so much damn grief.

Exhaustion settled in—from their training, from the

mental fatigue of trying to push his body, and from the sex. Hell, it had been good sex. He smiled as he drifted off, deciding to rest for just a minute before getting up to take the turmeric tablets Lauren was so darn insistent he swallow morning and night.

Chapter 13

LAUREN yawned as she woke, stretching her arm out and slowly opening her eyes. She was so warm and cozy, the bed so comfortable and . . . She gasped, realizing she was tucked up to Tanner's warm chest. How had she ended up spending the night in his arms?

She wriggled a little, but his arm tucked tighter around her. So much for sex only—she'd snuggled into him for the night like he was still the love of her life, not her summer fling.

"Morning."

Lauren looked up at the deep, husky voice and into Tanner's eyes as he blinked and yawned, his thumb brushing her shoulder.

"Morning," she murmured back.

Tanner stretched his arms up and she took the chance to scoot over a little, turning onto her stomach so her breasts were pushed into the bed. She tucked the pillow up tight to her chest as she looked over at him.

"So much for a quick rest," he said, laughing and reaching out for her.

Lauren froze at his touch, not sure what to do as he ran his fingers down her hair, still staring at her. When she'd locked herself in the bathroom the night before, it had been because she wasn't sure what to do, what all this meant, whether she'd be able to follow through with her flirtations. Well, she'd sure as hell managed the follow-through part okay, but she was feeling in need of that paper bag to breathe into again about now.

"Sorry, I didn't mean to stay in here all night, I just . . ."

He gave her a weird look. "Are we okay? You look worried."

She sighed when he reached for her, fingers on her shoulder, tugging her toward him. "I don't know what the rules are with this kind of thing. I mean, *is* this okay?"

His laughter was gruffer this time and he leaned in and claimed a kiss. "No idea, but we're the one writing the rules, so who gives a damn?"

His lips were as warm and soft as the bed sheets wrapped around her, cocooning her and making her forget everything else. She kissed him back, still keeping the pillow tucked to her breasts as a familiar flutter in her stomach told her she still wanted Tanner just as bad this morning as she had the night before.

"Oh shit, we'd better stop," he said, pushing her back a little.

"Why, did I hurt you again?" she asked. "I'm the worst therapist around!"

The humor in his gaze made her glare at him. "What?"

"It's just that I thought day time was for workouts and training. Not my PT taking advantage of me in the bedroom."

Lauren swatted at him, but he caught her wrist and placed a kiss to the inside of her palm.

"Until tonight then," she murmured.

"Oh, I have *no* problem being taken advantage of," he said, lying back with his arms above his head. "For the record, I'm all yours."

She refused to take the bait, deciding she'd damn well make him wait if he was going to tease her like that. "Well, if you're all mine then get up, get dressed, and be ready for a swim in ten minutes. Training starts now."

He laughed. "Oh, so it's like that, is it?"

She sat up and took the sheets with her, holding them tight to her body as she got up and walked out.

"What are you trying to hide? It's nothing I haven't seen before," Tanner called out as she headed for her own bedroom.

She giggled as she walked, feeling like a naughty girl caught out late with her boyfriend or trying to sneak back without being seen. This Tanner was like the one she'd fallen for all those years ago, the one she'd yearned for and mourned like he'd died. It couldn't last for long, but it was the rematch she'd needed, to get him out of her system once and for all, on her terms this time. She would walk away from him, but it would be because she wanted to this time, because it could never work between them, not because someone else was pulling the strings and forcing her hand.

Lauren washed and got into her one-piece, ready to swim alongside Tanner in the pool to help get his strength up. She liked the workout and it was good to be completely hands on with him, to see how far and hard she could push him.

"Lauren?"

She paused and wondered if she'd imagined Tanner's call. "Do you need me?" she called back.

"Yeah."

She picked up a towel and carried it under her arm, heading back into Tanner's room.

"Everything okay?" she asked, before seeing him sitting on the bed, still naked, with a grimace on his face that told her everything was definitely not okay.

"Sorry, I just don't feel right. My leg, it's, I don't know how to describe it, but when I put weight on it, it was weak."

She dropped to her knees and placed her hands on him, tugging at the tape she'd used to do the strapping with. "Let me take this off, see how you feel."

Had she pushed him too hard? Had something made him worse instead of helping him?

"I'm sore, but it's more than that. It's like my ankle or something is burning."

"Lie back," she said, hands resting on his skin and massaging more gently than she had been the day before. "You've got a lot of damage there to ligaments and soft tissue, so it was always going to be a slow recovery, but maybe we need to ease off a little, just focus on swimming, massage, and complete rest otherwise."

She glanced up at him and cracked up when she realized he was lying on his back, with his package on full display. Funny how she could totally ignore the fact that his gorgeous body was on show when she was focused on work.

"Whatever you say, doc," Tanner said.

Lauren frowned and kept working, knowing that he would never have called out to her and admitted his pain unless it was really bad.

When she'd finished, she stood and held out a hand to him. "Come on, let's just have a nice swim, and then we can order in breakfast and chill for the rest of the day."

Tanner took her hand and used some of her weight to pull himself up. When he was standing, at least a foot taller than her, he dropped a kiss to her hair, hand moving to her elbow.

"Thanks," he said.

She should have asked for what, but she didn't. She was here as a professional, and yet she wasn't sure if he was thanking her for the treatment or the booty call the night before.

Tanner hobbled into the bathroom and she went to place their order for breakfast, wanting it to be ready when they finished swimming. She was starving and she wanted Tanner to eat well while he was on her watch, with plenty of fresh fruit and protein.

Lauren went into the living room to make the call, ordering up fruit platters and omelets for two. She stood and waited for Tanner, looking out at the ocean and knowing that she'd never forget their trip for the rest of her life. They could never be together, not after everything that had happened, and they both had such different careers that consumed them, but being with him here, having him back just for a little while, was one hell of a feeling.

"I'm looking forward to that swim," Tanner said, and she turned to find the man who was consuming her thoughts standing in his swimming shorts, towel over his shoulder.

"Did that at least loosen you up a little?" she asked.

He nodded, but she wasn't convinced. "Come on

then, cowboy. Let's do a few slow laps and see how we go."

Lauren left her towel on a lounger, using the tie around her wrist to secure her hair into a ponytail. She watched as Tanner sat and then slipped straight into the water, and she dived in once he moved further into the middle of the pool.

She blinked when she came up and smiled at the man in the water beside her. "Come on, let's slowly do five laps of breast stroke then see how you're feeling," she said. "There's no better way to build up full body strength in a gentle way than swimming."

Tanner followed her lead and she let him set the pace, refusing to listen to the voice in her head asking whether she truly believed she'd be able to heal him. He would be fine—of course he would be—but would he be strong enough and fit enough to be number one again? She wasn't sure. But what she did know was that nothing was going to stop her from doing everything in her power to fix him.

"You look worried," he said as they turned and headed back in the other direction.

"I'm fine. Come on, let's switch to freestyle. But take it slow."

Lauren settled into a slow rhythm, focusing on her breathing, and wondering if she was truly cut out to be his physical therapist by day and his mistress by night.

Tanner sat outside, holding a beer and looking out at the ocean. He'd thought that sitting on his porch and looking over his ranch was relaxing, but the Fiji beach was something else. The light breeze, the temperature that was pleasant but not too hot, the white sand, the gently lapping ocean—there was nothing not to love about being cast away on a luxury island.

If his body slowly started to improve, and he was able to go home healed and ready to ride for the next season, it would end up being the perfect holiday. *And that was before he factored in Lauren.* He had no idea what the hell he thought he was doing with her, but what harm could it do? So they'd reconnected—so what? He wouldn't be second-guessing himself if he'd met some gorgeous brunette on vacation and spent a week having wild holiday sex with her, so why was Lauren any different? And once they boarded the jet to go home it would all be over.

He sighed and took a pull of beer. This was different because it was Lauren Lewis. Former love, the woman who'd ruined him for all others, the one human being in the world he'd genuinely thought he despised. Maybe he'd been fooling himself all along about that last part.

"How are you feeling?" Lauren's soft voice was warm, like arms being swept around him from behind.

"Good," he replied, taking another sip of beer before swiveling to look at her. She was dressed in denim cut-offs again and a pretty top, and he wondered if that was part of the attraction. That last summer they'd spent together had been all about her wearing teeny-tiny shorts, lying out in the sun turning dark shades of golden, and swimming. Fiji was turning out to be exactly the same, other than the recovery stuff.

"You want to eat in tonight or go to the restaurant?" she asked. "Or if you want some alone time then I'm happy to dine solo."

He laughed. "Solo? Not a chance. And for the record, I'd like to eat you."

Now Lauren was the one laughing, and when she moved closer he hooked his hand around her smooth leg and looked up at her. He didn't need to say anything, she seemed to know exactly what he was thinking and spun around, slowly sitting in his lap. She brought her mouth toward his, lips parted expectantly, and Tanner closed the distance, kissing her gently, enjoying the sensation of her weight on him, the feel of her silky, just-washed hair connecting with his skin.

"What the hell are we doing, Tan?" she asked, sighing against his mouth as she touched her forehead to his.

"Kissing," he replied, finding her lips again.

She kissed him straight back, but slower, their lips just grazing this time. "I mean us," she finally murmured. "I've spent my life—"

"I know," he said. "Work is work and pleasure is pleasure. I get it."

"So why am I bending the rules for you?" she asked. "It's a bad idea, I just know it."

"Because we're Tan and Lol," he teased. "We were voted most likely to be married, remember?"

When she laughed her head tipped back. "Oh my god, you've just given me a mental image of us at homecoming. And you're right, I think everyone had us pegged for being married in college and me barefoot and pregnant."

"Ah, it wouldn't have been so bad," he said.

"For you maybe!" She poked him in the chest. "I always wanted more than that."

They were both quiet for a while until Tanner ran his hands down her back. "Are you okay with this just being what it is?"

He saw her throat move as she swallowed. "Yeah, I am. You?"

Tanner nodded, looking into her eyes. "Me too. So what's wrong with two grown adults coming to an agreement about having some fun? This isn't something we should be beating ourselves up over."

He knew why he was okay with it, because she was gorgeous and he'd never stopped being attracted to her, but also because he was never going to let her get too close. If she wanted a relationship right now, he'd be running a mile. He couldn't trust her again, couldn't let go of the past enough to ever let that happen, but now that they were together, he couldn't see the point in being chaste.

"Come here," he said gruffly, reaching for her and coaxing her closer again.

Lauren didn't kiss him, she just tucked into his chest, cheek against him like she was listening to his heart. Maybe he'd regret getting up close and personal with her, but right now, it was his body begging him to give in, not his heart. His heart was still under lock and key, and as far as he was concerned, no one was ever going to find that key and hurt him. Not now, not ever.

"I'm sorry I hurt you, Tanner. I know it was a long time ago, but I don't think I ever said I'm sorry."

He stiffened, hating that he was a grown-ass man who could still feel the sting of betrayal from so long ago, so strongly.

"I'm sure you did already," he murmured back, knowing that it wasn't true. But it felt like the right thing to say. Besides, what else was he going to say: "It's about fucking time?" or perhaps "Yeah, nice to know you're finally admitting what a bitch you were back then." The past was the past, he needed to move on, and it was different this time. He didn't want a girlfriend or even a wife. He didn't have time for one and he didn't have any interest in settling down.

He forced his shoulders to drop, relaxing into the woman cocooned against him. He needed to enjoy this moment, because being with Lauren would make him forget all about the past. It had been the only negative thing holding him back in his life, and now it needed to be water under the bridge.

He looked down at her, felt a tightening in his chest knowing that in a couple of short weeks, their time together would be over and he'd never see her again.

Chapter 14

LAUREN was starting to get used to waking up with Tanner's warm body against her. She looked down at him as she silently rose, slipping away from him and leaving him among the rumpled sheets.

Saying goodbye was going to be hard.

She ran her fingers through her hair and headed to her room. The last week had passed by in a lazy blur of morning swims, stretches, food, massages, more food, and slow walks. Going back to her normal routine would be tough, but then it was always hard returning to long working hours after a couple of months off.

It was raining today, but they'd been told there was some wet weather coming, and it wasn't exactly the best time of year to be in the islands during their rainy season. She stood and stared out, before sighing and changing into her running clothes. Hopefully it would clear enough that she'd be able to get her run in regardless.

"Want to have breakfast then walk the mountain track?"

Tanner's voice surprised her and she turned, hands on her hair as she scooped it up, finding him standing in the doorway to her room, propped against the frame.

"How long have you been standing there?" she asked.

He shrugged but she could see the hint of a smile and knew he'd probably watched her dress.

"You feel up to the walk?" she asked. They'd been on the island for ten days, and although he was doing great, she didn't want to push him too hard yet.

"Yes, doc," he replied. "I think you've been doing a damn fine job on me, although it might have been all that sex rejuvenating me."

Now it was Lauren trying not to smile. Trust him to bring up the sex.

"Maybe we could grab breakfast first, then walk," she suggested. "Last thing I need is you slipping in the rain and having to carry you back."

They both laughed then, and Lauren could almost see herself trying to haul Tanner's six-foot-something body down the track.

"You been online yet this morning?" he asked, running his fingers through his hair. She liked it long, the way it fell forward and brushed his face. He'd had shorter hair back in school, but the length suited him.

"No, why?"

"The storm they've been worried about is looking like more of a sure thing," Tanner said, rubbing at his stubble now. Lauren's fingers itched to trace his jaw, loving how his shadow of a beard felt in the mornings, but she didn't move.

"You're worried?" she asked, grabbing her phone so she could read about it herself.

"Yeah, starting to be. I suppose they'll brief us if it's not safe to stay here, but I'd rather have a plan for getting out if we need to. I've emailed my travel agent to see if we can book somewhere on the mainland for a couple of days just in case."

Lauren skimmed through the news and could see why Tanner was so worried. "I hate the idea of being so close to the water here if it gets bad." She stared at him and saw that he was probably more worried than he was letting on.

"Let's just enjoy breakfast and go for our walk. I'm feeling good and I'm looking forward to pushing a bit harder today." Tanner walked toward her, his hands falling to her shoulders as he looked down at her before placing a slow, warm kiss to her lips. "If we need to leave, I'll have a helicopter sent over to collect us. We're going to be fine and they've probably got the forecast all wrong anyway."

She looked up at him. "What about all the people who live and work here?" she asked. "I hate that we can just get airlifted out but . . ."

Tanner placed a finger to her lips. "I'm as worried as you are, and if anyone here needs my help, they'll have it." His smile reassured her. "Now let's go and eat pancakes and bacon. I'm starving."

"Pancakes? Not a chance," she argued. "Fruit, omelet—"

"Sorry, sweetheart, but if I eat another goddamn omelet again I'll throw it back up. I'll swallow those turmeric tablets without complaining, but I'm eating pancakes and bacon and there ain't nothing you can do to stop me."

Tanner stole another kiss and slapped her butt, and it

was almost impossible to scowl at him as he winked and walked backward out of the room.

"Hey, I just noticed that you're hardly limping," she said.

Tanner looked down and she watched the recognition slowly pass over his face.

"Damn, you're right." He laughed. "I'm sore, but in a different kind of way. Like my muscles are aching but I don't feel like an old man so much."

Now it was Lauren's turn to laugh. "It definitely must have been the great sex then."

"Hell yeah."

She stood alone in her bedroom laughing as Tanner disappeared, wondering how the hell she was ever going to forget the man she loved for a second time.

Loved. There was no pretending otherwise, because she hadn't simply loved him once. She'd loved him then and she loved him still; she was playing with fire and she had no idea how she was ever supposed to extinguish it.

She decided to pick up the phone and call Casey, needing to just talk to someone else. Being here with Tanner had been amazing, it *was* amazing, but they'd been isolated and living in this little bubble of wonderfulness, and all she could imagine was how hard it would be when this island world of theirs started to unravel.

It rang six times and Lauren was about to hang up when a breathless Casey picked up.

"Lauren!"

She smiled into the phone, leaning against the glass to look out at the beach. It was so good to hear her friend's voice again. "Hey, stranger."

"How's Fiji? Are you ever going to come home or are you going to stay forever? It must be so gorgeous."

"It is. I don't think I've ever been anywhere like it before," she said honestly.

"And the company? I'm guessing you're all loved up with your sexy cowboy?" Casey teased.

"He's hardly *my* cowboy," Lauren said, lowering her voice. "But yes to the loved-up part."

Casey sighed. "Ohhh, I'm so jealous. You're on a beautiful island with a beautiful man, and I'm stuck here dealing with work and life."

She wanted to say *But you're not about to have your heart broken when it all ends*, but swallowed her words instead. "So tell me about home? Anything going on?"

"Well, my boss is still an asshole, and I keep fantasizing about leaving my job, but other than that? Not much different than usual."

Lauren smiled. "Well, maybe we should plan a girls' trip somewhere tropical," she suggested. "Something for us all to look forward to."

"Definitely! Hey, I have to go, but can't wait to hear more. Talk soon?"

"I'll call you another time. Bye."

As Lauren hung up and dropped her arm, phone clasped in her fingers, she wondered if she was ready for the fall that was coming. Having a fling was one thing, but letting Tanner go all over again was something else entirely.

Tanner looked up and smiled to himself as he saw how close they were to the top of the mountain. Today was humid as hell after the rain, and his skin was slick with sweat, but he loved the feeling of actually doing something more strenuous than swimming.

He glanced at Lauren walking beside him, wondering why she'd been so quiet all morning. He doubted she was worried about the storm—she wasn't the type to rattle easily—but she was obviously mulling over something in her head and she wasn't as talkative as usual.

"What do you say we jog the rest of the way?" he asked.

Lauren smiled and shook her head. "Easy, tiger. Remember what I said about not wanting to carry you back down?"

The idea of her trying to carry him was something he'd pay to see.

"I'm feeling great, but walking is killing me. Promise I'll take it slow."

She looked undecided.

"Come on, we're almost there."

Lauren sighed. "Okay, fine, but if you feel anything, *anything at all*, just stop. I haven't spent all those hours on you for nothing."

Tanner shook out through his shoulders and pushed off on the balls of his feet, springing forward into a light jog. His muscles bunched and pulled and he listened to his body, as cautious as Lauren not to push too hard and cause damage, but he felt good. Better than good, he was starting to feel great again. It was like he'd woken up this morning a huge step closer to having his old body back.

"You good?" Lauren asked, matching his pace.

"Keep your eyes on the track, sweetheart," he said. "I'm doing great."

Tanner focused on every footfall and jogged the rest of the way, his lungs full of air and his heart racing as he surveyed the island from above.

"Man, it's beautiful up here," he murmured.

"I know," she said, breathless as she stood beside him, shoulders almost touching. "It's why I've been coming up here every day."

"You know, I have you to thank for helping me to feel this way again," he said. "I couldn't have imagined actually feeling like this even two weeks ago."

She moved away from him and he tracked her, his attention on her instead of the view now. "You would have gotten to this point with or without me, Tanner. You've got a strong body, you're determined, and to be honest, any therapist could have helped you."

"But I didn't have just any therapist," he said, hearing the deep, gruff tone of his own voice. "I had you."

She turned and he saw tears in her eyes, the same kind of held-back, stuck-in-the-lashes big tears that he'd noticed that first time they were in bed together.

"I knew this would be hard, but . . ."

"What? Being here with me?"

She smiled, finally meeting his gaze head on. "I knew being here with you would be hard, but this, this whatever this thing is going on between us, it's hard knowing that we've gone back but . . ." She let out a big sigh. "I almost think we should just end this now. Today."

Tanner stood a little straighter, knowing what she was trying to say because he'd thought the exact same thing. "It's the island air, it's making us feel like we're kids again," he said. "Once we're back in the real world with other people around us, instead of being in this little bubble of paradise, we'll be fine. Trust me. It'll all be over and this will be the memory that stays with us when we think about what we used to have. And no, we're not ending this today. When we board the jet again, sure. But not yet, Lauren."

She nodded and he watched as she brushed her eyes with the back of her knuckles. He had no idea what she was thinking, her face impossible to read. "You're sure? Because . . ."

He felt a stabbing pain in his chest and he shook his head. "I'm sure, baby."

"Want to walk back down?" she asked, clearly trying to change the subject. "Or do you want to see how you feel doing a gentle run?"

Tanner grinned. "I thought you'd never ask."

"Just do some stretches with me first. I want your calves nice and limbered up."

"We've got awhile before we have to leave, so we can stretch for a while."

Her brows pulled together as she stopped, one leg stretched out. "Leave for where?"

"Did I forget to tell you? I know the weather's kind of crappy but we're having lunch on the private island." Tanner laughed. "And we definitely can't call this off between us before we have our island time."

"Just the two of us?"

Tanner winked. "I'm afraid so."

Lauren couldn't hide her blush as she looked down, pushing her leg out in front of her and holding a stretch. He copied her movement and wondered for the hundredth time what he was doing trying to be all romantic. He could say it was the sex as much as he wanted to, but if he did, he'd only be lying to himself.

When they eventually ran down the mountain, it took

all his willpower to go slow and not sprint to the end. If he could just get his wrist feeling right, he'd be one huge step closer to climbing on a bull again and showing that asshole Thunder Cat that he couldn't throw him like that ever again. And once he was back riding, he'd be able to forget all about Lauren—she could live on in his fantasies and that was all. Which is why he was going to make the most of having the woman who'd driven him crazy in his mind for so many years in his bed. Or on the sand. Or anywhere he could goddamn have her.

Lauren walked down to the boat, barefoot and with a bag over her shoulder. The sun was coming and going, and it was still incredibly warm, but it felt stormy. There was almost a smell, a coolness in the breeze that was indicative of something brewing from the weather gods.

She let the boat's skipper take her bag and help her onto the boat, and then she settled back and waited for Tanner to climb in.

"I'll come back to get you if the rain starts again," the skipper said as he moved them out into deeper water.

"Are you worried about the storm?" Tanner asked. "It looks bad on the weather radar."

"We'll decide tomorrow if we need to evacuate our guests," he replied. "Nothing to worry about."

Lauren sat back and enjoyed the short boat trip, loving the clearness of the ocean and the serenity of being somewhere so untouched by the rest of the world. When they got there she took the skipper's hand and slipped into the shallow water, amazed to see tiny fish swimming so close. She walked onto the island, marveling at how secluded it was, and sat down on the sand as Tanner joined her and their picnic lunch and towels were brought over to them. It was hard to wrap her head around the way they were behaving and what was happening between them, but she had to believe that Tanner was right. Once they were home, life would go back to normal—it was the tropical weather making them sex crazed.

Within minutes they were left alone and Tanner dropped to the sand beside her as the boat slowly disappeared from view.

"It's amazing here, isn't it?" he said.

She pushed her sunglasses up into her hair and continued to survey the ocean. "Amazing" seemed too much an understatement.

"Is it a bad thing that I don't want to go home?" she asked. "The idea of going back to work every day after this, it's rough. Maybe this is why I never take vacations, because it stops me loving my real life."

"By the time we leave we'll have island fever and be ready to rejoin the world again," he teased. "Trust me."

Lauren wasn't so sure she believed him. "Can we swim before we have lunch?" she asked. "I think there are snorkels and masks for us in that bag."

Tanner pulled out two masks and passed her one. "You planning on swimming naked?"

She laughed. "Not a chance. I don't need a fish thinking my nipples are lunch and taking a nibble."

Tanner reached for her, his smile wicked. "I'll fight any fish off. Those babies are mine."

Lauren stared at Tanner. He was grinning, the sun was just starting to peek properly through the clouds, and she couldn't take her eyes off him. How was he so handsome?

He was like a replica of what a big, hulking, sexy bull-rider should be, and it struck her that even without his plaid shirt or his hat, he still looked every inch a cowboy.

"Take off your T-shirt," she said.

Tanner raised a brow but did as she'd ordered without saying a word.

When he threw it down onto the sand, she licked her dry lips and lifted the hem of her dress up, pulling it up and over her head. She was wearing a bikini beneath it, and she glanced around to make sure they were completely alone before pulling the strings at the back and at her neck and letting it fall away. She saw Tanner's mouth fall open a little and she smiled, liking the way it made her feel.

She strode the few steps between them, stepping out of her bikini bottoms and pushing him back with the heel of her hand to his chest. He fell back, the smile never leaving his face as he lay back in the sand and she climbed on top of him.

"I guess that means we're not snorkeling before lunch?"

"Shut up and kiss me." Lauren kissed Tanner like it was the last time she was ever going to feel his lips against hers again. She opened her mouth and tasted his tongue, wishing they'd had this kind of send-off before they'd broken up. This was the moment she was going to hold on to forever—naked under the Fijian sun, on their own private slice of paradise, making love on the beach.

"Tanner!"

He flipped her, forcing her onto her back as he positioned himself above her. "You've healed me so well," he murmured, taking off his shorts, "I think it's time I took the lead."

She gazed up at him as he placed one hand on her knee and gently pushed it open. Lauren was waiting for him to lean in and kiss her, but instead he lowered himself and kissed down her leg. When he reached her thigh he traced it with his tongue, moving so slowly, then going back up again a little before running his fingers down her belly and making her quiver.

"Think of this as a little thank-you for all that cowgirl riding you've been doing."

Lauren held her breath as his mouth closed over her, the touch of his tongue so light she could barely feel it. He flicked back and forth and then delved deeper, pleasuring her with his mouth. She closed her knees around his head, fingers digging deep into the sand above her head as she moaned and bucked against him.

"Don't stop," she whispered.

Tanner clearly didn't have any intention of stopping, and when she rocked up to meet his tongue, heat pulsating through her, she shuddered as a wave of intense pleasure shocked her system. As she came down from her high, eyes shut, body thrumming with satisfaction, Tanner rose, smiling as he cupped both of her breasts. She was feeling lazy and satiated, but he was just getting started.

He edged closer, his big body hard up against hers as he kissed the side of her neck, the tickling sensation of his moist lips to her skin almost too much to stand. He'd had a shave after their run so his cheeks were smooth against hers, and she shut her eyes again and savored the feel of him, the touch of his lips and fingers, the smell of his citrusy cologne that lingered around his neck.

Tanner rocked into her then, gently at first, and she

lazily let him do all the work, smiling as he dropped his mouth to her breast. When he rose up higher, she finally opened her eyes, watching his face, liking the way he looked straight back at her as he moved in and out of her.

She locked the sight of him into her memory, lifted her hands to trace his face as she rocked up to meet him, not letting him stop, not wanting him to slow down. Tanner pulled her up then, scooping her against him. She sat on him as he held her, moving her up and down with his hands on her hips. She buried her face into his neck and his thrusting became more insistent, his hands firm on her, and she couldn't stifle her moan. She leaned back, folding onto the sand, and Tanner moved with her, covering her body with his own. She listened to him suck back a sharp breath and she bucked up to meet him again, fingernails digging into his shoulder as he let out a low groan.

When he finally lifted up, he looked down at her and kissed her, and she relaxed back into the soft sand. Tanner kissed her again before rolling over her and lying beside her, one arm flung out to touch her.

"You've definitely healed me," he said, laughing.

Lauren forced herself to sit up again and placed a hand to Tanner's chest. It was hot and wet, which was exactly how she was feeling.

"Come with me," she said.

Tanner had his eyes shut but it didn't stop him from grinning up at her. "I thought I already had?"

She play-punched his arm and then gave him a nudge. "Come on."

Lauren found her mask and snorkel and ran into the water, looking over her shoulder to check he was following. When she caught his smile she gave him a beamer right back, before diving into the water and basking in the sensation of the ocean against her naked body.

Tanner followed Lauren out into the water, chuckling to himself as her pert little butt breached the surface as she dived deeper. He put his mask on and pushed under the water too, wishing they were out on a better day. It was still nice, but he knew it would have been amazing on a hot, clear day with the sun burning bright above.

She gave him an underwater thumbs-up and he did the same back, watching as a school of tiny bright fish traveled past. When they both surfaced to blow out through their snorkels and get more air, Lauren reached for his hand, palm to palm, and they swam side by side, inspecting the underwater world. By the time Tanner let go and finally came up to the surface properly, taking off his mask as he kept treading water, he could see that they'd gone a long way.

Lauren emerged beside him and he pointed to the shore. "Think we'd better head back in."

She swam in a little circle around him. "I am getting kind of hungry."

Tanner swam back and into her way so she couldn't get around him, kissing her as she tried to dodge him.

"Eeek!"

He laughed. "What?"

"There's a snake!" She grabbed hold of Tanner and he just about went under the surface. "Ohmygod, why did we come out so far?!"

He turned and looked for it, seeing through the perfectly clear water and catching a glimpse of a black-and-white blur. It darted away so fast that it was gone before he had time to put his mask back on.

"Come on, it'll be fine," he coaxed, pushing her away slightly so she didn't drown him but keeping hold of her hand. "Let's head back."

"I hate snakes." She kept spinning to look for it. "What if it's poisonous?"

"I think they're called coral reef snakes," he said, knowing exactly what they were because he'd been flicking through a dive magazine while he'd waited for her to get ready earlier. "They won't bother us if we don't bother them." He had no idea if that was true, but freaking her out wasn't going to help.

He let go of her to put on his mask and snorkel again and waited until she'd done the same, and when she placed a hand to his shoulder he started to swim slowly in, kicking as he kept his eyes underwater to admire everything one last time.

As they hit shallower water he rose and took the mask off again, shaking his hair and frowning as he looked up at the sky. It looked ominous.

"I think we should get some clothes on," he suggested as he waded through the last of the water toward shore, loving watching Lauren squeeze her long hair out, and twist it in over her shoulder, covering one round breast. "I have a feeling our boat will be coming back soon."

Her eyes widened and she hurried up the beach, quickly drying herself and changing back into her bi-kini. As rain started to fall, the sky darkening even more, Tanner pulled on his shorts and grabbed the pic-nic basket, racing for the cover of the trees so they could set up camp.

Lauren ran after him, tucking up close as they set-tled down, rain dripping in big plops from the fronds above them. Tanner put towels over their legs as Lauren opened the basket before bursting out laughing.

"What?" he asked.

"It's nothing, I just—" She hesitated and passed him a sushi roll. "It's just that this has been one hell of a day. If it ends up being our last day on the island, I'm glad it's my last memory."

He hooked her chin with his fingers and held her still, staring into her eyes before looking down at her plump lips and kissing her slowly. A raindrop fell on his nose and dripped down to their lips, and Tanner pulled back and rubbed another drop from her cheek, noticing the tiny freckles that had appeared on the bridge of her nose.

"It sure has been one hell of a day, but if that boat doesn't come soon? We're in serious trouble."

Thunder rumbled in the distance and Tanner hoped it didn't come any closer, because sitting under a tree wasn't exactly his idea of fun if lightning struck.

Chapter 15

"THE storm has been upgraded," Tanner said, concern etched on his face as he stood in the doorway of her bedroom the next day. She hadn't been using it much since they'd started sharing a bed, but all her clothes were in her original room still and she'd already started to gather some of her belongings together. "We're leaving in a couple of hours."

Lauren had expected it. She'd known the news was coming but she'd been trying to pretend that it wasn't going to happen. She nodded and looked out through the big glass doors, at the trees blowing steadily as the wind lifted and the rain pelted down. They'd had rain in their time here, but it had always poured like a monsoon and then cleared and come out beautiful. This was different. There was a sense of danger in the air, an ominous change in the climate that told her Tanner was right—it was definitely time to go back to the mainland.

"Will we come back here?" she asked, still staring out. "If the storm passes?"

Tanner came up behind—she could hear his bare feet

padding over the tiles. "I don't know, depends on the destruction, and whether my doctor thinks I need to stay longer."

She sighed and when his arms encircled her, she leaned back into him. Tanner's lips found her neck and she shut her eyes for a moment, trying to forever commit to memory the feel of his chest and torso against her, his lips on her skin. It didn't matter how many times she told herself that he didn't meet the carefully selected criteria on her list for her perfect match—he was gorgeous and fun and charming and right now she was loving every second of being with him. Besides, finding a stable, serious man was never going to guarantee she didn't get her heart broken one day, so to hell with her damn list.

"Is it childish that I don't want this to end?"

Tanner stiffened behind her and she wished she hadn't said it.

"This as in *us*?" he asked. "Or the whole being on one of the most beautiful islands in the world?"

She stayed against him, knowing that both were true but that there was only one she'd to admit to.

"Being here," she finally said. "It's going to be hard going back to work and normal routines and things. I feel like I spend almost the entire year exhausted and then I limp through my time off and only just start to feel reenergized days before I'm due to start work again." Her sigh was loud. "Sorry, I'm not complaining, I love what I do, I just get tired of being so tired sometimes. And I had my heart set on spending more time here."

His sad smile told her he understood exactly what she was trying to say. "Can you believe it's Christmas tomorrow?" he asked. "Maybe we should have had the jet ready so we could fly home for it, since we have to leave early and all."

She actually just wanted to stay put. She wanted to enjoy more time in Fiji, she wanted to spend more time with Tanner, so she had enough new memories to last her a lifetime, even if they were in Nadi instead of Vomo. "I don't mind. Whatever happens is fine by me, and I can always continue your treatment back home if I need to."

"Hey, isn't your birthday close to Christmas?" Tanner moved to stand beside her as he spoke.

"Um, yeah." She smiled at the inquisitive look he was giving her. "It was actually the day we arrived here."

He froze. "You're kidding me."

"Nope." She laughed at the expression on his face, not letting on her surprise that he'd even roughly remembered when it was. "I celebrated a few days before we left—it's fine, so don't go feeling sorry for me. And I'm not a kid, so birthdays aren't that big of a deal, although I did plan this vacation so I was away for the big day."

"Now I feel like a complete shit," he said, reaching for her. "Happy birthday, beautiful."

When he spoke to her like that, his voice so soft and raspy, it broke away a little piece of her. She didn't want him to be sweet, she wanted him to be rough and arrogant, like he had been before they'd left Texas and when they were on the plane. She'd needed him to be like that, so she wouldn't fall head over heels in love with him all over again. Why did he do this to her when no other man had ever come close? Why did he have to be the one man on earth who had this effect on her, who made her question every decision she'd ever made?

He kissed her and she melted, opening her mouth and

kissing him back. She would have slipped her hands under his T-shirt and turned it into something more, but his cell phone rang and he groaned against her and kissed her one more time.

"Sorry. It might be the helicopter pilot."

He grabbed his phone off the counter and she watched him move, jogging a few paces, bending, leaning, walking. He was holding himself differently now, moving like he should be moving, and she was amazed at how quickly he'd managed to recover from his injuries. It had been just shy of two weeks and he was doing incredibly well.

"Everything okay?" she asked when he returned.

"Pack up fast," he said, brows furrowed. "We need to get off the island and back to the mainland as quick as we can. I've offered to pay for my own fuel and take supplies to some of the islands since they're so short on pilots. I'll bring anyone back with me who needs to come, too. Some of the workers leave their families for weeks on end to work at the resorts, and I'll bring back anyone who needs it, not just tourists." He gave her a pained expression. "Sorry, I'd rather be with you but I can't not offer to help, not when I can fly for them and help people."

Lauren moved to give him a quick hug, wrapping her arms around his neck and holding him tight. She rocked back to look up at him, knowing that no matter what she told herself, she'd never ever be able to forget the time they'd spent together. He was actually a really decent human being, she'd always known that, and she just wished the rest of the world could glimpse his kindness, instead of presuming he was some unfeeling, rich son of a bitch.

"You're a good man, Tanner," she whispered.

"I'm an asshole just as much as I'm good," he replied, his expression hard to read, eyes like big blue pools looking down at her. "Don't go thinking I'm anything special, Lauren. I only do what I have to do, what anyone would do in my position."

She knew a lot of wealthy guys. They'd been her clients for years, and some of them were lovely and some of them were assholes, and she doubted any of them would have volunteered to fly in a storm and offer to help like that. The difference with Tanner was that he didn't discriminate and he wasn't so worried about his own safety that he wouldn't help others in need. Maybe that came with the territory of bull riding—a job almost guaranteed to hurt him, but one he did anyway, not to mention the fact that most of the guys he rode alongside probably struggled to make ends meet, but they were still his friends.

Lauren left him and went to pack, wishing she had time to shower and put on some makeup. But after Tanner got her to the mainland, she'd have plenty of time to do things like that—in between worrying about him.

"You've got to be kidding me? Isn't there government relief for this kind of situation?" Tanner said, sounding angry.

Lauren poked her head out, wondering who Tanner was talking to. He looked frustrated as he paced back and forth, and she noticed again how strong he looked, how well he was moving.

"Yeah, I'm well aware I'm not in the United States right now," he said sarcastically, and Lauren wondered what the person on the other end of the line had said.

She guessed it had been pointed out that, luxury islands aside, Fiji was a third-world country facing a serious natural disaster if the storm intensified.

"Look, find out if they take Amex. Fill the goddamn helicopter with as much bottled water and whatever other supplies are needed before I get there, and I'll pay for it all when I arrive."

She ducked back into her room and finished folding her clothes. So much for calling himself an asshole. He might talk the talk of being tough, but when it came to walking it, he was sweet to the core. And that's when she realized why he'd been hurt so bad, because for all his macho talk and arrogant behavior sometimes, he was soft on the inside, and she'd gone and broken his heart. She only hoped that it hadn't made him weary of all women, because she knew he'd make some lucky girl one hell of a husband one day. She blinked away tears. And a darn fine dad to some kids, too.

It was less than an hour later that Lauren was running across the grass, head ducked low, about to get into the same helicopter that had brought them to the island. The wind was starting to whip up and she hoped it was safe enough to go up in the bird. She threw her bag in and got in herself as Tanner followed close behind, stowing their two larger bags safely and climbing in behind her. The door was shut and the helicopter was preparing for lift off almost instantly, needing to get them to safety as soon as possible. Other guests had left during the afternoon too, the island was going to be deserted of tourists soon, and it made Lauren sad to think of only the workers being left there. The beautiful restaurant no longer full of guests, serving delicious food and providing the most romantic of backdrops, and the pristine beach deserted.

She took one last look at the Vomo sign, reminding her of the time she'd gone up in a helicopter and seen the Hollywood sign when she was in la-la land with its enormous white letters.

She vowed to come back. One day she'd make that happen. Only the next time she came, she wouldn't be with Tanner, and the thought sent a ripple through her body that left her mouth dry and her heart empty. She thought of Casey and her sister and tried to smile, imagining them here with her. It would be different, but they were her best friends in the world and it'd be just as good. Or if not just as good, then close.

Tanner went to the Hilton Fiji Beach Resort with Lauren and checked in, but the moment he saw her safely to one of the little golf carts with a friendly porter, used for ferrying guests and luggage about, he prepared to turn straight back around and leave.

"You okay here on your own?" he asked, his arms wrapped tight around Lauren as he gave her one last hug and said goodbye.

"I'm fine. It's you I'm worried about," she said, kissing his cheek and stroking his shoulders. "Don't try to be a hero, Tan. Just stay safe. Promise me?"

He laughed, but he could tell she wasn't joking. Her eyes were too wide, her hands clenched at her sides already.

"I promise."

Tanner stared down at her and opened his mouth, stopping the words before they fell from his mouth. How easy it would have been to say "I love you." To tell her that he cared for her, that she meant something to him, something so deep that he'd never be able to stop thinking about her if he tried. And lord knew he'd tried! So many damn times over the years, and yet she'd always been there, lurking in his mind. *And his heart.*

"Goodbye," he said gruffly, instead of anything that he'd regret later. "Hunker down and I'll see you soon."

"Bye," she replied, folding her arms around herself as she ducked down into the golf cart. He blew her a kiss and watched her go, the little white vehicle speeding off and narrowly missing colliding with another one coming in the opposite direction.

Once she'd disappeared from sight, Tanner spun around and jogged the short distance across the open-air lobby and down the timber steps to where his taxi sat waiting. The sound of Fijian guitar music echoed behind him in the lobby as they pulled away, his window wound down, and within thirty minutes he was dropped back off at the airfield where the helicopters were being prepared. He'd flown almost as much as he'd driven a car, used to flying around River Ranch and helping out at muster time since he was a teenager, as well as flying for pleasure whenever he could. It was his happy place being up in the air, although today he was going to have to be extra careful. The winds were okay at the moment, but if they got any worse it would be too dangerous to stay up.

He introduced himself, talked to the other pilots preparing to head out—most of them Australian and New Zealanders working in Fiji—and then he was going through the checks as the big bird warmed up and he waited for clearance.

Within minutes he was lifting upward and then flying

forward, and he settled into pilot mode, trying to push all thoughts of being naked on a beach with the one woman he couldn't get out of his head, the one woman who'd always made him want more, made him refuse to accept anything less than what they'd had.

Back when they'd broken up, he'd started to sleep around, which was fun for a while, but he'd compare every girl he met to Lauren. None of them were as beautiful, as strong, as smart, or just as . . . He didn't know what it was about her, but no other woman had ever compared to her. But as the years had passed he'd never lost that pain deep inside, and he'd never forgiven her for ripping his heart out. Now, he knew it was dangerous to get too close to her—theirs was a rematch and it was just a fling, a blast from the past, which was why he needed to smarten up and stop letting his heart rule his head. No more thinking how much he could love her, how easy it would be to let her back in or to let down his own guard.

He had a ranch to return home to, and he had to get himself ready to reclaim his title belt and show the world that he was still the best goddamn bull rider in the whole of Texas. He didn't have time for anything serious, period, and he sure as hell wasn't going to let Lauren close again. Because he'd experienced losing her once, and he wouldn't ever put himself through that again. That was something he couldn't ever let himself forget.

The rain started to come down harder again as Tanner cursed the weather. They should have left the island earlier, and then he would have had time to help more people and get even more supplies where they needed to be. He'd been selfish not wanting to leave, and in doing that he might have jeopardized his chance to assist more people and communities in need.

Lauren sat in the restaurant that overlooked the pool on one side and the beach on the other. There were different-colored balls on each table that emitted a soft light, and the hum of a busy restaurant should have been enough to distract Lauren. But all she could think about was Tanner. Why wasn't he back yet? How many trips was he going to do? What if something happened to him?

She smiled at the pretty Fijian waitress who came past her table, a flower tucked behind her ear, and turned her attention back to her food. It was getting dark, so her worries for Tanner had trebled, but it was foolish not to eat. Her stomach let out a low growl as she finished her whole snapper and side salad. Once she was done she signed to charge to her room and gave the waitress a tip, before running to one of the waiting golf carts.

"Thank you!" She moved under the plastic side cover keeping the rain out and tipped the driver when he pulled up outside her room. She ducked for cover and let herself in, flicking on a light and noticing that there was a noise coming from the bedroom.

"Tanner?" she said quietly. She looked in and saw his big frame sprawled out on the king bed. He was still dressed in his shorts and T-shirt, but his tee was damp and he had shoes on still. Tears welled in her eyes seeing him sleeping like that, knowing how hard he must have been working, for the best part of the day, to go back and forth between the smaller islands, and she silently removed his shoes and found a blanket to place over him. Then she silently took her own shoes off and cuddled up under the blanket with him, shutting her eyes in a fruitless effort to stop the tears from falling.

She loved him so much, this big, strong, handsome cowboy, but they weren't meant to be. She'd hurt him too badly for him to trust her again, and she couldn't give him what she knew he'd want one day. Not to mention she was under contract with the Rangers and he was preparing to go back on the circuit and restart his crazy-dangerous career.

They'd had their chance and it hadn't worked out, and just because they'd had great sex didn't mean they were supposed to be together. When they were back home, old feelings would creep in, Tanner would start to resent her again for the pain she'd caused him. Her family would refuse to believe he'd changed, and maybe he hadn't? A bull-riding husband who regularly put his life in jeopardy probably wasn't her parents' idea of dependable, and to be honest, it wasn't hers either, and she wasn't about to tell him to stop doing what he loved. She wouldn't ask that of anyone, not ever.

She snuggled against him and breathed in the scent of him, tucked her leg over his to steal some of his warmth, cheek to his chest. Tomorrow they might be gone, and she wanted one last night of sleeping beside him before they sat on opposite sides of the Ford family jet and headed back to Texas.

The wind howled outside as Lauren held on even tighter to Tanner, listening to the rain pelt the roof as the storm intensified, leaving her wondering if they were going to make it until morning unscathed.

Chapter 16

ALMOST twenty-four hours later, at the end of Christmas Day, Lauren looked back one last time before walking up the steps to board the jet. She settled into the same seat she'd sat in on the way over and stared out the window, not able to shake the feeling that something wonderful had come to such an abrupt end.

"It looks terrible, doesn't it?" Tanner said, pulling her from her thoughts. "It was pretty violent last night and this morning."

She nodded and kept staring. They were lucky their plane had been on standby, and they'd only been cleared for takeoff in the last hour. Before that the conditions had been too dangerous, but they decided to leave instead of staying on, which meant it had been exactly two weeks since they'd arrived.

"I hate that this huge divide exists," she admitted. "Here we are being whisked away in a private jet, and yet there are so many people stuck here on this island. Their homes have been ruined, their lives destroyed by one single, cruel strike of nature."

Tanner reached for her hand across the aisle and she squeezed his fingers back. They'd made love that morning, but it had been different. Before, they'd been relaxed and slow; or, when it was intense there was that amazing connection, being held in Tanner's arms, nestled against his body as he thrummed his fingers across her body. But this time it had been different. He'd tucked into her from behind and they'd silently had sex, her rocking back into him, his mouth against her hair and his hand cupping her breast. After, he'd pressed a single kiss to her cheek and slipped out of bed and headed for the shower. It had been goodbye sex, and it was like neither of them knew what to say. Or how to behave.

"Every single worker we met at Vomo is going to be okay. I've left money for each and every one of them to help, and I donated a hefty amount to the Red Cross this afternoon. We've done everything we can, Lauren, and a damn sight more than most who've fled Fiji over the last few days."

She knew he genuinely wanted to help, and she appreciated everything he'd done, but she still felt guilty. Not to mention torn over leaving the place in her own selfish way, when she'd expected to be staying for so much longer.

"Tanner, when we get back, would you like me to stay on as your PT or would you like me to recommend someone else to take over?" It was the question she'd been waiting to ask him, not sure how to read his disconnect. Part of her wondered if he was worried about what he'd seen the day before, but the other part of her, the sensible part, knew that it was him carefully trying to distance himself from her. Just like she should be doing to him instead of holding out some stupid hope that they could keep their little charade going on a bit longer.

His hand fell away from hers and she wrapped her arms around herself now, suddenly feeling cold. It was as if he could read her thoughts.

"I think I'll find someone else to take over," he said in a low voice. "I think we're best to just . . ." He gave her a sad kind of smile. "I've had an amazing time with you, but I don't think I could go back to a professional relationship, seeing you all the time without . . ." He cleared his throat, his voice trailing off. "Nothing's coming out sounding like it's supposed to."

"What happens on Vomo, stays on Vomo," she said, bravely facing him and trying to sound more certain than she actually felt inside. They'd both agreed on this, and he was clearly finding the whole situation as difficult as she was. She didn't need to make this any harder on him—she'd known this was coming and it was best to be honest about what they'd had. And what was coming to an end.

The flight attendant came to check on them and gave them each a bottle of water before takeoff, and Lauren settled in and did up her belt. She wondered what he was thinking, whether he was as sad as she was about ending things, about getting off the plane and never seeing each other again. Their paths wouldn't cross— they hadn't in twelve years before now—and sadness hummed through her body as she thought about never touching, never kissing, never looking into Tanner's eyes again.

It was breakup pain all over again and she couldn't stand it. *So much for protecting her heart and keeping things casual.* This was why she was supposed to date serious guys who made sense on paper, men who she wouldn't fall completely head over heels for—she was supposed to be with the guy who wasn't capable of breaking her heart into a million pieces.

"Tanner, can you promise me one thing?" she said quietly, surprised by how easily she managed to say the words. She'd expected them to choke up in her throat.

He looked surprised. "Sure. Shoot."

"I'm worried about you, and I know that you're not mine to worry about, and I know you don't want to be told what to do or that your career is too dangerous, but just promise me that if you don't feel right, you won't ride. You can't mess with your body, and if your leg or your wrist doesn't feel right, you need to acknowledge that and sit the ride out. I wish we'd had longer here, because you still have a lot of rehab to go."

"Sweetheart, I'm not stupid," he said. "And I can always tape my wrist."

"And risk damaging it for the rest of your life?" she asked, incredulous. "Tanner, that's ridiculous—even you must know that. And for what? So you can win a few times, preserve your ego, and then suffer for years in arthritic pain?"

"Ah, and here we go again. Someone else telling me why I should give up now and spend the rest of my life behind a desk. Have you been waiting all this time to tell me that I'm never going to be able to ride again? Did my family put you up to this?"

"Tanner, stop," she begged. "Look, I'm not your mother and I'm not your girlfriend. I'm saying this to you as your physical therapist. I want you to look after yourself, and if that means sitting a ride or two out, then so be it. I'm not telling you to give up, I just think you might need a longer break from the sport."

"Yeah, you're right, you're not my girlfriend. You gave away that privilege without needing any encouragement."

"*Ohmygod*, are you kidding me?" She unscrewed the top off her water bottle and took a long sip. "What happened to the guy flying helicopters and making donations? The guy who made love to me on the goddamn beach?"

Tanner glowered at her and cleared his throat. "He's the same guy who likes to risk everything to feel alive on the back of a bull or a bronc," he said. "And anyone who can't understand that part of me can go to hell. I thought you got me?"

She felt her pulse start to race and took a deep breath and another sip of water. Where was the Tanner she'd just spent fourteen days with in Fiji? Hell, the past *twelve* hours with even? What had happened to the fun, warm, happy guy she'd been so close to falling for all over again? Or did he genuinely just have his back up all of a sudden because he thought she was no different than everyone else in his life? "You know what, you need to chill the hell out. As your PT, my aim is to keep you in the game for a long time. That's what I do, and if a player I worked with wasn't operating at a hundred percent, I'd be wanting him on the sidelines until he was ready. This has nothing to do with any personal connection we've had."

Tanner didn't say anything for a long moment, but when he did, Lauren was relieved that he didn't sound like quite such a jackass.

"Fair point, I guess I just don't think of myself as an athlete," he said. "I'm more of a one-man band and I'm not used to listening to anyone else." Tanner made a grunting sound. "I'm sorry."

She laughed. Well, that was damn obvious. "Well, one-man band or part of a team, we only get one body and we have to protect it. So get over your issues and remember what's important, and stop treating me like I'm not capable of making a professional recommendation."

There was an uneasy feeling between them as they were wheels up and away, and Lauren wished they were about to land on Vomo for the first time. She wanted to step back in time and experience those days on the beach all over again, instead of flying through the air on Christmas Day and wondering how the hell she'd managed to let Tanner back into her head—and heart—after vowing to never get close to him again.

"You want something to eat or drink?" Tanner asked. "I just"—he paused—"I didn't actually mean to be a total jackass before, it's just a sensitive topic. You know how it is with me and my family over this kind of stuff." He blew out a loud breath. "I am sorry."

Lauren had her back up now, and no amount of hearing him say sorry was going to change that. "Well, if I hadn't known then I definitely know now."

"Lauren, come on, I'm just sick of everyone jumping down my throat about what I do. I thought you were jumping on the bandwagon, that's all. Mia's the only person who's ever just accepted what I do and encouraged me to follow what I want to do instead of anyone else's expectations of me."

"The difference between me and everyone else is that I wouldn't dream of telling you what to do, Tanner. It's why we wouldn't have worked out, because I couldn't have stood by and been your groupie for the rest of my life, and I also couldn't have told you to stop." She stared at him, long and hard. "But there's a big difference between telling you what to do and trying to give you professional advice to ensure you can *keep* doing what you love. Your problem is that you can't see the woods for the goddamn trees."

Tanner shifted in his seat, and she listened to him move. "So you're saying we wouldn't have worked out, even if your old man had let me keep dating you?"

Lauren clenched her bottle of water tightly between her fingers, needing to be honest, to tell him the truth. "Exactly. What happened, it happened for a reason. We would only have ended up broken-hearted later down the track and it would have hurt a hell of a lot more. We're different people and we had different paths to take."

"Yeah?" Tanner grunted.

"Yeah," she said, yanking her iPad out of her bag and shoving her buds in her ears. She scrolled through to find a movie to watch and pulled out a cashmere sweater, not about to engage with Tanner for another second longer while he was being an ass. She didn't like this version of him, and it was like the moment they'd hopped aboard the jet he'd gone straight back to being the guy she didn't like, the one she'd been so cautious about going away with in the first place.

She'd been right to insist on things being casual between them. They'd had an amazing time, but it had also shown her why she needed to be with someone more levelheaded, someone who wasn't going to send her on a roller-coaster ride of emotions all the time. She needed a stable, calm, sensible man in her life. She was okay with career driven, they just needed to have the same goals and the same outlook on life. And she needed to be able to keep a little piece of her heart shut away, so the entire organ couldn't be ripped into pieces and stomped all over. Or maybe she just needed to keep that little piece locked away for Tanner, because no matter what she said or did, he'd always mean something to her, and he'd always have a piece of her that could never, ever be returned.

When their plane finally landed on the runway, Tanner was sore. He stretched out his legs and yawned, looking forward to crashing in his own bed. *Shame Lauren wasn't coming home with him.* As if she knew he was thinking about her, she looked over and he gave her a tight smile, wishing he hadn't been such an asshole when they'd boarded. He knew she was only trying to help, but something about her telling him what to do, when he'd listened to people doing that to him all his life, had grated him up the wrong way. It was like after so many years of being backed into a corner about his choice of vocation, he was hardwired to snap whenever someone brought it up. The Zen-like feeling being on an island had started to fade the moment it had become clear they were going to have to fly home early.

And he was trying to deal with the fact that what they'd had, their little holiday fling, had come to an end. He wanted to hold her tight and ask her to stay with him, to tell her they were perfect together if they would both just give in to the damn attraction between them. But he clenched his jaw tight instead and didn't say a word. It wasn't worth it and he sure as hell wasn't about to beg her. She'd made it clear she wanted fun not a future, that she wouldn't date someone her parents didn't approve, and that her career was the most important thing to her.

He knew which battles were worth fighting, and he didn't back a losing horse. What he'd never confess to her or anyone else was that he would give up his career for the right reason, that what made him prickly was other people in his life thinking they knew best about what he should spend his time doing. He loved the adrenaline rush of bull riding, he loved the money, and he loved the lifestyle. He'd succeeded on his own terms and he was damn proud of it.

"There are two cars waiting, Mr. Ford," the attendant announced, coming to stand by his side. "Is there anything else you need me to organize for you?"

He raised his head and smiled. "Thanks for asking, but I'm fine. Lauren?"

Tanner watched as she unbuckled her seat belt and stretched. "Thanks, I'm fine too."

They both gathered their things and Tanner stood, waiting for Lauren to exit the jet down the stairs before following her. There were a hundred things he could have or should have said, but the words that had flowed so easily between them on the island had all but disappeared.

Lauren turned on the tarmac, her bag in one hand, the other shielding her eyes from the sun. The air was cooler here, so different than the humid, constant warmth in Fiji.

"I guess this is goodbye," she said, as the drivers from each car collected their bags and put them in the trunks of their respective sleek black vehicles.

Tanner didn't know what to say. Lauren's eyes were

shining and he wanted to sweep her into his arms and tell her it was stupid, the whole thing. What they'd done, both being too stubborn or too scared to at least try to be together—but he couldn't see the point. They'd had an agreement, and their time was up.

"Can I kiss you goodbye?" he asked, suddenly feeling like he needed permission to touch her, to press his lips to hers in the same way he'd been doing whenever he wanted to while they were away.

She smiled, her nod barely noticeable. Tanner took the few steps separating them and bent to place a single kiss to her lips, hesitating, their mouths connected for all of two seconds. Tears trickled down her cheeks and he raised a thumb to gently brush them away.

"Goodbye," she murmured. "Call me if you need me."

"I'll miss you, Lauren," he whispered.

She held up her hand. "Me too."

He stepped back and watched her go, one of the drivers waving her over and opening the rear door of her car.

It was over. They'd had fun, but it was back to reality now. Lauren Lewis was firmly in his past again. And he didn't like it one goddamn bit.

Lauren sat in the car, grateful that the driver had the dark tinted pane up between the front and rear seats. She tipped her head back and swallowed down the choke of emotion in her throat, eyes squeezed shut tight as she tried to stop the tears from freefalling down her cheeks as pain cloaked her.

Seeing Tanner standing there, feeling that final, lingering kiss, knowing it was over again when it had never really even started, was rough. Tanner had been her first love and he may always be her biggest love, as well as her biggest regret. She regretted finishing things with him when she loved him so deeply all those years ago, even though she knew it had been the right thing to do, and she regretted going back and giving in to temptation all over again.

Tanner would always be her weakness—and for a girl who hated not being in control and being any kind of weak, that was a hard pill to swallow.

She was going back to work in a few weeks, and once she was focused on her team and her job again, she'd be able to move on. She'd be too busy and too exhausted to dwell on what could have been. All she needed was to get through the next month.

A silent, shuddering sob erupted from deep inside of her and she stuffed her fist to her mouth as she buckled forward, struggling to breathe as emotion consumed her. Why had she put herself through this? Why had she ever said yes to treating the one human being on the planet who affected her like this?

She cried and cried, wiping frantically at her cheeks only for more tears to fall. Lauren sucked back gulps of air, as if her lungs had been deprived of oxygen, as if she was on the verge of a panic attack.

She just needed to get home. She needed to crawl under the covers and hide from the world, sleep for a day and stay in her cocoon until she was ready to brave life again. Tanner was gone. She wasn't going to see him again and no amount of crying was going to change that.

She'd survived losing him before and she'd survive again. The only other option was to die of a broken heart, which meant that she was only allowed to wallow for a few days at the most before pulling herself up by her boot straps and putting one foot in front of the other. Eventually the pain would heal to a deep thud inside of her that she could keep hidden away, that only she would know about. After all, she'd managed to live that way for years, so it was going to be hard but not impossible.

Lauren rummaged in her bag and found some tissues, blew her nose, wiped at her cheeks, and dabbed her eyes until she felt human again. Once she was cleaned up, she stared out the window and watched the world pass by, turning so her cheek was against the seat. Fiji was already a distant memory, and the sooner it disappeared from her head altogether the better.

She quickly picked up her phone and tried to keep it together.

"Hey!" Casey answered after the first ring.

"Can I come over?" Lauren asked, holding her breath before bursting into tears again.

"Wine or hot chocolate?" Casey asked.

Lauren gulped. "Just a shoulder to cry on and a sofa to curl up on."

"Love you," Casey said.

Lauren wanted to say the words back, but she couldn't get them out. Instead, she hung up the phone and cleared her throat, pulling herself together enough to tell her driver the change in address.

Chapter 17

Two Weeks Later

"LAUREN, what's going on? I've never seen you so . . ."

Lauren paused, staring across the street. She forced herself to take a sip of her cappuccino.

"What?" she asked.

"So blue."

Lauren smiled and touched her sister's hand to reassure her. "I'm fine. I'm just thinking about the upcoming season and the new players." She'd sworn Casey to secrecy, not wanting Hannah to know how heartbroken she was—the last thing she needed was it getting back to her mom and then having to deal with her on the phone. But sitting across from her sister, it was hard to keep her poker face on.

"Sorry, honey, I call bullshit. What's really going on? You've been like this ever since you got back from Fiji. Did Tanner do something to hurt you?"

Lauren almost choked on her coffee as she spluttered her reply. "No! No, he didn't do anything to hurt me, not like that. This has nothing to do with Tanner, I'm just tired. And I have the holiday blues I guess."

Hannah was silent as she finished her coffee and ate a forkful of the slice of carrot cake they were sharing. But when she looked up, her eyebrows were arched and Lauren knew that her sister's intuition meant she wasn't about to give up.

"I don't believe for a second that's all that's going on, Lauren." She sighed. "If you don't want to tell me, that's fine, but don't lie to me."

Lauren looked into her sister's eyes. She'd been wanting to tell her, from the moment she'd arrived home, but confessing what had happened, actually saying it out loud meant she'd have to admit that it had happened. Keeping it in her head meant she could pretend it was a dream, a fantasy like the millions of fantasies she'd had over the years about Tanner.

"Lauren? Oh shit, don't go crying on me! I didn't mean to be a pushy–"

"I didn't want to tell you. I mean I did, but I . . ." Lauren's voice trailed off.

"Holy shit, you actually did sleep with him, didn't you? You guys were back on the entire time!"

"Shhh," Lauren hissed, looking over her shoulder. "It wasn't—well, just stop!"

"*Ohmygod*, you've been holding out on me! I can't believe it!"

Lauren felt her cheeks ignite; all her skin flaming like it was on fire. She took a big breath. "He was such as asshole to start with, but you know how we always were together, there was that spark between us and we couldn't keep our hands off each other. But it was just supposed to be a fling."

Hannah rolled her eyes. "Yeah, I remember. I think we *all* remember what you and Tanner were like."

Lauren flushed all over again at the memory of Tanner's touch, of his kisses, of running her fingers down his back as they made love, being tucked up in bed against his chest afterward. "One thing led to another and we just, well . . ."

"Ended up naked?" Hannah hissed. "I've got two kids, I know what happens, silly."

Lauren burst out laughing and her sister joined in, and soon she was wiping away tears as she hiccuped and put her hand over her mouth. Trust Hannah to make her open up and get her smiling again.

"So what happens now?" she asked.

Lauren's eyebrows shot up. "What do you mean *what happens now*?"

"Well, are you guys back together? Or are you just taking it slowly?" She hesitated and frowned. "Or did you break up? Is that the problem? What the hell is going on to make you so glum?"

Lauren shook her head. "No, we're not together. It was just a holiday fling—you know, getting it out of our systems once and for all. There was no breakup because it was never a relationship to begin with."

Hannah didn't look convinced. "Hold up. You reunited with the love of your life, you had crazy hot sex," her sister laughed. "Hold up. It *was* crazy hot, right?"

Lauren sighed. There was no point in lying. "Yeah, it was crazy hot."

"So all that and you just, what, said goodbye at the airport and that's it?"

"Yeah, that pretty much sums it up." It sounded stupid now that she was saying it out loud, but having fun had seemed so simple at the time. "We'd agreed to go separate ways when the vacation was over, and that's what we did."

"That's ridiculous. You guys were made for each other and if Mom and Dad hadn't forced you apart, you might still be together."

Lauren could have pointed out that they were kids back then, that she was happy with her job and the way things had turned out. Yeah, she would have liked to look into a crystal ball and see if she might have been happy with Tanner, but chances were he'd have tired of her, or his friends would have given him shit for only being with one girl. She wasn't about to start wallowing in what could have been, not now. And besides, she wasn't about to make her mom feel guilty about potentially keeping her away from the man she could have loved for the rest of her life. That was the exact reason she hadn't told anyone in her family.

"You're sure you've done the right thing? I mean, what does he think?" Hannah asked.

"He thinks I broke his heart back then and he wasn't going to let that happen again." Lauren drained the last of her coffee, even though it was almost cold now. "Seriously, he wasn't interested in anything more than having some fun, and it was fun, so I can't complain. We were both on the same page about what we wanted, and I told him the exact same thing—that I didn't want anything more than a fling."

"You just didn't expect to fall in love with him all over again, did you?" Hannah asked in a soft voice as she reached over and took her hand, squeezing her fingers gently.

Lauren bit down on her lip, trying not to think about how much she missed Tanner. He'd been such a jackass on the plane when all she'd been trying to do was look out for him, but it didn't change the fact that she still cared deeply for him. She always had and there wasn't a switch that could be flicked to just turn off feelings like that.

"It doesn't matter how I feel," she said, squeezing her sister's fingers back and using her other hand to wipe away her own tears, using the back of her knuckles to brush them off her cheeks. "There are so many reasons that we're not right for each other—it's too complicated and we're just not supposed to be."

Her sister gave her a long, worried stare. Lauren was certain it was probably the same look Hannah gave her kids when they hurt themselves or when she was fretting about them when they were unwell.

"Does he know why you ended things?" Hannah asked. "It seems only fair that he find out after all this time."

Lauren nodded. "He knows. I think part of him realized all along that they had something to do with it, but he was still so angry about what I'd done. I just wish he'd known how much it hurt me, too."

"Honey, he'd never have let you go if that was the case and you know it."

She did know it, and she wasn't sure if that made it worse or was somehow reassuring.

"And you're sure you can't make it work, or at least give it a try? Do you really want to walk away from him without giving things a chance?"

Lauren had turned that question over and over in her mind so many times, but there was no way around it. "It's just not meant to be," she repeated. "I love my job and he's happy doing what he does, not to mention the fact that Mom and Dad will still think he's a badass given our history and everything else. There are so many reasons why we just don't work. Trust me, I've thought of them all!"

Hannah caught her eye and held it, not letting her look away. "Loving what you do for work is one thing, Lauren, but job satisfaction isn't enough. It doesn't keep you warm at night and it doesn't give you someone to love when you're old. There's this little thing called 'balance' that most sensible people believe in. You heard of it?"

Lauren laughed. "I'll meet someone one day," she said, trying to convince herself as much as her sister. "But for now, just let me be, okay? Even if I was interested in something more, Tanner isn't, so can we please just talk about something else?" And if he was, he'd had his chance and hadn't said a damn word to make her think otherwise.

"Like how much I want to finish that piece of cake?" her sister asked.

Lauren grabbed her own fork and stabbed a mouthful. "Not a chance. I'm the one with the broken heart."

Hannah waved to the waiter, laughing as he came over. "Can we have another piece, please? And cream on the side with the next one."

Lauren smiled across at her sister, loving that she could sit and pour her heart out to her, and then commiserate by eating cake. She'd done the right thing in telling her, and she felt lighter already from sharing her pain.

Tanner was a great guy in so many ways, but it just wasn't meant to be, and she had to admit that in order to move forward. He was handsome, they'd had great sex, and they'd always had that explosive chemical re-action to each other, but that didn't mean they were sup-posed to be in a relationship together. That ship had sailed long ago.

"So any hot new players joining the team this sea-son?" her sister asked.

Lauren gave her a deadpan stare. "You know I don't look at the players like that."

Now it was her sister giving her a serious stare in reply. "Well, now that you've breached your work eti-quette with Tanner, him being a client and all, I thought maybe your rules had relaxed."

Lauren reached for the plate of cake as it was placed on the table. "You know what, I think I'll eat this all myself now."

If looks could kill, her sister would be long dead.

Tanner checked the weight of each bull as it passed through the weighing machine and read it out to be re-corded. He'd been helping out Stretch, foreman at River Ranch, all morning; the day before he'd mustered the bulls in; and the days before that he'd helicoptered around his family's ranch double-checking all the stock and doing an aerial survey of their fencing.

And now he was so damn exhausted and sore from being on his feet all day he was wishing he'd just left the ranch workers to it.

"Tanner, what the hell are you doing down here?" He groaned when he heard his father's loud voice boom across the yards at him. "Don't you have some place else to be?"

"Just giving the guys a hand," he called back. "You know how I like to keep busy."

His dad moved closer, but Tanner stayed focused on reading the weights.

"You trying to prove that you're the heir to take over the ranch? Is that what this is?"

Tanner laughed. "Didn't know I had anything to prove. Who the hell else would take over?"

He glanced at his old man and was surprised to see him raise his eyebrows as if in question.

"Mia? You think *Mia* should take over the ranch? Dammit, this day is turning out worse than it damn well started." Was that look he was giving him serious or was the old man just trying to get a rise out of him?

"Settle down, son," his father muttered. He was standing closer to him now, and Tanner let one bull through before opening the chute for the next, still doing his work as they talked.

"We've got some good weights recording today, you'll be impressed," Stretch called out from the other side of the wooden chute. "Might be one of our best years yet."

"Good, I'm happy to hear it," Walter replied. "But tell me, did you ask my son for help or did he come down here looking for work? Hope he hasn't been getting under your feet."

Stretch made eye contact and Tanner just nodded. He wasn't about to ask the man to lie for him, but his body rippled with anger at his father's comment. He might have thought he was being funny, but one thing Tanner was not was a nuisance—children with nothing better to do and no skills got under a man's feet, not a seasoned rancher.

"Seems like he wanted to keep occupied," Stretch

said. "And we were pleased to have the help. It's always good having one of your boys lending a hand."

Tanner owed him a beer for that reply.

"Ain't no one better flying the helicopter around the ranch, either. He's been a mighty good help these past few days."

Tanner groaned. Maybe he didn't owe him a beer now that he'd gone and told his father how long he'd been there for. But it was true, he was damn good up in the air, because he'd been flying almost as long as he'd been driving a car.

"So let me get this straight, while I was away you moved in and you've been working here like a madman? I thought you were supposed to be resting up? Wasn't that the point of all the physical therapy?"

Tanner stretched his back out, sore and wishing to hell he was resting up. But resting and staying still meant his mind would start wandering again, and that was the last thing he needed. Long dark hair, brown eyes, golden skin begging to be touched—he pushed another bull through. Why couldn't he get her out of his head?

"Come on, son, we need to walk," his dad said. "Can you spare him?"

Stretch laughed. "Well, I've been enjoying the time off to tell you the truth, but sure. He's all yours."

Tanner took the last recording then climbed over the railings, holding his hand up in a wave to Stretch and the other ranch hands. It'd been nice spending time with them, just hearing them talk shit and being part of a team—he missed the banter from the guys he traveled around with and saw at all the competitions he rode at. They might compete against one another but there was a real sense of camaraderie once the competition was over for the day.

"Son, we need to talk."

Tanner wiped at his brow with his forearm, the plaid shirtsleeve removing the layer of sweat and dirt. Being in the pens all day was hard work, and it was dusty as hell. "Sounds serious."

"The last thing I need is you getting all hot under the collar, but I've had some news and I want to talk through some options with you."

Tanner stopped walking and looked at his dad. He noticed the lines on his face, noticing how much he'd aged, wishing the clock would stop ticking so damn fast. His father drove him nuts sometimes, but he couldn't imagine not having him around any longer.

"You're worrying me, Dad. I thought you were going to ask if I'd stop riding for you, but it's something more, isn't it? What happened in New York?"

Walter sighed and walked over to the closest fence, hitching his boot on a rail, elbows bent and resting on the timber. Tanner joined him and waited for him to get whatever it was off his chest.

"I wasn't in New York. I was in Dallas getting some tests done."

"Tests? What kind of tests?"

"I've got cancer," he said. "I've kept it quiet because I didn't want to alarm you kids, but I'm going to need to start treatment and I need to get my affairs in order."

"Christ," Tanner swore under his breath. "How could you go through that and not tell us? Does anyone know? I would have come with you, I would have dropped everything and been there for you. We all would have."

His father looked calm, but Tanner's heart was racing, his head full of questions. The old man had clearly had time to process all this but . . . dammit! He was not ready to lose his father.

"I'm sorry," Tanner said, clearing his throat and trying to swallow away the lump that had formed there. "What do you need me to do?"

"The cancer's in my prostate, but my urologist and oncologist are both optimistic," Walter said. "I'm a strong bastard and I damn well told them so, so don't go expecting me to die on you anytime soon."

Tanner laughed despite the somber topic, knowing that his father would face any treatment like a battle and be determined to win it. He was like that with everything in life, and he had no reason to think he'd treat cancer any differently than he would a business competitor.

"What is it you want to ask me? You want me to give up bulls, is that what this is about?" Tanner felt his pulse ignite but he balled his fists, forcing himself to stay calm. This was different, this was his dad's health, and he needed to keep a clear head instead of being reactive.

Walter shook his head. "I'm not telling you what to do with your life, Tanner. We've had that conversation too many times already." He turned to look at him. "I'm also not planning on being ten feet under any time soon, but it's made me think a lot about things. Your brother deserves his seat on the board, but he's not a rancher like you are, and Angelina's the same. She's an amazing businesswoman but she's no rancher, either. Mia loves the land and I'd like you two to work something out when it comes to living on the ranch or dividing the land up, but it's you I need running things here when I'm gone." His father clapped a hand on his back. "This is *you* making the call, Tanner, not me. But you need to decide whether you want to make your own way in this world once I'm not here, or if you want to step into my shoes and take up your birthright. That's your decision to make, not mine, and I won't pressure you into anything."

Tanner gulped. This was way too real, talking like his dad was already gone. "You talked to the others about this yet? About any of this?"

"You're the first to hear of it, other than my attorney. What I need from you is your word that you'll put this ranch first when I'm gone. I'm going to see my lawyer next week, put all my affairs in order, and I want you managing the ranch and overseeing all our property, as well as being my power of attorney. Cody can manage the finances and reinvestments and your sisters will keep their seats at the table, but I see you running the show. If that's what you want to do, then the offer is there, son." He placed a hand on Tanner's shoulder, his bright blue eyes locked on his as he spoke. "There will come a time when you'll need to decide between bull and bronc riding, and running the Ford dynasty, Tanner, and I need to know that you're levelheaded enough to make that call when the time comes. I don't need an answer now, but you're going to have to chew it over and give me an answer sooner than later."

Tanner didn't hesitate. He held out his hand, clasping his father's palm when he did the same. "I love what I do, and I was never going to stop because I was told to, but if this family needs me? If this ranch needs me? You can count on me, no questions asked. I'm proud of my namesake and I'll never turn my back on what you've built here, and that's a promise."

His father pulled him in for a hug, a rare display of affection that took Tanner by surprise. He wrapped his arms around his dad and held him straight back, blinking away tears as he considered the thought of his father not being around for much longer. It didn't seem so long ago that they'd all had to confront death when their mom had passed away, even though it was almost fifteen years ago.

"You know, your brother might have been the conventional success story," Walter said, letting Tanner go and giving him another friendly slap on the back before stepping back and starting to walk again, "but you? You've made it on your own. You've earned millions doing something that gives you a buzz, and that's no different to the way I feel doing property deals. I'm proud of you, son, and I want you to know that we're not all that different. I should have told you years ago, but you know how I am sometimes."

Tanner fell into step beside him, trying to stop his jaw from hitting the ground. It was the nicest thing his father had ever said to him, and the first time he'd ever heard the words *I'm proud of you*. He also got how hard it was to pay someone a genuine compliment or talk about feelings—maybe they weren't so different after all.

All these years he'd been like an angry bull himself whenever anyone in his life had suggested he give up what he loved. Until now. He wasn't giving up anytime soon, he was so damn determined to climb up again, clasp his fingers through the rigging and feel the buck of a bull beneath him, but when the time came, he knew he could walk away. If it meant stepping up and taking over the reins of the Ford family ranch and property portfolio, he'd do it. In a heartbeat.

"Don't tell me that after all these years you're going to admit to being the rebel in your own family?" Tanner asked, teasing his dad.

"You'd better believe it," he said, rumbling with laughter and making Tanner crack up laughing too. "Your granddad wanted me to be some fancy attorney or doctor or something, wanted me to have the education he'd never been able to have, but that wasn't for me. We all have to follow our own path, no matter what everyone else thinks."

All these years of thinking they were at odds—it was a strange feeling seeing how similar their choices had been.

"Well, looks like we both picked the right path, huh?"

His old man laughed. "I guess so. Now tell me about Fiji. You think it'd be a good place for an old man to recover from cancer treatment? I kind of like the idea of taking a pretty nurse with me, and I'd get to see what it was like for you traveling with your gorgeous therapist."

Tanner wasn't ready for cancer jokes yet, not after just finding out, but he braved a smile for his father's sake. It was nice to spend time with him like this, even if the circumstances weren't exactly ideal.

"Fiji was amazing, I'd highly recommend it," Tanner said. The part he wouldn't recommend was hooking up with an old flame and driving yourself stark raving mad over her.

"So if it was so amazing, why are you working yourself to the bone out here with the boys? Why the hell aren't you training and focusing on your recovery? And don't give me some bullshit about wanting to do hard labor for no good goddamn reason."

Damn, his father knew him too well. Better than he'd realized. He was about to open his mouth and give him some bullshit answer when the old man chuckled.

"She got you all hot under the collar, didn't she? That old flame of yours?" He was still smiling to himself as he nudged his shoulder into Tanner's. "Take some advice from an old man, would you? If she's driving you this crazy, then do something about it. We don't get enough time above ground as it is, and if I were your age again, I'd be making the most of it. What the hell have you got to lose?"

Tanner wasn't going to have this conversation, not now, and he wasn't going to explain why he was keeping as much distance as possible from Lauren. "Thanks for the advice, Dad."

They headed for the house, walking side by side, Tanner glancing at his father every now and again. He hoped he wasn't in pain, and he sure as hell hoped he'd tell Mia soon, because there was no way Tanner could keep this a secret from his little sister. She'd know straightaway that something was wrong and that he was hiding something from her.

Tanner lay in bed that night, his mind split between worrying for his dad and playing over his advice. What the hell was he doing pretending like he didn't have feelings for Lauren? He'd never stopped having feelings for her—he'd just hated her for what had happened.

Maybe he should call her. What the hell was wrong with seeing if she'd come take a look at him? Maybe see if she could massage away some of his stiffness? Run him through some more exercises?

He groaned and shut his eyes. *Or slip between his*

sheets and remind him just how much he wanted her skin against his.

Tanner reached for his phone and stared at it. He should text her. It was late but he could still send her a message and see if she'd come by the ranch. The season hadn't started yet, she'd have time if she wanted to, and maybe seeing her on the ranch, on his home soil, would be the catalyst he needed to get her the hell out of his head.

He scrolled through his contacts then groaned as he realized he didn't even have her number. Mia had been the one in contact with Lauren before their trip, and Tanner had never thought to ask her for it. They weren't supposed to be hooking up once they were home, so there hadn't seemed to be any point.

He looked her up on Facebook, clicked Friend Request then noticed she hadn't posted a picture for almost two years. Clearly she wasn't into social media—another thing they had in common. So he begrudgingly texted Mia instead, asking if she wouldn't mind forwarding him Lauren's contact info.

A text pinged back almost instantly.

Why do you need it? Are you in pain?

Tanner laughed to himself. *Yes*, he replied. Only it wasn't his injuries that were causing him pain, not this time.

Hope you're ok. I'll forward the contact through in a sec.

He never fooled his sister, yet the one time he actually had something to hide she hadn't even picked up on it. He lay back, trying to figure out what the hell it was about Lauren that drove him nuts. She was beautiful, but there were plenty of beautiful girls out there in the world and none of them had ever made him feel like she did. Maybe it was their past, but there just seemed to be something about her, something that made him want to caress her cheek one moment and slam his fist into a wall in frustration the next.

Tan, did you really think I was going to fall for that? I want all the details, and I want them now, so get your butt over here in the morning. It's the only way you're getting her number.

He threw his mobile across the room and punched his pillow, bellowing like an angry bull. Damn her! The only other woman to ever drive him nuts was Mia, and this time she actually had something he wanted.

He tossed and turned and then got up, deciding to see what was on television. What was it with women making his life hell?

Chapter 18

LAUREN was laughing at something her sister was saying when she grabbed her ringing phone and saw an unfamiliar number. She held her finger to her lips and backed out of the room, hoping the kids wouldn't follow her. They were little rascals and they had their only aunt wrapped around their little fingers, although she had to admit that staying with them had been a nice distraction. Being in a house full of little people and helping her sister out had been cathartic, especially given how she'd felt since she'd arrived home, and she wasn't exactly looking forward to leaving in the morning and going back to her empty house.

"Lauren Lewis," she said, poking her tongue out at her niece and carefully shutting the door behind her while trying not to laugh.

"Lauren, it's Tanner."

Lauren braced her hand against the door. Tanner? What the hell was he doing calling her?

"Lauren?"

"Sorry, I'm here. How's the old body doing?" She

cringed. Why had those words come out of her mouth? She slapped her forehead and wished she could just hang up the phone and start the conversation over. Or maybe fall into a hole and never emerge. Surely she could have come up with a better question than that!

His deep, low laughter echoed down the line. "It's not too bad. But I tell you what, that other PT you sent me to? He could learn a thing or two from you."

Now it was her laughing. "You went to see him?" she asked. "Sam Winstone?"

"Yeah, that's the guy. I can tell you right now that you're a much better therapist."

She sunk down to the floor, back against the wall as she trembled with stifled laughter. "Funny, but Sam's a woman, Tanner. You sure you went to the PT I recommended?"

Tanner's groan was too much to bear and she burst into laughter, wiping tears from her eyes as he muttered expletives.

"You know, this is not how this conversation was supposed to go," he grumbled.

"Okay, how about you tell me why you're calling and we can start over," she suggested, liking the sound of his voice as she pressed the phone harder to her ear. She'd been missing him, but she hadn't known quite how much she'd missed the rich, warm timbre of his voice. The tightness in her chest eased and she felt her shoulder un-bunch—maybe she didn't need the massage she'd booked after all. She'd expected any future conversation they had to be difficult, but this was, this was *nice*.

"Look, I know we agreed to part ways when he touched down," he said. "And I also know I agreed to use a different PT on home soil."

Lauren held her breath. Oh, hell no. Was he going to ask her out? Was he going to ask for a second chance? Or was he just seeking her professional advice? She was about to speak when he beat her to it.

"It's just that you were a miracle worker in Fiji and I'd do anything if I could book you for another session. Any chance you could come here to the ranch, even for a couple of days?"

She cleared her throat. So he wanted her professionally, not personally. She should have guessed. In fact, she should have been relieved instead of feeling like she'd just been sucker punched. Thank heavens he hadn't been standing in front of her when he'd asked because she would have found it impossible to keep a straight face.

"Oh, of course. I mean, if you really think you need me, then I'm sure we can make something work." Why were these words coming out of her mouth? She was supposed to hold strong and refuse to treat him, to recommend someone else and insist that he follow the plan she'd set for him!

"I'm staying at home, River Ranch I mean, while my dad's away for a while. Keeping an eye on the place and helping out where I can. Any chance you can come here this weekend?"

She sighed. She was officially a pushover. "That sounds great. How about I come by on Saturday morning?"

"Thanks, Lauren. See you then."

She said goodbye and dropped her phone to the floor and her head between her knees. Why hadn't she just said no? Why was it so impossible to say no to Tanner? She could have said she was busy or that there was preseason training going on, anything other than yes would have been preferable.

The sound of the door opening made her look up, and she found her sister standing there, a worried expression on her face.

"You look like you've seen a ghost," Hannah said, coming closer and dropping to the ground across from her.

"I just spoke to a ghost, that's why," Lauren mumbled, dropping her head back between her knees.

Hannah rubbed her back in big circular motions. "Tanner?"

Lauren exhaled. "Yeah."

"It's okay to love him still, Lauren. We can't choose who we fall for."

She knew that, but up until a couple of months ago, she hadn't heard the name Tanner Ford in years. She'd moved on, created a life for herself that she loved, and now here she was acting like a lovesick teenager. Why was he so hard to get out of her head? And her heart? Why did she feel so affected from just one conversation with him? And why was she tingling all over at the thought of seeing him again?

"I thought he wanted me," she whispered. "I thought he was calling because he felt the same, but it seems I actually was only a vacation fling for him." She should have been relieved, but instead she felt defeated. A little part of her had believed that he'd come looking for her, that he'd fight for her and demand that she give them a chance. That he wouldn't let her walk away. It had been a silly fantasy, but it had been in her head anyway.

Her sister didn't say anything and Lauren just sat

there, head down, counting to fifty before finally hauling herself up.

It was time to admit to herself that her fantasies about Tanner were just that—*fantasies*. There were so many reasons keeping them apart, and the sooner she stopped thinking that something could miraculously change that, the better.

Tanner was about to bite into his sandwich when Mia walked into the kitchen, hands on her hips and a look on her face that said she was not in a mood to be messed with. He'd been avoiding her for days, ever since he'd managed to find Lauren's number all on his own without having to divulge a thing to his sister. But now she was on the warpath and he doubted he'd emerge unscathed.

"Where's Dad?" she asked.

Tanner blew out a breath and set down his sandwich. "He's started his treatment," he said, annoyed that he was the one to have to tell her. Why hadn't he told her before he'd left?

"Already? Why didn't he tell me? I could have made arrangements and gone with him so he didn't have to do it on his own."

Tanner smiled at Mia, knowing how hard it must be for her not to be involved with what was going on. When the old man had told him, he'd processed it and respected his wishes that he wanted to do it all alone, but he knew firsthand that women didn't find that quite so easy—well, women like his sister anyway. She had a heart of gold and she'd step across burning coals to help anyone in their family, but that was exactly what Walter didn't want. He didn't like a fuss.

"Mia, he wants to do this solo, you know how he is. I'd probably be the same."

She looked exasperated as she stood, hands on hips. "He might say that but I'm sure he'd rather have me there. I could have taken care of him afterward and made sure he was eating enough, that he had everything he needed and—"

Tanner chuckled. "Mia, everything you just said is why he went alone. He wants to deal with it on his own, he needs his space, and if he needs us, he knows we'll be there in a matter of hours. He promised me that the oncologist has all our details, okay? He has the best team treating him and we need to trust in the decisions he's made."

Mia let out a loud groan and sunk down onto one of the bar stools. He opened the fridge and got her a juice, pouring it into a tall glass and sliding it across the counter. Then he leaned down and picked up his sandwich again, thinking he'd dodged a bullet. She was so distracted with their dad she'd forgotten all about wanting to meddle in his life.

"You still want that phone number?" she asked as she raised the glass of juice to her lips.

Tanner finished his mouthful. Maybe he'd been wrong about that. "No."

"So you got it from someone else so you didn't have to confess your sins to your sister?"

Tanner ignored her and kept eating. She'd always managed to do that—it was like she could read his mind.

"Come on! What happened with you two? It's obvious that something is going on."

When he finished eating, he stayed propped on his elbows and gave Mia a long, hard stare. "I have no sins to confess. I have no idea what you're even talking about."

"Bullshit! You're the biggest sinner of all!"

He didn't even bother answering her; he just brushed his crumbs onto his hand, tipped them onto the plate, and turned around to the sink. He preferred to have the house to himself, so he'd given their housekeeper a few days off, and he knew that Mia would notice that soon, too. He wasn't about to admit that he didn't want *anyone* here when Lauren turned up in the morning.

"Don't tell me you're trying to get back at her for what she did to you, Tan. I know she hurt you and you've never really let go of that, but you guys were so young and way too intense."

Maybe he was trying to get back at her, but not in the way Mia was meaning. He wasn't trying to punish her, he wanted to see her again, he wanted to look into her eyes and see if there was something more between them. Right now he had no idea if it had just been the combination of being isolated on a balmy island together with a history that made them know exactly what they were missing out on, or if it was actually something more. All he knew was that he couldn't get her out of his head and it was driving him insane.

"I just wanted her professional help again, that's all. You were right about her being good at her job. She's amazing."

Mia's narrowed her gaze as her hands fell to her pregnant stomach. "If it was just for physical therapy purposes, you would have just come over and asked me for her number, Tan. It's more than that, I can tell."

He shrugged like he didn't give a damn. "So what if it is?"

"You're playing with fire, that's all I'm going to say. Don't go breaking her heart just because she broke yours."

He didn't reply, because he was fairly sure that if anyone's heart was going to be broken, it'd probably be his.

"I'm going out for a walk and then I have to do stretches," he said, changing the subject and offering his sister a smile. "I might head down to the bulls and then make my way up past your horses if you want to come?"

Mia frowned but she didn't mention Lauren again. "I'm good, thanks. I'm exhausted from working two horses this morning. Catch you later."

He watched her go and wondered why he didn't just get everything off his chest and be honest with her. Trouble was, he didn't know what honest was—he had so many feelings, so many possibilities, circling through his mind, he wouldn't have even known where to start.

One more weekend, that's all he needed with her. One more night, one more night of being intimate with her, to see her on his home soil and prove to himself that it was just sex and memories. Then he'd focus on his next ride. He'd already missed the season kickoff and he wasn't about to sit out the year's second major, so once the weekend was over, he was going to train and train and focus on his first big performance. If he had to ride that damn bull again that had thrown him, then he needed to be ready, mentally and physically. Thunder Cat would not take him down a second time.

He headed for the door, pulled his boots on, and strode across the grass. Screw going for a walk. There was a mechanical bull sitting in the shed with his name on it, and he was damn well going to take it for a trial run to show himself he was rearing and ready to join the circuit again. That was his problem—too much thinking time and not enough work. Maybe once he was focused again instead of so goddamn idle, he wouldn't think about Lauren ever again.

Lauren's knees were knocking when she stepped out of her car and looked up at the imposing Ford residence. She'd spent a lot of time on the ranch when she'd dated Tanner, and he'd snuck her into his bedroom a few times, but mostly they'd liked being outside together. He'd taught her how to horseback ride and she'd surprised herself by how much she'd enjoyed it all—there had been something so peaceful about being on the ranch and seeing Tanner on the property he'd grown up on. Around the other kids at school he'd always been the daring one, always trying to outdo the other guys or make people laugh. And he'd always been the one knocking back shots when the other boys were drinking beer, the one with a cigarette hanging out the corner of his mouth, the kid with the roaring motorcycle and the fast car who liked to show off.

But as much fun as that Tanner was, it had been Tanner the rancher that she'd truly loved.

She pushed the memories aside and walked up to the front door, knocking and then waiting. When no one answered she raised her hand again, but a warm voice from behind stopped her.

"Hey."

Lauren spun around slowly and exhaled as she set eyes upon Tanner. "Hey yourself," she said, sounding a whole lot more together than she felt inside as she looked him up and down.

"Thanks for doing a house visit," he said. "You have an overnight bag I can carry in for you?"

"Well, my patient won't be carrying it in for me," she joked.

"You want to go for a ride?" Tanner asked.

She almost choked on her own tongue. A ride? "I . . ."

"Dammit, I meant a horseback ride. I, shit. Sorry."

Lauren laughed. "If these jeans and sneakers are okay, then sure thing. I'd love to."

It wasn't that she'd have said no to the other kind of ride, she'd be lying if she didn't admit to thinking about the fun they'd had every moment of every day when her mind started to wander. But horseback riding was a whole lot safer.

"How are you feeling?" she asked, walking back down the steps and falling into step beside him. She looked at the way he was walking, impressed with his movements and the fact it was almost impossible to detect a limp now.

"I'm getting there. By the end of the day I really start to feel it, especially in my leg, but it's my grip that I'm worried about the most." He made a face. "I think you were right about having to go easy on my wrist."

She was pleased he was taking his injury more seriously. "I think I'll show you how to strap it correctly before you compete. It'll give you more strength there, but I still think you need to be careful about riding at all if you think it's too weak on any given day."

"I hear you loud and clear, doc, and I'm not arguing. Not anymore."

She stopped walking. "Sorry, are you a new patient? I thought you were Tanner Ford?"

He laughed. "Haha, very funny. Maybe I've realized these past couple of weeks that I'm not invincible."

Lauren smiled as she walked alongside him, itching to brush her fingers against his as their hands swung dangerously close. Was she really just here on business or was it something more? Because right now, she couldn't tell.

She admired the ranch as they walked—the big oak trees, the immaculate grounds, the perfectly stained wooden fences and the pretty horses grazing on the other side.

"Are these yours?" she asked.

"Nope, they're Mia's. Some of her horses are turned out having a nice break while she's pregnant," he replied. "That's her house over there. You can just see the roofline past the stables."

She took a good look as they walked—the spot where Mia's house was had just been a field back when she used to visit the ranch. It didn't take long for them to reach the yards where the ranch horses were kept—same as they'd always been. Most things about River Ranch hadn't changed at all. There were two horses already tied up and she guessed Tanner had been the one to secure them and start getting them ready for their ride, presuming she'd say yes.

Lauren leaned on a fence post as Tanner quietly saddled up the horses, disappearing for a short time to offer her a helmet, despite the fact that he'd reappeared wearing a Stetson.

"Thanks." She took it and put it straight on, happy to be playing it safe, especially since so many years had passed without her ever getting up into the saddle.

"Come on, I'll give you a boost up," Tanner said.

He led the horses out and stopped beside her, the shorter of the two, a beautiful rich red color, sniffing her hand and dipping her head low.

"Give me your leg," Tanner said.

She picked up the reins, remembering what to do, and lifted her left leg for him to give her a boost. His hand closed around her knee as he counted to three and then lifted her high above the saddle. When she landed with a soft thump she grimaced, realizing how out of practice she was.

"Sorry," she said, patting the horse's neck before pushing her feet into the stirrups and sitting up straight with her shoulders back.

"You'd make a great cowgirl," Tanner said with a wink from the other horse, already mounted up and with his heels pushed down. She noticed that first because it was the one thing she'd been worried he wouldn't easily be able to do given his ankle injury, although she bet he'd have his foot hanging free of the stirrup before too long.

"Let's go, gorgeous," he said.

Lauren almost fell off the horse. So much for her professional services being required—she was starting to feel like this was more first date than therapy.

The horse she was riding obediently followed along behind Tanner's, and she tried to relax into the saddle, worried the animal would feel her anxiety and think that her rapid heartbeat was because she was nervous of riding. In reality the only thing she was scared out of her wits about was the man riding in front of her.

"Where are we heading?" she said, almost scared to ask the question.

"Thought we'd take a walk down memory lane and

ride to the river. Maybe we could do some stretches there?"

Lauren gripped the reins a little tighter. Stretches? There was only one thing they'd ever done at that river spot, and *stretching* wasn't exactly what she'd call it.

Tanner had no goddamn idea what he was doing. Why had he decided it was a good idea to take her down to the river? It was as if he was trying to sabotage their weekend, trying to recreate something that could never be again because they were adults now, not teenagers sneaking off to make out away from prying eyes.

He dismounted when they reached the spot and held out his hand for Lauren's reins. But as she swung her leg over, looking unsure, he let the reins go and moved to catch her, his hands to her hips helping to guide her to the ground.

Dammit. Now his hands were on her slender hips and he could feel the warmth of her through her skinny jeans. He held on too long, frozen, until she slowly spun around to face him. Lauren was breathing fast, and her eyes were wide as she looked up at him, so clearly filled with uncertainty.

"Why are we here?" she whispered.

Tanner didn't answer her. Instead he bent, removing one hand from her hip so he could take off his hat, discarding it to the ground, and then carefully unclipping her helmet and taking if off her head. He let that fall from his fingers to the ground, too, landing with a soft thud.

Lauren hadn't moved, but her lips had parted, and when her tongue darted out to moisten them he slowly lowered his head, waiting, giving her the chance to move away, before covering her mouth with his in a long, slow kiss.

She moved into him, her arms finding their way around his waist as she tugged closer, head back as he kissed her over and over again. He ran his hands down her back then up and under her T-shirt, wanting to feel her bare skin, needing to connect with her warm, soft flesh.

"What are we doing?" she murmured, pulling back, hands flat to his chest as she stared up at him. "We can't do this."

He groaned. "Yes. Yes we can."

"No." She pushed back more firmly, her hands finding his as she stood a foot away from him, her eyes still trained on his face. "We can't keep doing this. It's, it's . . ." She looked exasperated. "It's too hard. I should never have said yes to coming here."

"Why can't we just keep it casual? It worked for us in Fiji." He pulled her closer again, hips against hers as he lowered his body again and placed a light, teasing kiss to her lips, tongue against hers. She kissed him back, hands under his shirt now, caressing his chest. But when he skimmed his palms to her butt, grinding into her, she pushed him away again. "I've missed you, Lauren. The last few weeks have been goddamn impossible."

"It doesn't matter," she protested. "It's too hard, Tanner. I can't do casual and I can't be around you like this again. It's not fair to either of us and you know it."

"Not fair?" he repeated. "Sweetheart, we're both having fun, no one's getting hurt."

She wrapped her arms around herself and backed into the horse picking at some grass while he waited for her. "*I'm* getting hurt, Tanner. *I'm* the one who can't handle this. Maybe you can, but I can't. I'm finally starting to move on and, and I can't go back. I just can't."

He stared at her, finding her words hard to digest. "*You're* hurting? Honey, I was hurting for years and I doubt that caused you to lose any sleep."

He saw the hurt register the second the words had come out of his mouth. Why the fuck had he said that? Why, when she was here with him right now and he was trying to convince her that they should be hooking up, would he have snapped that at her?

He swallowed. He'd said it because it was the goddamn truth and the words had been festering for years, that's why.

"Shit, I didn't mean to sound like that," he said, cringing at the fierce look on her face now. "I'm sorry. I shouldn't have said—"

"Yeah, well, you did," she interrupted before he could finish, "and I'm not about to remind you that I hurt myself, too. Can we just go?"

He faltered. "Go?" She wasn't serious, was she?

"Yeah, as in get going. Leave," she replied. "You're fine, Tanner. You've got great movement and you need to keep up your stretches. Be careful of that wrist and be sure to get it strapped before your first competition. You don't need me here and you know it, because this wasn't about your recovery, it was about us."

He watched as she gathered up her reins again and lifted her leg, waiting for a boost. When he didn't comply, she managed to stick her foot in the stirrup and haul herself up into the saddle on her own.

"It's over, Tanner," she said, looking down at him. "Whatever this was, whatever *us* part two was, it's over, and we're not doing this again. I can't put myself through this again. It's not fair to either of us, and it's definitely not fair to me."

He'd hurt her, just like he'd always wanted to all those years before, to make her feel what he'd felt, only now the last thing he wanted to do was see tears in her eyes, to hurt the only woman he'd ever truly loved. And he hadn't even realized, back then, that she'd hurt herself just as bad in the process.

"I'm sorry," he said, his throat thick with emotion. "I'm so sorry, Lauren."

"Yeah, me too," she said somberly. "I should have known better than agreeing to come here in the first place."

He remounted his horse and they rode silently back toward the yards. He kept glancing over at her, at the way she was holding her chin high, sitting in the saddle like she'd been doing it her entire life.

"You know, once upon a time, I couldn't have imagined a life without you," he forced himself to say, knowing he needed to get what he was thinking off his chest while he could. He needed to be honest with her. "I could see us on the ranch together, with a brood of kids cantering around on ponies or climbing trees." He took a deep breath. "I've got my own place now, but I still see myself here."

She met his gaze, just briefly. "Me too, Tanner. I used to see that too."

When they eventually reached the yards, having ridden the rest of the way in silence, she dismounted on her own and he didn't offer to help—he could tell when a woman wanted her own space, and Lauren was giving off that vibe a hundred times over.

He took the reins from her as she stepped toward him, one hand to his shoulder as she stood on tiptoes and brushed a kiss to his cheek.

"Goodbye, Tanner," she said, her smile sweet as she stepped away. "I wish things could have been different between us."

He swallowed a lump in his throat as she turned and walked away. She was walking out of his life again, and this time he knew he'd never see her again. He stood there for as long as he could stand it, then led the horses into the yard, taking off their saddles and bridles, calmly giving them a rubdown and then letting them go, not wanting them to feel his anger and be scared of his temper. It was only once the horses were away from him that he let out a roar that made him sound more animal than human.

Goddamn it!

He shut his eyes and smacked his palm into the fence as he buckled forward and struggled to breathe. Telling himself she'd been the former love of his life? That had been utter bullshit. He loved her as much now as he had then, he was just too chickenshit to put his heart on the line again and admit the truth. Instead he'd let her walk away all over again.

Lauren had no idea what she'd done. She slapped her hand against her mouth as she sat in her car, in shock, her entire body shaking as she tried not to scream. What was so different about being with Tanner now? Tears burned her eyes but she refused to let them fall, frantically blinking them away as she let her forehead drop to the steering wheel.

Why had she ever agreed to see Tanner again? Why

had she ever thought she could have a fling with a man she'd once loved so deeply? Why had she been stupid enough to say yes to him on the phone the other day instead of refusing to go near him again?

Because she was too weak when it came to him. So weak it made her sick. She should never have come here, and she'd known it before she'd even stepped foot on the ranch.

Tap, tap, tap.

Lauren looked up, mortified when she saw Mia Ford standing outside her car, looking worried on the other side of the glass. She went to put her window down, then realized the key wasn't in the ignition so she pushed the door open, quickly wiping at her eyes. Why hadn't she just gotten in her car and driven away? If she hadn't sat here, then Mia wouldn't have seen her and she wouldn't be about to have a discussion with the sister of the man she'd just turned her back on. Again.

"Hey, is everything okay?" Mia's face was the picture of concern, and it made a fresh wave of emotion clog in Lauren's throat. "What happened?"

"Sorry, I was just leaving," Lauren managed, clearing her throat and trying to act like she wasn't falling to pieces. She took a deep breath and forced a tight smile that she was sure wouldn't fool anyone. "I'm fine."

"Lauren, what's going on? You're not fine," Mia said. "Do you want to come in for a coffee or something?"

Lauren coughed, still trying to breathe and stop the sobs that were waiting to erupt in her chest. "I need to go, I'm sorry."

"It's my brother, isn't it? I knew something was going on with him." Mia grumbled. "I'm sorry I ever asked you to treat him. He's obviously been behaving like a jerk and it's my fault you even had to deal with him in the first place."

"It's fine, he's fine, I mean," Lauren stumbled over her words. "He didn't do anything, it's both of us. We're just, there's been stuff going on between us but it's over now."

Mia pulled the car door open a bit further and leaned against it, looking down and straight into Lauren's eyes.

"If you need me to talk to him, you just say the word." Mia looked up and then sighed, like she wasn't sure she should be saying whatever she was about to say. "He loves you, Lauren. I think he always has."

She couldn't believe that. He lusted after her, that much had been obvious, but it wasn't love, not anymore. "I don't think so," she said, struggling to keep her composure. "Anyway, things are complicated between us, they always have been."

"I'm sorry, Lauren. For whatever's going on between you guys, I just—"

Lauren blinked through her tears. "This is between me and Tanner, it's not your fault at all." She should have told her that their time in Fiji had been the happiest and most content she'd felt in a long while, but she couldn't get the words out. It was time to drive away from River Ranch for the last time.

"Goodbye, Mia."

Mia held up her hand and stepped back, hand falling to her rounded stomach. Lauren looked at it, imagined the brood of kids Tanner had talked about, and burst into tears. She wanted that; it wasn't a past fantasy for her, she wanted that still. Trouble was, the guy only wanted her for a good time, not a long time, and she might not be able to give him one child let alone a brood, even if he did want her. And she had to stick to her guns on this—Tanner was not right for her. This emotional roller coaster that went on whenever they were together was too intense, and that kind of intensity could only ever result in heartache. Pure and simple.

Lauren started down the drive, blurry eyed as she navigated the entrance and turned out onto the road. She had to get herself together. She'd walked away from Tanner and survived it once, so there was no reason she couldn't do it again. She was a professional woman with a great career, a great home, and a supportive, loving family. She didn't need Tanner, or any man, to make her happy—she had enough as it was.

So why did it feel like her heart was breaking into a million tiny pieces and her lungs were being constricted, making every single breath feel impossible?

She brushed her tears away and gripped the wheel, focusing on the road. Tanner was her past, not her future, and the faster she got her head around that, the better.

The Rangers were about to go into their full training program again soon. She had a busy season ahead of her and she needed to focus on her job. It was what she loved, it was what she'd dedicated her life to. And it was what she'd given up Tanner for in the first place.

The players were counting on her, their partners relied on her to keep their men in top condition to avoid injuries, and she had a hefty mortgage to pay—those were the things she needed to focus on.

Her family had been right—Tanner wasn't the man for her. Loving him wasn't enough, it never had been.

Chapter 19

One Month Later

TANNER had never been so nervous in his life. He was pacing, his heart was racing, and he couldn't draw in enough air to fill his lungs. What the hell did he think he was doing? What was he trying to prove?

"You look scared as hell," a voice said from behind him.

Tanner looked over his shoulder, wondering who was getting in his space when he was trying to prepare. Then he realized who was standing with his hands shoved into his jean pockets, watching him.

"Well, if it isn't the old man," Tanner teased. "Ryder *goddamn* King. You're lucky you weren't mobbed coming back here."

Ryder was grinning as he strode over, hand outstretched. "Couldn't miss the chance to see a good comeback," he said, clasping Tanner's hand and slapping his back at the same time. "They're calling you the second-chance cowboy."

Tanner stared at Ryder. "You're fucking with me."

"Nope. There's even some cute-as-hell college age girls out there with a sparkly sign stating exactly that. I kid you not."

Tanner's chest tightened again and he flexed his wrist, grimacing. He knew he shouldn't be competing if he didn't feel right, but hell, half the guys out there were bandaged up to their eyeballs. He wasn't ready to give up the sport he loved, and if he didn't get back into it now, he wasn't sure he ever would.

"You're all healed up, or that wrist still giving you hell?" Ryder asked.

It was one thing lying to his family and dodging their questions, but when a former pro like Ryder King asked the question, knowing exactly what it felt like to be staring down the barrel of a ride like he was? Lying wasn't an option.

"It's—I don't even know how to describe it—it feels sticky in the joint," Tanner said, flexing it again and making a fist. "I don't have full strength there like I used to."

Ryder looked around. "You got a bag with tape in it? I can strap it up for you, get it good and tight, and you can powder and glue up."

Tanner jogged over to his bag, pleased with how easily he was able to move now. The wrist was the only thing left still bothering him.

Ryder studied his wrist, feeling it and turning it over, before putting the tape between his teeth and pulling it out.

"I'll do it nice and tight, but you know you're only asking for trouble if you keep at it without healing properly first, right?"

"Yeah, I know." Tanner listened to the roar of the crowd, knew the clock was counting down until his ride and he needed to get ready. His head was all over the place and he needed to sort his shit out before he stepped anywhere near that damn bull.

"You're on that mean bastard Thunder Cat again today, aren't you?"

Tanner had been seeing that damn bull in his sleep and it was driving him crazy. "That's the one." He'd been mighty unlucky to draw him again so soon.

"He's just a bull, no different than any other out there. Don't overthink it, and get the hell away from him when you come off."

Tanner met Ryder's gaze. Ryder had been the best bull rider around in his day, and he appreciated the pep talk.

"And then come find me for a beer afterward," Ryder said.

"So we can commiserate?" Tanner asked with a laugh.

"No, so I can tell you that the best part of being a bull rider is retiring, you fool." Ryder tipped his hat and pointed toward the action. "Quit while the going is good, that's my advice. Now get out there and have the ride of your goddamn life."

"You're serious?"

"Deadly." The set of Ryder's face told him he wasn't kidding around. "I'm no saint, but being home with my girl and being on the other side of the ring is a damn sight more enjoyable. Once you give up the adrenaline rush, anyway."

Tanner blocked out what Ryder was saying, not wanting to even hear the word "retirement" with the battle he was facing. And when he walked toward the chute, the roar of the crowd in his ears as they cheered for whatever poor bastard was riding for his life in the ring, everything disappeared from his head. He climbed up and looked down, hearing the heavy, snorting breath of the bull that had almost killed him.

Thunder Cat looked up, throwing his head, and Tanner caught his eye.

"Time for second chances," he murmured, waiting for his name to be called, clapping powder between his hands, before slowly easing himself down onto fifteen hundred pounds of mad, wild flesh.

The accident flashed through his mind; the stabbing pain; the bite of torn flesh; the searing, vomit-inducing crack that still echoed through him whenever he thought about that day. And that goddamn bull spinning around and staring at him before goring him on his way past.

Go away, he ordered.

"And next up we have former PBR grand champion and one of the highest-earning bull riders of all time, Tannnnnn-er Ford!"

Tanner sucked back a breath, his lungs on fire as he eased down. His legs were shaking until they were against the bull, fingers tight through the rigging as he settled in, ready for the fight of his life. His body was feeling good, his pulse was racing, and he was as pumped as he'd ever been—it took him back to his first ride when he'd believed he was invincible and couldn't wait to climb aboard a big goddamn bull and show the crowd watching exactly what he was made of. He'd hated the Ford tag when he was growing up, and bull riding had been his way to prove to the world that he could make it on his own, that he was stronger, tougher, and more talented than anyone gave him credit for. And to show his family that as much as he liked his trust fund and the perks that came with being part of the Ford dynasty, he didn't need family money in order to survive. *To thrive.*

The signal went and the chute opened, and all Tanner could hear was the huff and puff of the wild-as-hell beast beneath him. He spun and whipped around, bucking wildly, and Tanner counted in his mind, ready to scream as he held on like he'd never held before. His body was flung back and forth and he dug his fingers tighter, refused to loosen his grip, refused to let the bull get the better of him a second time. He could do this—this was his comeback, and no one, not even this son-of-a-bitch bull was going to take his moment away from him.

Eight. The last buck sent him flying, but he'd done it! Tanner flew through the air and landed roughly on his feet, stumbling as he tried to correct himself. The clown was doing his job, but Tanner looked back and saw him charging, knew the bull wanted to smash him into the ground and gouge him all over again if he was given half a chance.

Tanner was hauled back and he leapt up, scrambling up the wooden side fence and tucking his boots up high.

Fuck you, Thunder Cat, he thought, watching the sleek black bull charge around the arena as the crowd went crazy. *You didn't get me today, and you won't get a goddamn chance to get me again, either.*

Tanner inhaled the familiar rodeo smell, absorbed the addictive feeling of being in the arena with thousands of fans screaming and clapping and watching the sport they loved. He flexed his hand and experienced the familiar, jolting pain. It wasn't bad most of the time, but he could sure as hell feel it right now after the stress he'd just put his entire body through.

He might love being a bull rider, but Ryder was right. The best thing for a guy his age, after so many years at the top, was bowing out on a high. He had never wanted to accept defeat before, but it was time to retire. And it was no one's decision but his own, and that's why it finally felt like the right thing to do. When he'd been asked before what else he had left to prove, it had rubbed him up the wrong way fast, but faced with his father's mortality and what he'd decided he wanted from the future? It was time.

Before he climbed down on the other side, Tanner waved to the crowd and fist-pumped the air. The announcer was running through his ride, hyping up how well he'd done, and Tanner hoped he'd done well enough to win. If this was his last ride, it had better have been enough to beat the young riders who'd been chasing his tail for the last couple of years. He'd always loved seeing the new up-and-comers, the way they didn't give a shit and believed they'd bounce when they hit the ground. Hell, they probably did bounce the first few times, their bodies more lithe and unbreakable than the older guys on the circuit, but only the odd one ever climbed the ranks and managed to succeed big time. But it was time to move aside and let someone else take his place, and he was ready to cheer them on instead of gritting his teeth and competing alongside them.

Bull riding had been his everything, but he'd had a change of heart, and if he'd learned anything over the years, it was that following his heart, not his head, was always the better decision.

"Dad?" Tanner called the second he'd pushed the big oak front door open at River Ranch. "Dad?" he repeated, kicking his boots off and heading into his father office. He wasn't there. He heard the faint sound of a television down the hall and smiled. His father was definitely home.

"Hey, Dad," he called out, not wanting to startle his old man.

"Tanner? Aren't you supposed to be riding a bull?"

He laughed. "I rode him already."

"And instead of having a night out you decided to come back home? How did you even get back here so fast?"

Tanner poured them both a drink, whiskey on ice, and passed one glass to his father as he sat on the chair opposite him. His father took it and reached for the remote, turning the TV off and facing him. He'd been single-minded about getting home as fast as he could, and now he was here, exhaustion was starting to gnaw at him and his ankle and wrist were killing him, so it was a relief to be sitting with his legs stretched out. He was also hoping the drink would numb the pain and discomfort a little.

Tanner held up his glass and leaned in to clink it against his father's, before taking a small sip. The familiar burn in his throat put him at ease as he sat back.

"What are we drinking to, son?"

"My retirement," Tanner replied, not missing a beat and surprising himself how quickly the words came out.

"Your *retirement*?" Walter repeated.

"I've been thinking about it a lot, ever since your diagnosis, and the timing feels right. It's been a long time coming and it's taken me awhile to get my head around it, but I'm ready."

He watched as his father took another sip, shaking his head as a smile slowly spread across his lips. "You know my treatment was successful, don't you? I might not be around as long as I'd like to be, but I'm not dying. You're not getting rid of me that fast!"

Tanner held up his drink again. "To your health," he said. "And you'd better stick around for a while yet, because I'm planning on doing my MBA first before joining the family business. Thought I'd better add some letters to my name to make me sound more legit."

Walter grinned. "Well, damn, I'll drink to that!"

Tanner slowly sipped his drink, feeling like a weight had lifted from his shoulders that'd been pushing him down for weeks. He'd made the right decision, and it had never been so clear as right now.

"What're you watching?" he asked.

Walter picked up the remote again and tossed it to him. "Nothing much. Find us a movie or something decent to watch, would you?"

Tanner couldn't remember ever sitting in his father's den and watching a movie with him, hell, he couldn't remember spending a Saturday night in with him period, but it was nice. He laughed to himself as he flicked channels. Maybe he was finally growing the hell up.

Lauren sat at her parents' dinner table, smiling as her father finished pouring the champagne for his girls, and lifted her glass high. She loved nights like these. Her sister's family, her mom and dad, all gathered together eating great food and drinking something equally as good—it was her perfect kind of night.

"When does work start to get busy for you?" her father asked. "Do you have time for a game of golf with your old man?"

Lauren and Hannah exchanged glances, like they had when they were girls and their father had suggested something deadly boring or had forgotten what they liked and didn't like to do.

"Sure thing, Dad," she said. "But how about we just go for a hike instead?"

"Patience, my love, patience," he said in his dad voice. "Once you stop rushing and start enjoying the game, you'll learn to love it."

"Seriously, being a mom doesn't give you an automatic card to get out of golfing," Lauren hissed to her sister.

"Oh, Lauren was just telling me the other day that she was starting to love the games with you. Perhaps you should do a few extra holes next time?" Hannah said.

Lauren kicked her sister under the table, ready to kill her. She loved spending time with her dad, she did, but golf? She took a gulp of champagne to commiserate.

"What courses are you enjoying?" Fred, Hannah's husband, asked.

Lauren turned to Hannah and was about to chastise her when there was a knock at the door. Her mother looked as surprised as she was that someone had come by to visit.

"You expecting anyone?" she asked her mom.

"No, not tonight. Would you mind seeing who it is?"

"If it's someone wanting money or selling something, tell them to take a hike!" her father said. "Unless it's a neighborhood kid. I always give them a few dollars if they're fundraising."

Lauren got up, drink in hand, to answer the door, smiling at her dad. She bet he always bought the kids' fundraiser chocolate bars in particular—he had a mighty sweet tooth that her mother was always trying to discourage. She pushed aside a big silver balloon that was in the doorway she had to pass through, with HAPPY WEDDING ANNIVERSARY emblazoned across it. Her parents had been married forty years to the day, and they'd been having a wonderful time looking at their old wedding photos and listening to stories about their early years together.

There was a soft knocking again as Lauren reached for the door handle. "I'm coming," she called out.

She yanked the door open and her glass almost slipped straight through her fingers. Tanner was standing there, wearing slim-fitting dark jeans, a dress shirt with the top collar undone, and a tailored jacket. Compared to the clothes she was used to seeing him in, he looked like he was heading somewhere special.

"Hi," he said.

"Hi," she repeated, not sure what else to say.

"I'm sorry to intrude, I know it's a special night for your folks, but would you mind if I came in?" His smile was sweet but she could tell that he was nervous, and she had no idea why he'd turned up at her parents' house.

"How do you know it's their anniversary?" she asked, still standing in the doorway, trying to decide whether to let him in or try to convince him to go back to his car. The last time they'd seen each other hadn't exactly gone well.

"Your sister posted it on Facebook," he said. "I took

a shot that they lived in the same house, and that you'd all be here celebrating since it was a Saturday night. I remember how much your folks preferred to stay in rather than dine out."

Lauren should have told him that they'd just sat down to dinner and were in the middle of toasting their marriage, so now wasn't a good time, but instead she stood back and waved her hand into the house. She didn't know what she had to lose and it was probably easier having him come in than walking him back to his car and having to be alone with the man. "Come on in then, I guess."

Tanner stepped in and looked around, waiting for her and touching the small of her back to let her go first. He was a true Texan, his manners faultless when he was on his best behavior—only right now she wished he wasn't. It was like his eyes were burning into her from behind, and her body was tingling from his touch, still craving what it had been denied.

"Cute photos," he said as they walked past framed pictures of her and her sister as toddlers.

"You'd have seen them before if you'd ever bothered to come in when we were dating," she pointed out. "I recall your preference was to sit outside lounging on your motorcycle, smoking a cigarette that you'd eventually drop and grind beneath your boot in my dad's driveway—which drove him nuts by the way. And I'd be inside begging to go out with you." She spun around. "You know, I'm pretty sure he still hasn't forgiven you for all that stuff, so don't go expecting Mr. Nice Guy, okay?"

Tanner groaned. "Okay, well, let's not mention any of that tonight. It's been a long time and I bet he's forgotten at least half of the shit I put him and your mom through."

She had no idea why he was even in her family home, but something told her this was no casual drive-by. He looked so handsome all dressed up—she was used to seeing him in his work clothes, which consisted of a simple rotation of plaid shirts and jeans, or his vacation attire, so either he was going somewhere after this or . . . she was puzzled. Would he dress up like that just to come here? His hair was combed back off his face, still too long on the ends but it suited him, and she saw that his boots were polished, too. For some reason he'd made a big effort with his presentation and attire. Some reason that was starting to make her uneasy, whatever it was.

"Ah, Mom, Dad," Lauren said, as a hush fell over the room and every face at the table turned to Tanner. "We have a visitor."

"Mr. and Mrs. Lewis," Tanner said in a loud, clear voice. Something wasn't right, she still had no idea why he was here or what was going on, but her anxiety was starting to build. Big time. He looked like he was about to ask her to prom.

She saw the shock register on every face, but it was her sister who frantically looked back at her, searching her face, dying to know if Lauren had known he was coming. Lauren shook her head ever so slightly and mouthed *no*, and her sister nodded, understanding in only the way a sister could.

"Tanner," her father finally said, pushing out his chair and coming around the table to shake his hand. "It's been a long time. Good to see you."

Was it? Her dad had never been happy to see him

before and she'd been so certain that wouldn't have changed. Ever. Why would he feel differently now, or was he just being polite because Tanner was a man now and he was technically a guest in their home?

"Happy anniversary, sir," Tanner said as he clasped her father's hand back. "I hear congratulations are in order. Forty years is no mean feat."

Her father had already downed a couple of drinks— they all had—so if there was ever a time for Tanner to get away with turning up at their house unannounced, it was probably now. She was surprised by how relaxed her dad's body language seemed to be.

"I read that you were competing yesterday," her father said. "Sounds like you had a good ride, is that the right terminology?"

Tanner laughed. "Yes and yes, it was a good ride. Climbing back on the beast that had thrown me and done its best to kill me took nerves of steel, I can tell you that. But I'm sore today, damn sore!"

"I didn't know you'd been following Tanner's bull-riding career," Lauren said, trying to hide her shock.

"You'd be surprised what I know, sweetheart."

Clearly she would be. After he'd as good as marched Tanner out of her life, she hadn't expected her dad to have given him a second thought. But to find out that he'd been *following* him?

"Mr. Lewis, I know I've interrupted your evening so I won't take long, but I wanted to show you that the boy you knew, back when I was dating your daughter, well, he's all grown up now." Tanner cleared his throat. "I understand now why you asked Lauren to end things with me, because to be honest, if I was a girl's dad, I'd have been holding a shotgun and marching me the hell away, too. I was a bad influence on her and I needed to grow the hell up before I had any right to be laying claim to her."

Lauren tried to stop her jaw from falling open as she looked from her father to Tanner. Surely this wasn't actually happening? Did Tanner come here looking for forgiveness? Why the hell would he even care what her father thought of him now that he was a grown-ass man? And what was this talk about *laying claim* to her? Any other time she'd have jumped up to defend her rights as a woman, but right now she was too shocked to say anything. And curious—she was deeply, painfully curious to know why this conversation was even taking place.

Her father made some weird hand gesture, shaking it like he was clearing the air. "Tanner, the past is in the past, and to be honest, maybe I was a little hard on you."

Tanner grinned. "Seriously? Because with all respect, I think you were probably right about me."

They both laughed, and Lauren went to sit beside her sister, legs shaking as nerves set in. It was like she was in a dream, watching what was going on without actually being a part of it. She felt like she was back in high school.

"Sir, the reason I'm here," Tanner said, looking more serious, his face more somber now, "is to ask for permission to date your daughter, with the intention of making an honest woman of her one day. I've gone about this all wrong in the past, but this is me trying to do the right thing so you know my intentions right from the outset."

"Holy shit," Lauren murmured, her hand quivering as she reached for her glass of champagne. She slowly, quietly polished off the rest of it, not setting her glass back down until every last drop had been consumed.

Hannah suddenly had a hold of her other hand but Lauren couldn't look at her. Her skin was on fire, her body was still shaking, her tongue wouldn't move. She couldn't have gotten a word out even if she wanted to. Why was this conversation going on as if she wasn't even in the room?

"Tanner, maybe we were wrong to break you up, but we only did what we thought was right at the time." Her father turned, and Lauren watched as he exchanged glances with her mom. "I'm done telling my daughter what to do though. If you want permission, then you'll have to ask Lauren. It's hers to give, not mine."

Her father, Tanner, her mom, her sister, and Fred all turned to look at her. Lauren balled her fists and dug her nails into her palms.

"Lauren?" Tanner asked, and suddenly as his gaze warmed her, it was like they were the only two people in the room. She stared back at him, wishing she knew what to say, wishing she wasn't so terrified of what she didn't know, of having her heart broken.

"I . . ." she murmured, so genuinely lost for words.

Tanner came closer and dropped to one knee in front of her, taking one of her hands and holding it in his. "I'm sorry for the way I behaved, but if there's one thing I've realized, it's that I can't let you slip through my fingers again. I'm so, so sorry I hurt you."

"I honestly don't know," she whispered. "I'm sorry, I . . ."

"Tanner, why don't you join us for the evening?" her mother said, taking the attention from her. Lauren would be eternally grateful and hoped she remembered to thank her later. "There's plenty of food and we have another bottle of champagne waiting to be opened."

Tanner smiled in response, but it was *her* answer he seemed to be waiting for.

"Lauren?" he murmured. "I'll walk straight back out that door and leave you to your evening if you want me to, you just say the word."

"Stay," she croaked, before summoning all her courage and reaching out, hesitantly, to touch his cheek. "Please stay." She couldn't answer his questions or figure out how she felt or what she wanted, all she knew was that she didn't want him walking out that door and away from her right now. *Maybe ever.*

Tanner leaned a little closer and Lauren's heart skipped a beat, waiting for him to kiss her, expecting it. But instead he pulled back and took her other hand, pulling her to her feet. He was definitely on his best behavior, trying to impress her parents.

Tanner sat at the table, beside Lauren and across from her father. It was a strange feeling. All these years of blaming Lauren for ending things, and suddenly he could see so clearly why she'd done it, and he could see why her parents hadn't wanted him near their daughter. Hell, he'd have probably sent his daughter to a university on the other side of the world if he had any say in the matter, so the fact her father had sternly told her to call things off probably wasn't a bad call.

But he was here now, and he wasn't about to let Lauren just disappear from his life again, not now when he could prove why he deserved her.

He noticed Lauren's glass was empty and reached for the bottle of champagne, refilling her glass. Her hand came to rest on his thigh, so lightly he might not have even felt it if he hadn't seen the movement.

"It's nice to have you here," she whispered as her head dropped to his shoulder.

Tanner's body stiffened, but he let it go, forcing his shoulders to relax as he took in a big breath. His natural reaction was to rebuff this kind of thing in public, he was so used to not having a girlfriend or being close to anyone, but this was the intimacy he'd craved for so long. With the woman he'd been craving.

"I can't believe I was allowed in the house," he murmured to her, kissing her head affectionately and stroking a hand through her long hair. "I'm thinking I'm not as hated as I thought."

"So Tanner, tell us about your comeback," her father said. "You've had one hell of a career to date."

He kept an arm around Lauren, thumb brushing her shoulder as he smiled over at her dad. This was nice. This was a close-knit family who'd invited him into their embrace, and it struck him why Lauren had been so adamant that she wouldn't be in a relationship that they didn't approve of. Her family were kind, decent human beings, and they clearly all loved one another very much; he wouldn't give up family gatherings and relationships like this for anyone either. Her mom was so kind and full of smiles, despite the past, and he smiled straight back at her when she made eye contact, clearly happy enough to have him seated at her table.

"My first ride back was on the bull who tried to end me, but I've been thinking a lot about second chances lately, and I think that helped to get me in the right head space."

"And my gorgeous sister managed to get your body back in tip-top shape, I'm guessing?" Hannah asked.

Tanner laughed and squeezed Lauren's shoulder. "She sure did. I'm betting she's one of the most valuable assets on the Rangers," he said. "Am I wrong?"

They all had a laugh, and Tanner pushed his knife and fork together on the plate after taking his last mouthful of dinner.

"You are a wonderful cook, Mrs. Ford."

She swatted the air at him. "Honey, it's about time you called me Julie. You're not that naughty boy any longer, so no more need for formalities."

"I try my best not to be," he joked. "And I truly am sorry for what I put y'all through back then. I might ride bulls for a living, but other than that I'm a pretty straight up kind of guy."

"Well, that's good to hear, but I have to confess I didn't cook a thing. Lauren and her sister ran down to my favorite Italian restaurant and ordered the lot as a treat."

"Well, it was still good, whoever made it. It's been a great night."

"Do you want to help me clear the table?" Lauren asked, rising beside him.

"Sure." Tanner filled his hands with plates and stood back to let Lauren go first. Her brother-in-law had disappeared to put the kids down, letting the girls have a good catch-up at the table, and Tanner wondered how he'd get on trying to wrangle kids. Bulls were one thing, but kids? He wasn't so sure about that.

He set the dishes down at the same moment as Lauren, and she stepped in close to him, shoulder to shoulder. He heard her big inhale and when he turned to her, she did the same, her cheek against his chest, her arms around his back. Tanner held her tight, not saying a word, just enjoying the feel of her in his arms, her warm, slender body wrapped so firmly to his. When she finally looked up, her head tilted back and her deep brown eyes locked on his, he slowly kissed her, taking his time, wanting her to know how much he loved her.

"I can't believe what you did tonight," she said, pushing back as she smiled up at him. "You've got balls, I'll say that."

"I wanted your parents to know that I cared for you enough to man the hell up," he told her. "It was time I started behaving like a man instead of the boy who didn't know how lucky he was to have you."

She sucked in her bottom lip and he knew she wanted to say something, and she was trying to figure out how to say it.

"What is it?" he asked. "Whatever it is, I don't want there to be secrets anymore."

"Did you mean what you said about making an honest woman of me? Does that mean what I think it means?"

He dropped another kiss to her lips and brushed her hair from her face. "I lied when I told you I didn't want anything more a fling," he confessed, forcing himself to open up. It was now or never and he wasn't about to ruin his one shot at being real with her. "I've only ever wanted you, Lauren. It just took me awhile to get my head around, I don't know, my own shit I guess. I was still hurting from something that had happened so long ago."

"I never stopped loving you," she said, holding him tight. "But is that enough for this to work? I mean, one of us has to give something up or we'll never see each other, and I don't even know if I can give you what you want."

He stared down at her. What he wanted? "I want you, it's as simple as that," he said. "What is there that you couldn't give me?" He saw tears well in her eyes and raised his hand immediately to brush them away. "Hey, why are you crying?"

She sighed and shut her eyes, but a tear escaped from the corner and ran slowly down her cheek. "You said at the ranch that you wanted a brood of children, and I used to want that too, but I don't even know if I can have kids now."

He wrapped his arms around her tight, pulling her to him and wanting to keep her safely cocooned against his chest forever to protect her. She looked so sad, full of so much hurt, and he'd have done or said anything to soothe her.

"I'm not here because I want your babies, Lauren. I'm here because you're the one for me, and I don't want to waste another day pretending I don't love you."

Shit, the word had slipped out. It was the first time in his life he'd said the L-word and he could feel the change in Lauren, the way her breathing became shallow and her hands stopped moving against his back.

She didn't say it back to him, but she didn't need to. The fact that she was giving him a chance right now was enough. More than enough.

"So you don't mind? If we can't fill your ranch with children?" she asked. "Hand on your heart it isn't a deal breaker? Or the fact that I'm working eighty-hour weeks during the season?"

"Sweetheart, I'll take however much you're willing to give me. I promise that'll be enough," he said honestly.

"And trust me, I think Mia will be filling the ranch with enough kids all on her own. Maybe we can just be the awesome aunt and uncle, which will mean me getting a whole lot more time alone with you anyway."

"I have endometriosis," she said quietly. "I would love kids one day, but it might make things tough, or maybe even impossible. I want you to know that I'd want them if I could though."

He grinned down at her. "Whatever you want, baby." Tanner said as he rocked his hips forward, kissing her when she leaned into him. "Whatever you want."

"Huh-hmm," Lauren's father made a noise in his throat to announce himself.

Tanner pulled his lips from Lauren's and looked sideways, jumping back when he saw her dad standing in the entrance to the kitchen.

"Hands off my daughter," he said with a laugh. "It'd be embarrassing to have to throw a grown man out my front door for getting frisky with my youngest girl."

Tanner gave her dad a salute and took a step back. "Speaking of your girl, would it be rude to steal her away before dessert?" Her dad shrugged and pointed to his daughter, making it clear that the decision was hers to make, not his. "There's somewhere I'd like to take you, if you don't mind skipping out of here early."

Lauren looked curious and nodded, giving her dad a quick kiss on the cheek before taking Tanner's hand, their palm and fingers intertwined.

"Where we going, cowboy?"

He winked and brought her hand up to his to kiss. "You'll have to wait and see."

Chapter 20

TANNER hadn't been this nervous when he'd eyed up Thunder Cat and prepared for his last ride. He wiped his shirtsleeve against his brow, wondering why the hell he was sweating so much when it wasn't even a warm evening. He reached for Lauren's hand and liked the fact she pulled him in and tucked her arm around him, her hand finding the pocket of his jeans just like she'd used to do so often.

"Just because you've turned into Mr. Romantic doesn't mean we can just slap a Band-Aid on and fix everything," she said, leaning deep into him. "I hope you realize that."

"The only Band-Aid we needed was for my head," he joked. "And trust me when I tell you I've got my head straight."

"You're sure about that?"

He laughed. "Yeah, well, when it comes to you I have." He hadn't mentioned his retirement to her, but then she hadn't asked and he liked that about her. He had kept thinking about what she'd said about them both being dedicated to their careers and loving what they did. She hadn't liked the thought of either of them losing out on what they loved. If she'd insisted he give up riding, he would have bucked against it and probably dug his heels in and refused. But this was his decision, and he'd made his peace with it now. Over beers he'd listened to Ryder tell him that the best thing in his life was his family, and it had made Tanner think long and hard about his future. There was only so much pleasure he could get from riding, and now with his father unwell and so many other things going on, the timing seemed right.

It was like the time he'd given up smoking. His sisters had told him it was a disgusting habit, the girl he'd been seeing on and off kept telling him to quit, and he wouldn't, *couldn't*, quit. But the day he'd decided to put his health first on his own terms? He'd smoked his last cigarette and never, ever picked one up again.

"Tanner, where are you taking me?" Lauren asked. "It's cold out here."

"Come on, it's not far."

He'd driven them most of the way, but there was an elevated spot that overlooked the river that he wanted to walk the rest of the way to. When he'd planned this, he'd had no idea whether her parents would even let him in their house, let alone Lauren saying yes to coming with him or even feeling the same way he did. But she had, and he wasn't going to miss the opportunity to show her how much he'd thought about her and how great they could be.

"This won't take long," he told her as his lips brushed her hair. "It's just up there."

He tugged her along, knowing that she must think he

was absolutely nuts to have her out in the dark. But the moonlight was enough to go by, and the lights from his truck had illuminated part of the way, too.

"Is this where we rode the other day?" she asked, stopping and looking around like she was trying to get her bearings. "This is—"

"Our place," Tanner said, finishing her sentence. "Down there is where we had our first kiss," he said, holding her close to his side as he stared down into the darkness. "It was where I got to second base, then third." He kissed her when he paused this time, then let go. "And whatever other bases there are," he murmured.

She returned the kiss, reaching for him when he stepped backward. "What's that there?"

Tanner walked backward a few more steps then squatted down, feeling around for the switch he'd left on the ground. He waited a moment, in the dark, wondering if he'd gone too far, before flicking it. Lights twinkled on the low grass, sparkling in a huge, magical square, and Tanner stood and went back to get Lauren.

"What is this?" she asked, taking his hand and walking back over with him. "It's beautiful."

"This is the where I want to build us a house one day," Tanner said simply. "If I can prove myself to you and we can make a life together, I want to live here, overlooking the one place in the world that means something to both of us."

"Tanner," she said, her voice a low hum in her throat as she parted from him and stepped inside the square. "I don't even know what to say."

He let her walk around a moment, watching her, imagining the house they could build, the home they could create there one day.

"I was a show-off a lot of the time when we were seniors, but when we were down there, together, I was able to let my guard down and just be me," he told her. "Over here, we could have our kitchen, looking down over the river, and our bedroom over there. It can be something we dream about and plan for years before we even do it, if you want to, but this is where I see myself in ten, fifteen, hell, even thirty years' time."

She came up behind him and wrapped her arms around him, and relief passed through Tanner. Lauren held him so tight and he stayed still, eyes shut.

"This is so perfect. I can't even believe you did all this for me," she said, voice mumbled against his back.

"Is there a *but* coming?" he asked, turning in her embrace and tucking his arms around her, too.

She didn't say anything for a while, just stared up at him in the dark, the fairy lights like a halo behind her, twinkling away as he waited for her to say something.

"I want this to work, Tanner. I really do," she said, but there was a catch in her throat, an uncertainty in her tone.

"But?" he asked softly.

"But I don't think I can deal with a broken heart again," she said. "I've protected myself all this time and kept myself in this bubble I guess, and I know I can't live in that bubble forever, but it's kept me safe."

He relaxed, knowing exactly what she meant because he'd thought it himself a thousand times over. "I know. But we're both risking it all here, Lauren. You know how we are, we were always all or nothing, and I don't expect it to be any different this time."

They stood in silence, wrapped in each other's arms

as Lauren moved closer to him and turned her head to look back at the lights.

"I can't give up my career for you," she said. "One day, I'd step back from my crazy schedule if we had a family, but not right now. It's too important to me."

"But I can," he said, surprising himself by how easily he'd said the words he'd been thinking.

He felt the stillness in her body. "You can what?"

"Give up my career," he said. "But right now we just have to figure out a way of giving this, *us*, a real chance."

"You're thinking about giving up bull riding?" Lauren asked. "Tanner, don't do that for me, you'll only resent me for it later and that's not the way I want so start over."

"I'm not doing it for you, I'm doing it because I want to," he said honestly, kissing her on the upturned tip of her nose. "Someone wise once asked me what I had left to prove, and I've decided that I want to do what makes me happy, and sometimes those things change. Remember I told you how I'd like to do an MBA one day? Well, this is that day."

Lauren leaned back in Tanner's arm, ready to pinch herself to see if she was dreaming. Was this actually happening? Since when had Tanner been so romantic and . . . she ran her hands down his thickly muscled arms and exhaled. The boy had been fun and reckless, but this was Tanner the man. This was Tanner who'd let go of all the hurt and baggage from the past and asked her for a fresh start. Hell, he'd been bold enough to show up at her folks' place on their anniversary and ask for a second chance, and she had to admire him for that. And was he really giving up riding and going to settle down and study?

"Are we really going to do this?" she asked, standing on tiptoes to taste him, to kiss Tanner and inhale the scent of him and lock this exact moment into her memory.

"Build the house?"

She play punched his arm. "No doofus, this, *us*?"

He kissed her, lips murmuring so softly against hers it made her melt against him, pressing her body to his and grinding into him, wanting more. *Needing* more.

"Yes, sweetheart, we are," Tanner told her, with so much sincerity, so much depth in his voice, that it melted something inside of her that she hadn't even known was frozen. "If you want a house in town, too, I'll build you one there or buy something for us. There's nothing I won't give you, and there's only one thing I expect in return."

She hesitated before answering, not sure if she wanted to hear what that one thing was.

"What?" she asked, the word rushing out of her like a big exhale of air.

"You," he said simply. "I just want to know that we're solid, that if there's a problem you'll tell me instead of walking away like you did last time. You might not want my help, but we're stronger together, okay?"

She nestled against him, looking down, knowing how happy she'd be here one day. Not yet, because she had a life that required her to be in town and to travel and work like a dog for, but one day. For now, just being with Tanner would be enough.

"Can we go back to your place now?" she asked. "I'm beat."

He nodded and she ran her fingers across his cheek, his stubble tickling her skin. She stood high on her toes and nibbled along his jaw line until he let out a low groan that sounded more like a growl.

"Leave the lights though," she whispered. "Can we just turn them off but not take them in yet?"

"For you?" his lips whispered against hers. "Anything."

Lauren bumped against him, hip to hip, thigh to thigh, as they walked back in the dark to his truck. There had been a time she'd never thought she'd step foot on River Ranch again, that she'd never imagined a second chance or even a stolen moment with Tanner in her lifetime after walking away from him the last time.

Life was full of surprises and she couldn't believe how things had changed.

"We have two weeks until my work load explodes," she told him as they walked.

Tanner bent down and grabbed her, throwing her over his shoulder as she screamed and squealed, slapping her on the butt as he jogged the rest of the way.

"Tanner, stop!" she pleaded as she bobbed along, laughing so hard she couldn't fight him.

"If we don't have long, then we'd damn well better make the most of it."

When he put her down, his hard body against the length of hers and the cool metal of his truck behind her, she grabbed the back of his head, fingers kneading into his hair as she raised her mouth, and kissed him. Tanner kissed her back just as hungrily, pressing her down, crushing her against him as he ran hands down her sides, holding her hips as she lifted a leg and tucked it tight around the back of his legs.

His breath was hot against her neck when he finally released her, his head still dipped as his lips whispered against her ear. "Come on baby, it's time to go home."

She kissed him again, slowly this time, running her hands from the back of his head all the way down his back. They were together again, and nothing had ever felt so right.

Chapter 21

TANNER clapped his hands together, sending powder puffing up from between his palms, and breathed in the familiar smells of being part of the action at a rodeo. It had been a couple of months since he'd made the decision, but actually working up to a big event, knowing it was his last professional ride? That was something else entirely.

He'd started riding when he was tiny, when his dad had thought it was a bit of a laugh to put his brave young son on top of a calf and let him pretend he was in the rodeo. Then he'd started riding horses and breaking in the wild ones, riding broncs and going on to watch his heroes who won title after title staying on top of the meanest bulls around.

The bug had bitten early, before he'd even left school, and despite all the rows and threats from his father, Tanner had refused to give in and done what he wanted to do. His father had been furious with him for turning his back on a more stable career, but when he'd started earning more and more money, eventually becoming the highest earner on the PBR circuit, as well as earning his degree, his father had eased off. Until the fall. Then everyone had been on his damn back.

But today was the end. It was a celebration of what he'd done and the man he'd become, but he also knew it was about growing up and moving on. This was a young man's game, and he'd survived and lasted longer than most.

"And next up we have *Taaaaaanneeeeerrrrrr* Ford," the announcer trilled, making Tanner's name last at least a few seconds longer than it should have. "Ford is one of our most popular riders on the circuit, and injury hasn't stopped him from being called the second-chance cowboy!"

Tanner channeled all his energy into the ride, lowering himself down onto the back of a bull that he'd probably been drawn to ride three times in his career. He wasn't a standout bull, but he'd do the job.

Tanner signaled that he was ready and within an instant they were propelled out into the ring, the bull giving it his all and spinning, bucking, and kicking to get his rider off. Tanner loosened his body, let it go with the movement of the beast beneath him. He nudged his spurs in, his left arm raised high as the bull gave one hell of a buck, tossing himself around as Tanner did his best to stay on and give the crowd one hell of a ride to remember him by.

Then just like that, he was flying through the air, stumbling to his feet and leaping up onto the railings to avoid the charge of the angry bull. *It was over.*

Tanner waved to the crowd as they cheered and bellowed, some of them die-hard fans who'd seen him ride countless times, some who probably saw or heard about the agony of his big fall, and others watching him for the first time. He was sure going to miss it.

"Good ride," one of the guys said to him as he climbed over and down to the other side.

"Thanks," Tanner replied, recognizing the young man who'd spoken to him. "Bobby, is it?"

He received a grin in response. "Yeah it is. Didn't expect you to know me."

"You've got a lot of talent," Tanner said, straightening his hat as he talked. "I'll be seeing you from the other side of the fence next time."

"You're retiring?" Bobby asked, sounding incredulous.

It took Tanner a second to reply. It was a hard word to get used to saying. "Yeah, this is my last one. I'll see you around."

He walked slowly and looked at the bulls, waiting for their time in the ring. He loved the sound of them, the way they moved, their big, thickly muscled bodies. Bulls were in his blood, but there were so many ways he could stay involved in the sport he loved. He leaned on the railings, seeing Thunder Cat, the bastard bull that he'd expected to hate so much. Turned out he wasn't so bad at giving second chances after all.

Maybe he could mentor someone, a young ambitious rider who needed a hand up. He could breed bulls. Hell, he could take over operations of the entire beef side of Ford Ranch if he wanted to right now. But all that mattered to him now was being happy, and he'd finally seen the forest for the trees—riding bulls wasn't the only way to feel that buzz of adrenaline that he'd become so addicted to.

Lauren popped a light, fluffy pink piece of cotton candy into her mouth, grimacing as she watched Tanner half leap, half fall from the bull he was riding. She slurped back a big sip of cola, trying to settle the frantic, twisting sensation in her stomach as she waited for him to leap up on to the railings. Thank god he was about to retire. There was no way she could stand to watch him doing this more than once—her heart had been in her throat the entire time!

She breathed a sigh of relief when he leapt up onto the railings and waved to the crowd who were busy cheering and clapping for him. It was insane how many people were watching. She wondered where he'd gone and how he was feeling.

He was probably trying to absorb the moment and commit it to memory, so instead of going to look for him, she stayed put and kept watching the show. Respecting his space and giving him the time to process what he was doing was the least she could give him right now.

She leaned forward to watch a rider being hurled through the air, cringing as he hit the ground and the clown ran in to distract the bull. She gasped when the bull spun around and came back for him, just as the rider was pulled to safety. This was not something for the fainthearted! She wondered if the guy had a partner or family watching on.

"Hey, beautiful."

Arms slipped around her from behind, big hands warm to her stomach as lips found her neck and dipped against her collarbone. She relaxed into his touch, loving the softness of his fingers and the deep whisper of his words against her skin when he spoke.

"Are you sure you're done?" she asked, rocking back into him and wishing her hands weren't full of cotton candy and cola.

He leaned over her shoulder and sipped through her straw. "You really should be drinking beer, not cola," he scolded. "And only you would eat cotton candy instead of a corn dog."

She laughed. "Only *me*, meaning because I'm a girl?"

"Come on," he said, tugging at her waist. "It's time to go."

"Go where?" she asked, taking a long, final sip of her drink before dropping it into a trashcan.

"Anywhere, I don't care," he said, smiling at her as he placed an arm around her.

"Can I have an autograph?!" A young boy raced over, and soon Tanner was surrounded by kids jumping up and down.

Lauren stepped back, watching him and loving that he was so friendly with his young fans. He laughed and signed posters and programs, talking away and admitting that today was his last ride as a professional bull rider. She knew how hard it must have been to admit that, to actually confess to someone other than her that he was officially in retirement now.

"Come on," he said, grabbing her hand and waving goodbye to the crowd that had gathered behind them.

"Tanner, I'd love a drink and something decent to eat. Want to check out a cool little restaurant I read about online?" she asked, trying to play it cool so that he'd never guess what she had planned. He wouldn't expect her to know anywhere to eat or drink in Georgia, and she didn't want to give anything away.

"Ah, sure. Whatever you want."

He no longer had his chaps and spurs on, but he was wearing his worn-in jeans and a plaid shirt, a few buttons undone at the front and his sleeves rolled up to show off deeply tanned forearms. He had a bag slung over his shoulder, and his hair was curling slightly around his ears. Lauren walked beside him, holding his hand, unable to take her eyes off the handsome man at her side.

"I love you," she said, her voice barely a whisper as she pushed up to kiss him, nipping at his plump lower lip.

"I love you, too," he replied, his smile starting at one corner of his mouth and slowly spreading to the other as he looked sideways at her.

She giggled and dipped her head to his, before falling back into step beside him and heading for the exit.

Tanner kept his arm tucked firmly around Lauren as they walked toward the restaurant she'd chosen. They'd taken a cab there, and he'd noticed how overly talkative she was. Maybe she was still on a high from attending her first PBR event or seeing him ride? It didn't really matter why though, he was just pleased to have her by his side, happy as hell and talking a mile a minute.

He still found it hard to believe that they were together. That his career had just ended. That life was about to change forever, and that he surprisingly was fine with it all.

She tugged on his hand for a moment and he stopped, trailing a hand down her arm and wondering why she was giving him such a strange look.

"Kiss me," she said, her smile infectious.

He bent to kiss her, hovering over her mouth once he'd finished. "Why do you look like the cat that got the cream?" he asked.

"Maybe you're the cream," she replied, sucking in her lower lip between her teeth, the way she always did when she was nervous or unsure.

He slapped her playfully on the bottom and grabbed her hand back, glancing up at the sign for Stone's Cuisine & Cocktails. She was up to something, he just didn't know what.

Tanner pushed the door open, holding it for her, and she hurried past him before stepping aside. Tanner went to say something, had opened his mouth, when he froze as the door shut behind him.

What the hell?

"Surprise!" Lauren murmured, sidling up beside him and pressing a warm kiss to his cheek. "Happy retirement, baby."

Tanner was speechless as he looked at his family—all of them—sitting at a table, all sporting big grins and waving at him to come join them.

"You brought everyone here?" he asked, incredulous. "How did you convince them? How did you keep this a secret from me?"

She nudged him toward his family. "The secret was easy, and so was getting them all here. I don't think you realize how much they all love you."

He laughed. "Or how much they're all thrilled I've retired."

Mia was on her feet first, arms extended, and Tanner bent to give her a big hug.

"That was a great final ride, Tan," she said, squeezing him tight. "I'm so proud of you."

"Of course you are," he replied, "you were always my number-one fan!"

Sam stood up beside his wife, hand extended. "Great ride."

"You all bothered to come to Georgia for me?" Tanner said, shaking his head as he clasped his father's hand. "Hell, I thought pigs would be more likely to fly than get all of you to watch me on a bull."

"Not all of us, me and Ange have been propping up the bar and drinking cocktails!" Cody called out.

Tanner dodged around his dad and bear-hugged his brother, slapping him hard on the back. "Typical that you've been the one sitting in here drinking while I say goodbye to my career. I don't even think you remember what it's like to be a real rancher and go to rodeos. Too busy being a city slicker."

Cody punched him in the arm and he howled, pretending to nurse his arm.

"And you, unbelievable," he said to Angelina, kissing his sister's cheek and embracing her. "I can't believe you came all this way."

She hugged him, kissing his cheek back. "That gorgeous girl of yours is demanding. She wouldn't take no for an answer," Ange said. "But I like her—she's definitely a keeper."

"Hell yes, that's one thing we won't ever be arguing about," he said, giving his sister a wink as he turned to the rest of his family.

Lauren was standing across from him, on the other side of the table, and he noticed that she was slightly apart from his family, looking unsure. Was she worried what his reaction would be to having all his family here?

Thank you, he mouthed, hoping she could tell what he was trying to say.

He would have kept wondering, too, if her smile hadn't lit up her entire face.

"Anyone ordered champagne yet?" he asked, still grinning at Lauren.

His father waved a waiter over and Tanner moved around everyone else to Lauren. Her smile was wide as he wrapped his arms around her and dipped her backward, kissing her as she giggled.

"Thank you," he said, not caring that they were in the middle of a restaurant or that his entire family was watching. "For future reference, I hate surprise parties, but this"—he sighed and kissed her again—"this is about as perfect as it damn well gets."

"Good," she replied, pushing him back a little and hauling him toward his family, her grip on his hand firm. "Now stop kissing me and start drinking. We've got some celebrating to do!"

Tanner pulled out a chair for Lauren and took the bottle of Veuve Clicquot from the waiter. Another waiter was placing a tray of oysters on the table as Tanner popped the champagne, grinning when everyone started to clap.

"To my last bull ride!" Tanner said.

"To finally getting rid of the rocks in your head!" Cody added, holding up his glass.

Tanner poured Lauren's glass first, bending to whisper in her ear. "To the most beautiful, perfect woman I could ever have wished for," he said quietly, his words spoken only for her.

Her cheeks tinged pink but she touched his hand to stop him from rising.

"To our second chance at love," she whispered back, staring into his eyes.

"Hurry up, lovebirds! We're getting thirsty over here!" Cody called out.

Tanner ignored his brother, discarding the bottle on the table and kissing the hell out of his girl instead.

Epilogue

LAUREN walked in and flopped down on the sofa. She was exhausted. Mentally and physically, absolutely beside herself kind of exhausted.

"Tanner?" she called out.

She had no idea if he was in the house, but his truck had been in the garage and he hadn't mentioned anything about going out. Usually if she was going to be home at a decent hour, he was waiting, surprising her with his new-found culinary skills, but she couldn't smell anything cooking tonight and there wasn't a sound in the house.

Lauren shut her eyes, deciding that he mustn't be home. She didn't mind. He was probably out having a drink with friends, and she could shut her eyes and catch up on some sleep before he got home. Her stomach was growling and she was thirsty, but it was worth starving for a bit longer if she was able to lie still.

She breathed deep, like she did in yoga, in through her nose, holding it a second, then slowly letting it out.

She repeated it a few times and started to drift off, sleep slowly cocooning her as her body relaxed.

"Surprise."

A low whisper was followed by something wet touching her cheek. What the heck? Her eyes popped open and she looked straight into the darkest brown eyes, so pure and innocent, followed by a tongue darting out to smear her with a big lick.

"Why are you holding a puppy?" she mumbled, wriggling back to a sitting position and rubbing her eyes, wondering if she was dreaming.

"Don't you love him?" Tanner asked, holding up the pup and giving him a cuddle.

"Of course I love him, he's a puppy," she said dryly as Tanner passed the dog to her. She cradled him close and inhaled his sweet puppy smell, trying to keep him still as he wriggled and tried to get back to her face for more licks. He was chocolate brown and felt as smooth as silk.

"I thought it was about time we made a commitment," he said. "We're co-parenting now."

Lauren laughed. "Co-parenting? Do you have any idea how much your old rodeo buddies would laugh if they heard you talking like that?"

Tanner laughed straight back at her and flopped beside her on the sofa. The puppy leapt straight out of her arms and scooted over to Tanner, lavishing him with love as her man pretended to fight him off then gave in to the attention.

"Getting jealous?" he asked.

"Of a puppy?" Lauren nudged him with her toe. "Please don't tell me you did this to make me jealous and get more attention."

"Shit, is it not going to work?"

They both laughed and she moved closer, snuggling up to him, head on his shoulder as she stroked the puppy's silky soft head.

"He's gorgeous, Tan," she said. "He looks like he's going to be huge though."

"I might have picked the biggest puppy in the litter," he confessed, kissing the top of her head. "Growing up we used to have a German Shorthaired Pointer, and when I saw this little guy for sale, I thought he'd be perfect. He'll be great on the ranch, and they're a great breed."

Lauren didn't mind. She loved animals, she'd just always been too busy to have a pet with the hours she worked. But if Tanner wanted a dog, then she was happy to share a home with it.

"So long as you get up in the night to take him out, he can be our fur-baby," she said.

"Does that mean I'll have to get up in the night for our human babies, too?" he teased.

She groaned. "Don't even talk about it," she said, hating the topic. "It makes me worry that you've got your heart set on kids." There was a decent chance she could get pregnant one day, but there was just as good a chance that she couldn't, and the thought still twisted her into knots.

"Hey, if we decide we want kids, we'll find a way to have kids. There's more than one way to have a baby."

She reached for the puppy to give him a snuggle, holding him to her chest and kissing his warm little head. It was actually quite a nice idea to have a dog around the house—so long as he didn't chew all her shoes.

"Do you know we've been together a year now?" Tanner asked.

Lauren smiled down at the puppy who'd just fallen asleep on her lap, then leaned into Tanner without disturbing their new baby. "It's a year from our trip to Fiji," she said. "I don't know about you, but I'm not convinced that's our anniversary, Tan. We didn't actually get together properly for a while after that." She laughed. "A long while."

He kissed her, his lips moving so softly over hers and making her moan. He knew just how to kiss her, just how gently to brush his lips over hers to turn her to liquid.

"It's a year since I first laid eyes upon you again," he murmured. "And a year since I got to see that gorgeous body naked again."

She stifled a laugh. "Honey, the baby's listening! You can't talk like that anymore."

The look Tanner gave her was wicked. "Screw the fur-baby."

He carefully lifted the puppy and placed him on the sofa on the other side of Lauren, pausing to kiss her on the way past and stroke his fingers down her arm to her hand.

"Come with me," he said. "I have our anniversary present waiting on the table."

She wasn't going to argue with him about whether or not it was their anniversary, because so long as there was food waiting on the table, and maybe wine, then she was happy. Lauren happily took his hand and let him haul her up, still tired but feeling more alive than when she'd stumbled in. It had been another crazy busy season for her, and right now she'd be happy if she never had to work another day in her life.

"Oh," she said, seeing papers stretched out over the table. Her heart sank—clearly he was excited about showing her something, but she wanted food!

"I was expecting dinner," she said, trying not to register her disappointment.

"Dinner's on its way," he told her, pulling her forward. "I ordered Italian."

Her stomach growled in response. "Okay," she said, still not sure what he was giving her as she edged closer. And then she focused on the huge sheets of paper that were laid out.

They were blueprints of a house.

"The plans have been finished," Tanner said, his voice lower, huskier than usual. "If you give them the green light, then they'll start work on our house as soon as we're ready."

Lauren's hand dropped from his as she leaned forward, fingers reaching for the papers and tracing every line as slowly as her eyes were. *Holy shit.* Every single thing she'd asked for, every little thing she'd ever mentioned to Tanner, had been included. There was her big wardrobe, the bathroom layout she wanted with the huge bath, the big ranch-style kitchen and nook area, the library with two walls of bookcases and the big veranda so she could sit and look out at the river. Every single thing was there.

"It's perfect," she whispered. "It's absolutely perfect."

Tanner's arms closed around her from behind. "Does it look like home?"

Lauren took a deep breath as she studied the plans

again, soaking in every part of the design and imagining herself living there, seeing herself sipping wine at the counter while Tanner cooked or sitting out on the veranda and admiring the sprawling ranch with him. It couldn't have been any more perfect.

"It looks exactly like home to me," she finally replied. "I couldn't be more in love if I tried to be."

"With me or the house?" he asked, cocking an eyebrow as she spun in his arms to face him.

"Both," she said earnestly, surprised that he pulled back when she leaned in to kiss him.

"Lauren, there's something I've been meaning to talk to you about," he said, running a hand through his hair and instantly alerting her to the fact he was nervous about something.

She waited, shoving her hands into her jeans pockets as she waited for him to continue. She was worried for a split second, until she saw a smile start to play across his lips. He was up to something!

"I just don't feel comfortable moving in with you yet," he said, hand on his heart and making her laugh. "Until you make an honest man out of me, I'm not sure I can do it."

She planted one hand on her hip, playing along with his silly charade. "So the fact we share a bed at least five nights out of the week doesn't bother you, but officially moving in with you is off the table? What exactly are you suggesting we do about it?"

Tanner's face morphed into a smile the size of Texas. "It just so happens I have a solution, darlin'," he said, reaching into his back pocket.

"Oh yeah?" she replied, breathless as she watched him, wondering what he was about to do.

"Yeah," he said, dropping to one knee and reaching for her hand. "I had this crazy idea we could get married. What do you say?"

She slapped the hand he wasn't holding over her mouth as he slid the biggest, sparkliest ring she'd ever seen onto her finger. The diamond was huge, the platinum band covered in smaller diamonds that caught the light and dazzled her.

"I'd say that's no way to ask a girl," she whispered.

Tanner rose and kissed her fingers, his eyes never leaving hers. "Lauren, will you marry me?"

She took a second to stare at the ring, to absorb what was happening. Little over a year ago, she'd never ever thought she'd cross paths with Tanner again, let alone marry the man!

"Yes," she said, her voice shaking as she smiled and stepped into his chest. "Yes, Tanner, I'll marry you."

He dipped his mouth to hers in the warmest, softest, most gentle kiss of her life. His fingers trailed down her back as she cupped her hands around his neck, drinking in the taste and scent of him, and grinning against his mouth at the weight of her new ring on her hand.

"What's so funny?" he asked.

She lifted her hand to admire the huge square diamond.

"Nothing, I just"—she kissed him and tucked tight to him—"I just can't believe that after all these years, after everything, that we're here."

Tanner kissed her again. "Well, you'd better believe it," he murmured against her lips.

"A wedding and a fur-baby," she whispered, glancing behind her at the now-sleeping puppy on the sofa.

"And a husband-to-be who wants to see you out of those clothes and wearing only that ring," he teased as he tugged her back again for another kiss.

"Oh really?" she asked, fighting against him as he grabbed her wrists and held her still, making her giggle.

"Uh-huh, and he's getting really impatient."

Lauren broke free and ran, bolting away from him and down the hall. But Tanner's heavier footfalls were interrupted by a yipping noise as the puppy suddenly woke up and joined in the chase.

"I'm having second thoughts about the fur-baby!" Tanner called out, as Lauren spun around in the hall in time to see him scoop up the puppy.

"Tough luck," she said, taking the dog from him just as the doorbell rang. "Looks like you're out of luck, *husband*."

Tanner growled as he stormed back down the hall to the front door, and Lauren smooched the pup while he greeted the delivery guy. Italian takeout, a puppy, and a diamond ring—it was the perfect evening.

She blew a kiss at Tanner when he turned around to face her and he dropped the paper bags and ran down the hall, scooping her and the puppy up in one swoop and carrying them into the bedroom as Lauren's laughter echoed around them.

The puppy barked when Tanner tried to kiss her, and he picked him up and gave him a hard stare.

"Look, scrappy, this ain't gonna end well if you block me from kissing my girl."

The puppy let out a yap in response, making them both burst out laughing.

"Whoever said they wanted children?" she asked, grinning up at Tanner.

"Beats me. I just want a wife."

Lauren lay back and Tanner collapsed beside her, the puppy in between them. It might not be everyone's version of perfect, but Lauren couldn't have been happier if she'd tried.

"I love you, darlin'," Tanner declared.

She grinned over at him. "I love you too, but I'll love you even more if you go get that Italian for me. I'm starving."

Tanner laughed. "Your wish is my command."